10/14/14 B+T $25-95

Ghost Wanted

Ghost Wanted

Carolyn Hart

BERKLEY PRIME CRIME, NEW YORK

THE BERKLEY PUBLISHING GROUP
Published by the Penguin Group
Penguin Group (USA) LLC
375 Hudson Street, New York, New York 10014

USA • Canada • UK • Ireland • Australia • New Zealand • India • South Africa • China

penguin.com

A Penguin Random House Company

This book is an original publication of The Berkley Publishing Group.

Berkley Prime Crime Books are published by The Berkley Publishing Group.
BERKLEY® PRIME CRIME and the PRIME CRIME logo are trademarks of Penguin Group (USA) LLC.

Library of Congress Cataloging-in-Publication Data

Hart, Carolyn G.
Ghost wanted / Carolyn Hart. — First edition.
pages cm. — (A Bailey Ruth ghost novel; 2)
ISBN 978-0-425-26615-1 (hardback)
1. Mystery fiction.   2. Ghost stories.   I. Title.
PS3558.A676G55 2014
813'.54—dc23
2014021907

FIRST EDITION: October 2014

PRINTED IN THE UNITED STATES OF AMERICA

10 9 8 7 6 5 4 3 2 1

Cover design by Jason Gill.
Interior text design by Laura K. Corless.

To Trent and Adrienne with love

Ghost Wanted

Chapter 1

Bobby Mac and I don't spend every moment aboard our cabin cruiser, *Serendipity*, on jade green waters reminiscent of the Gulf. Heaven knows that where you wish to go, there you are. It might surprise you that a rough-and-tumble oilman like Bobby Mac knew his way around art museums on earth. His tastes—and mine—were eclectic, from Gustav Vigeland's sculptures to Mary Cassatt's *Breakfast in Bed*. It was Heavenly now to see one of our favorite artists at work. Sunlight-dappled water lilies in the pond. Bobby Mac and I stretched on a blanket, quiet as stone cherubs, watching Claude at work on a new painting.

A telegram sprouted in my hand. My eyes widened. I will admit to a thrill of excitement. I waggled the stiff yellow sheet at Bobby Mac. He gave me a thumbs-up, as he always does. What a guy. We met in high school when he was a dark-haired, muscular senior and I was a skinny redheaded sophomore. We've been having fun ever since.

I blew Bobby Mac a kiss and went at once to the Department of Good Intentions, arriving immediately. That's the beauty of Heaven—here can immediately be there. It's all in the spirit.

Oh dear, you are already puzzled. Bobby Mac? Sunlight-dappled pond? Do I mean Giverny? Claude? Telegram? From there to here in a heartbeat?

Perhaps I should begin with me. I am Bailey Ruth Raeburn, late of Adelaide, Oklahoma. Yes, *late*. As in *dear departed*. *Dear departed* has a lovely ring, though I'd be the first to agree that not everyone in Adelaide had adored me. There was the high school principal who hadn't been pleased when I flunked the coach's son. All endings lead to new beginnings, and I loved my years as the secretary at the Chamber of Commerce, which provided a front-row center seat for both public and private shenanigans. There was the time . . . Oh, sorry. I am easily distracted.

Back to my departing . . . Bobby Mac Raeburn, the captain of my heart and of the *Serendipity*, steered us out into the Gulf of Mexico seeking a recalcitrant tarpon despite lowering clouds and a whipping wind on what would be a fateful day. For us. Suffice to say, after a valiant battle with the elements, the *Serendipity* was lost in the Gulf and Bobby Mac and I arrived in Heaven. Now the *Serendipity*, as bright and fresh as on the day she was launched, rocks in a tranquil Heavenly sea and provides a haven for me and Bobby Mac.

Those who dismiss the idea of Heaven as balderdash will flee from my narrative. Isn't *balderdash* a lovely word?

I am in good company—of course, given my current location, that surely goes without saying—in choosing *balderdash.* No less than Thomas Babington Macaulay, the great nineteenth-century historian, once said, "I am almost ashamed to quote such nauseous balderdash."

Heaven is no more balderdash than I. However, to convince the skeptic is not my task at the moment. I remain confident that there is, however feeble, a spark of yearning within each earthly soul for all that is holy.

Don't be put off by a mention of holiness. Heaven isn't solemn. You enjoy laughter? Holiness does not preclude humor. Saint Teresa of Ávila combined a deep sense of ineffability with a laughing heart. As she once said, "Lord, if this is the way you treat your friends, it's no wonder that you have so few!" Laughter is always to be found. Just the other star-spangled night, Bobby Mac and I loved every minute of Danny Thomas's new special, and Saint Jude was in the first row, cheering him on.

Claude Monet? He remains a genial fellow and doesn't mind at all when admirers gather to watch the progress of another masterpiece.

As for the telegram from Wiggins—more about Wiggins in a moment—the dear fellow remains a man of his times, the early nineteen hundreds. I'm sure if I were associated with an up-to-date department, there would be e-mails and texts galore, but my heart belongs to Wiggins's delightful Department of Good Intentions, which is housed in an old-fashioned train station, a replica of Wiggins's earthly train station, where he served as stationmaster.

As for my swift arrival upon receipt of the telegram: There are no barriers in Heaven. From there to here is as quick as a thought. Have a yen for a swoop down a snowy mountain? Even better than Vail and no smashups. Or perhaps your taste runs to bird-watching.

All God's creatures have their place. Yes, all those companions we cherished through the years, tabby cats and Labs for us, are here, as loving as the day they departed earth. Sometimes, if you feel that you have a glimpse of Heaven when you see an eagle on the wing or the ineffable grace of a prowling panther or a swirl of monarch butterflies, you are quite right. All the beauty on earth that makes your breath catch and eyes mist is only a foretaste of Heavenly extravagance with color and motion and being. Just this morning I saw an Eastern Rosella, gloriously red and white and gold with touches of green and blue. Look them up the next time you're in Australia.

I paused to admire Wiggins's redbrick country station with its wooden platform. Shining silver tracks stretched into the sky. Immediately I was eager to swing aboard the Rescue Express, the train Wiggins dispatches to earth with emissaries to help those in trouble.

I paused near a crystal arch outside the station to gather my thoughts and consider my appearance. The telegram—I fished it from my pocket—seemed somewhat overwrought for steady, resolute Wiggins. I read it again: *Bailey Ruth, Dastardly deeds in Adelaide. Come at once. Posthaste.* Wiggins urged quiet, behind-the-scenes action by the department's emissaries. After returning from my last jaunt to earth, he had said rather plaintively, "Becoming visible always leads to complications." Yet surely my summons meant he appreciated my willingness to assess a situation and do what needed to be done, even if I broke a few rules along the way.

Wiggins is devoted to rules, i.e., the Precepts for Earthly Visitation. I know them now by heart and have no need to carry with me a roll of yellowed parchment with elegant inscriptions. I can recite the Precepts quickly if asked.

4

I cleared my throat, took a deep breath. I spoke clearly. With resonance. Any former English teacher can always be heard from the last row.

PRECEPTS FOR EARTHLY VISITATION

1. *Avoid public notice.*
2. *Do not consort with other departed spirits.*
3. *Work behind the scenes without making your presence known.*
4. *Become visible only when absolutely necessary.*
5. *Do not succumb to the temptation to confound those who appear to oppose you.*
6. *Make every effort not to alarm earthly creatures.*
7. *Information about Heaven is not yours to impart. Simply smile and say, "Time will tell."*
8. *Remember always that you are* on *the earth, not* of *the earth.*

A prefect rendition, if I did think so myself. If I had a moment, I would no doubt delight Wiggins by enunciating each and every Precept. The Precepts were now ingrained in my inner being. That is possibly an exaggeration. Truth to tell, and that is a Heavenly requirement, I often fail to adhere to the Precepts, which makes Wiggins doubt that I am qualified to be a Heavenly emissary. I know Wiggins never questions my intentions. As he's often told me, "Bailey Ruth, you mean well, but . . ."

I hoped he understood that I not only had the best of intentions, I was admirably serious and devout.

Scratch the last.

I can't claim saintliness.

Didn't that better equip me to help those still on earth? Level playing field and all that, one imperfect being aiding another. Though of course, once in Heaven . . . Ah, but I mustn't violate Precept Seven. I offer my fragmentary descriptions of Heaven only to establish my identity.

In a moment of self-appraisal, I also scratched *serious.* Unless we were speaking of having a seriously good time. All right, I couldn't present myself as serious or devout, but I could always cling to good intentions. With that reassurance, I was ready to pop inside the station; then I paused.

Wiggins was not au courant with fashion. I considered my attire, a fetching white linen suit with faint narrow charcoal pinstripes. White is always flattering to redheads. Had I mentioned that I have flaming red hair, curious green eyes, and a spattering of freckles on my face? My age? Well, let's say I was on the shady side of fifty when the *Serendipity* went down, but in Heaven you are what you want to be. Twenty-seven was a very happy year for me, so that's the Bailey Ruth you see. However, perhaps my white suit and white strap sandals were too stylish. I wasn't as fine as an Eastern Rosella but satisfactory, assuredly satisfactory.

I glanced at my reflection in the crystal.

Flamboyant?

I do not, Heaven forbid, spend time dwelling on how I look.

Well, not much time.

Perhaps I should appear a trifle dowdy when I met with Wiggins, as a counterbalance to shiny flyaway red curls and bright green eyes and bubbly effervescence. I can be restrained. Yes, I can.

As for my costume, I'm afraid Wiggins sees pleasure in gorgeous clothing as evidence of intrinsic frivolity. What is life without an appreciation of beauty?

This was not the moment to reinforce his view of me as well-meaning but prone to flouting regulations with wholesale abandon, not with a telegram clutched in my hand. I sighed as my reflection in the crystal swirled from loose red tresses—think Maureen O'Hara—and crisp linen suit to hair drawn back severely in a knot, an undistinguished tan blouse, and, painful though it was, brown twill trousers. I gritted my teeth, added brown ankle boots. I was suffused with a sense of nobility at my sacrifice for the cause.

I hurried toward the station steps, remembering my shy arrival when I'd first come to the Department of Good Intentions to volunteer. At least now I knew I was welcome. A tiny doubt flowered. Wiggins was a welcoming man, but that last adventure—well, surely he knew I'd done the best I could despite huge challenges. It wasn't my fault that I appeared, and there I was, unable to disappear. But that's another story.

I was reassured when Wiggins burst through the open doorway. The lack of doors is another lovely aspect of Heaven. All may enter and depart without hindrance.

I beamed at him. "Wiggins, I came at once."

Wiggins looked just as I'd seen him on my initial visit to the Department of Good Intentions—thick, curly reddish brown hair; genial, broad face beneath a green eyeshade; robust walrus mustache; stiffly starched white shirt with sleeves puffed from black arm garters; heavy black woolen trousers held up by wide suspenders in addition to a broad leather belt; high-top black leather shoes buffed to a gleaming shine.

His first words destroyed any illusion of Wiggins as usual. "Bailey Ruth"—his voice was near despair, his spaniel-sweet brown eyes beseeching—"you're living proof that appearances can be deceiving."

I stared in surprise. Had my brown wren ensemble shocked him? Did he instead prefer the more au naturel Bailey Ruth, red curls bouncy, new fashions on display? Happily, I swirled back into my white linen suit with the faint charcoal gray stripes that added cosmopolitan flair and the cunning white sandals. I fluffed my liberated hair.

He stared in return, but I realized he didn't see me. His eyes looked through me. There was anguish in their brown depths.

I came nearer, touched his arm. My fingers traced through the ethereal Wiggins, yet I sensed a spirit tensed against pain. "Tell me, Wiggins."

"I shall. I must." He inclined his head, then, ever the gentleman, stood aside for me to precede him. I led the way to his office. I waited until he settled behind his golden oak desk in a bay window that afforded an excellent view of the waiting room and the station platform and silver tracks winding away into the sky.

He clasped his strong hands together. Words came in disjointed bursts. ". . . disgracing her name . . . can't abide this . . . although I shouldn't intervene . . . her choice not to come yet . . . thought she wanted to stay near Charles . . . but he's here now. . . ." He looked perplexed, then said firmly, "Of course, there's no time in Heaven. Passage of earthly time is of no importance. Except, of course"—his tone was kind—"to those on earth. I understood she wasn't ready to come for some reason." He tugged at one side of his walrus mustache. "She's brought much happiness these past years. To see the legend of the Rose Lady forever linked to ugliness would break my heart. I know no one can—or should—believe her spirit is behind the occurrences this week, but there is a deliberate effort to connect Lorraine's roses with vandalism and theft. Yet how can I justify a mission to protect her reputation when there are many people in truly dire straits?" He was clearly in misery.

To say I was bewildered put it mildly, though clearly Wiggins was despondent because someone he cared about was in a pickle. I grappled with the fact that time seemed paramount to him. "No time in Heaven. Certainly not, Wiggins." I made a huge effort to appear comfortably knowledgeable. Of course there was no time in Heaven. Everyone knew that. Right, and maybe everyone but me understood the concept. In my defense, I never understood how those little pictures got in our TV set when I was on earth. I turned on the TV and there was Lucy. Click a switch and the lightbulb burned. These things happened. Did I need to understand the physics of the phenomena? I am similarly ill equipped to explain the relationship between Heaven and Time. However, the matter seemed of great import to Wiggins. I made soothing noises. "Certainly, Wiggins. Absolutely understandable. No time in Heaven. Absolutely not."

His glance was pathetically grateful. "You grasp the point. There are those who are drawn to remain and do good. But now . . ." His golden brown eyes filled with dismay. His mustache quivered. "Surely she will see that she must finally depart earth. I can't approach her directly. I wish I could." The yearning in his voice touched me. "To speak with her . . . But that would never do. What I need is tact. Empathy. Behind-the-scenes"—sharp emphasis—"exploration to discover the miscreant, bring an end to this dreadful exploitation of her good name."

Behind the scenes. I was hearty, as if there could be no doubt that I, of all emissaries, would remain behind the scenes. Wiggins has a horror of his emissaries appearing on earth. Regrettably, in the past, I sometimes felt forced to appear. "You can count on me. Behind the scenes." I admired my resolute tone.

It would be nice to say my words reassured him. Nice, but inaccurate. In fact, he sighed.

"Wiggins, I always try to do the right thing." I might have sounded a little defensive.

He looked stressed. "If it weren't Adelaide, I wouldn't have summoned you."

Adelaide was my home when I was alive, a lovely small town in the rolling hill country of south-central Oklahoma. Although there is no time in Heaven, I'd been pleased on my return visits there to see what the passage of earthly time had wrought in Adelaide in the years since the *Serendipity* went down. Adelaide was prosperous, growing, vibrant, thanks in large part to the accomplishments of the Chickasaw Nation.

I'd now completed four successful adventures in Adelaide on behalf of the department. Scratch that. Four missions. Wiggins abhors the idea of ghosts having adventures. Oh, there I go again. He also abhors the use of the term *ghost*. He equates the noun with the popular picture of ghosts as scary creatures rattling chains. Why chains, I wonder? In any event, I don't see that saying *tomahto* makes the fruit any different than *tomayto*. Emissaries are invisible visitants (except when circumstances arise, as I have indicated) from Heaven to earth. If that doesn't mean ghosts, I wasn't standing here in a white linen suit with a delicate gray stripe. As for his stricture against equating a mission with adventure, I firmly believe adventures are good for the spirit. Especially mine.

"Adelaide." I beamed at him. "Wiggins, you know I can help."

Dot. Dot. Dot.

True to the early nineteen hundreds, the latest intelligence reaches Wiggins via Teletype.

Dot. Dot. Dot.

He whirled at the urgent sound and rushed to the telegraph key fastened to the right side of his desk. A sounder amplified the incoming messages.

Wiggins dropped into his chair, made rapid notes, his face creased in concentration. Once he drew a sharp breath. The clacks ended. He swung in his chair to me. "You know Adelaide. You could help her." But he sounded anguished. Clearly he was conflicted. "Precept Two. I have always insisted that Precept Two be observed."

Dot. Dot. Dot.

"Oh, Heavens." Wiggins took a deep breath and gazed at me with a mixture of hope and shamefacedness.

Shamefacedness? Wiggins? Whatever could be upsetting him? I hastened to help. "Precept Two," I repeated firmly. I knew the Precept, of course: "No consorting with other departed spirits." "Wiggins, don't worry. That's the last thing I'd do." I hoped, of course, he was too distracted to remember that was exactly what I'd done on my last visit to Adelaide.

Wiggins didn't appear consoled. If possible, his expression grew even more doleful. "Right." His tone was hollow. "Absolutely. Definitely, you must observe Precept Two." He appeared completely demoralized.

Clack. Clack. Clack.

He gave the sounder a desperate look, bounded to his feet, and dashed to the ticket box. He pulled down a bright red ticket, stamped the back, and thrust the ticket toward me. "Go. Try. Do what you can. She—oh, Bailey Ruth, she needs help."

She? In the past, when Wiggins briefed me on a mission, he explained who I was to help. Last time was an exception, of course. But now as I grabbed my ticket, I knew only that *she* was in trouble. There was no time for more, because the rumble of iron wheels on the silver track was deafening.

I rushed out to the platform as the Rescue Express thundered on the rails. The train paused long enough for me to swing aboard a passenger car. I stood in the vestibule, held tight to a hand bar, and leaned out as the Express picked up speed.

Wiggins's frantic shout followed me. "Dark dealings being blamed on her. Her portrait . . ." His words were lost in the rumble of the clacking wheels.

Chapter 2

I stood in darkness on a wide central landing of wooden stairs. To my right and left, flights led from the landing to the next floor. Golden-globe wall sconces shone at the top of the upper stairways and at the bottom of the central steps. I sensed without seeing much of my surroundings that I was in an old building. Years of use had hollowed the wooden treads. The wooden railings were ornately carved. Should I go up? Left or right? Or possibly down? Wiggins had sent me in such a rush. . . .

Brisk footsteps sounded below.

I looked over the handrail.

A flashlight bobbed. I dimly saw a stocky shape behind the beam. There was no attempt at concealment. Footsteps thumped loudly on the wooden treads.

I was careful to stay out of the way when he reached the central landing. It startles earthly creatures if they bump into an emissary. The concept of an invisible entity with substance may be as puzzling to the reader as my difficulty with time and Heaven. Take my advice—don't trouble yourself trying to understand the inexplicable.

The newcomer stopped on the landing. His arm swung up and the flashlight beam illuminated a portrait in a fine gilt frame. "No problems tonight, Miz Lorraine." There was a defensive edge to the gruff tone, as if he were making an apology of some sort. "I do my best. I can't be here and there and everywhere at the same time. I'm sorry as can be I mentioned you to that student reporter. But when there were roses everywhere, I thought maybe you were doing something special. Everybody on campus knows you loved giving out roses. I'm sick about those headlines in the student newspaper—"

I recognized both the portrait and the name. The beautiful woman in the portrait with sleek blonde hair and gray blue eyes was Lorraine Marlow, and she had been dead long before the *Serendipity* went down in the Gulf. I'd often admired this regal portrait on the landing of the central staircase in the college library. I felt a prickle of unease. The man with the flashlight addressed the portrait in a familiar way. I was sure this was not the first time he'd spoken to her.

"—and I'll keep looking every night 'til I find out who's behind the trouble. I shouldn't have shot my mouth off to that reporter. I wish I'd never talked to him. I thought Joe Cooper was a good man, been to Afghanistan and come home to go to school and make something of himself. But he's disappointed me."

My eyes had adjusted to the dark. The speaker was bear-shaped in a dark cotton jacket, dark trousers, and work boots. The left sleeve of the jacket was pinned to the shoulder. I wondered how he had lost that arm. He moved uncomfortably from one foot to another. "Miz Lorraine, I'm doing my best to get to the bottom of it, but there's so many ways in and out of the library. If only I hadn't talked about you. I can't believe what he wrote. I'm going to tell him what I think about him."

"Everything will work out. Joe's a nice young man." The voice was high and clear with a bell-like tone, a kind voice, yet definitely that of a woman accustomed to deference.

I looked wildly about. But there was only the man with the flashlight looking up at the portrait.

"Miz Lorraine, did you see what he wrote? About the rose in his office?"

"I did leave that particular rose." The light musical voice sounded happy. "I'm glad. I was there when he talked to that young woman. They are meant for each other. But like so many of the young, they think careers are more important. But I had nothing to do with the other roses."

I looked up at the portrait, managed a silent swallow. I had no doubt the woman's voice belonged to Lorraine Marlow, who had been dead for many years.

"He didn't deserve a rose." The deeper voice was resentful, angry. "Not when he's acted the way he has, writing you up in the same way he wrote up the gargoyle and that book."

"Dear Ben." There was laughter and affection in her voice. "Everyone deserves a rose. Love is all that matters. Anyway, none of this is your fault."

I scarcely breathed as I listened. The beautiful high voice, full of light and grace and kindness, was encouraging. Nonetheless, I was listening to a disembodied voice with no visible speaker and I knew without doubt I was at the right place at the right time. I had found Wiggins's damsel in distress.

In my excitement, I blurted out, "You must be *she*!"

Wiggins was upset because *she* was in trouble. He'd let slip that he'd always paid particular attention to Adelaide. Because of Lorraine Marlow? How could he have known her?

I reached out, touched the edge of the portrait frame. "Lorraine, can you tell me—"

"Who's there?" His flashlight beam flipped up the stairs, down, over the railing to the dark rotunda below. "Nobody there. Must be upstairs." He clattered up the steps, shouting, "Stop! Whoever you are. Trespassing. Stop." Obviously Ben hadn't confused my lower husky voice with Lorraine's, and he was in full pursuit of an unseen interloper.

Now the portrait was in darkness, but I remembered Lorraine Marlow's long, delicate face framed by soft golden hair, her smooth forehead, aristocratic nose, high cheekbones, and delicately pointed chin. There was an elfin quality to her beauty, a haunting sense of gentleness and kindness lost too soon. Her widowed husband endowed the library with much of his fortune after her early death, and the portrait was hung in her memory. At his death, Rose Bower, their fabulous estate that adjoined the far side of the campus, was left to Goddard College and became the site of the college's most elegant parties and receptions and served as well as guest quarters for distinguished visitors.

Thoughts tumbled in my mind. Wiggins's summons. His distress. Precept Two. My bewilderment when my promise to strictly adhere to Precept Two—"No consorting with other departed spirits"—made Wiggins even more miserable. *Dastardly deeds in Adelaide.* Well, why didn't he just tell me I was supposed to help Lorraine Marlow and to heck with Precept Two?

Ben was too far away to hear me, but I kept my voice low. "Wiggins sent me."

Silence.

Words are not always necessary. Emotions communicate without a whisper of sound. I knew Lorraine Marlow listened, breath held, amazed, surprised, shocked. Wiggins meant something to her. Yet I felt resistance. It was as if a door had closed solidly, firmly.

I plowed ahead. It always amazes me how often everything could be made right if people spoke honestly. However, no one has ever accused me of pussyfooting around. "I'm Bailey Ruth Raeburn. I grew up in Adelaide." I was trying to remember some of her history. I thought she had come to Adelaide after she married Charles Marlow.

No response. The only sounds were slamming doors on the second floor and Ben's gruff shouts. The silence on the landing was sentient, wary.

Was there sadness in her silence? Or dismay? Or fear?

I said gently, "How did you know Wiggins?"

A quick intake of breath.

Train travel dominated the country in the late 1800s and early 1900s. Women in long skirts alighted from carriages to enter bustling stations, accompanied by hatted men in dark suits. Wiggins was a product of his times in a stiff white shirt, suspenders, black woolen trousers, and high-topped black shoes. I knew him in his Heavenly station. I didn't know anything about his life on earth except that he had loved being a stationmaster. "Wiggins has a train station in Heaven. He sends emissaries to earth on the Rescue Express to help people in trouble."

"Ooh." Her voice was soft. "How like Paul. He loved his station. He planned to go back—" She broke off.

Paul? Go back? Lorraine and I both were making discoveries. Wiggins's first name was Paul. She hadn't known him as a stationmaster. "When did you know"—I paused. I scarcely felt it proper to call Wiggins by his first name—"him?"

"Paul sent you here?" There was a wondering tone in the light, high voice.

"I just arrived." I put two and two together. "Wiggins wants you to come to Heaven."

Abruptly, the silence was empty. I was alone on the landing. The portrait was only a picture.

Heavy steps announced the watchman's return. He was a little breathless from his exertions. He lifted the flashlight, and the lovely portrait was again revealed. "I didn't find anyone. I don't know about that voice. Maybe it was the wind and I got it mixed up in my mind. Sorry if I worried you, Miz Lorraine. I guess everything's okay tonight. But something happened three nights in a row. Why not tonight? Maybe"—hope lifted his voice—"I got 'em too scared to come back." A pause. "Whoever's coming knows all about the library and when I make my rounds and, like I said, I can't be everywhere at once. I'm going to mix things up the next few days, spring some surprises. Now"—he tucked the flashlight under his arm, touched his cap with two fingers in a respectful salute—"you rest easy. I'll see to everything."

He turned and stumped down the steps, flashlight beam flicking from side to side.

I was sure I'd know if Lorraine Marlow heard him. I had no sense of her presence. I was a bit miffed at Lorraine's recalcitrance. She needn't think she was going to keep me from my appointed task. I was here to help her and, by golly, she was going to be helped. Obviously she felt it wasn't any of my business how she'd known Wiggins. I'd counted on her to explain why Wiggins was so upset, but I was sure I could find out on my own.

I flowed alongside Ben as he swung his flashlight beam between bookcases. He checked the main stacks, painstakingly opened the doors to the large reading rooms, made sure no one was there, even took time to peek into darkened individual carrels. The clock in the library tower struck eleven as we came out the main door and started down wide marble steps.

Occasional lampposts, all gleaming a soft gold, were placed every twenty-five yards along the main walk. Ben made a circuit of the library, flashing his light into shrubbery, then up to illuminate arched windows. The gothic redbrick building was topped with a crenelated parapet. He thudded down short steps to check a basement door, swept the beam of his flashlight along a wide loading dock. Finally, apparently confident that everything was secure, he left the sidewalk and took a path that angled through a grove of trees to a nondescript one-story brick building.

The light above the entrance revealed the legend on a frosted front door panel: *Campus Security.* He entered, lifted a hand in greeting to a young man lounging behind a counter.

"Yo, Ben. All quiet tonight?"

"All secure." Ben stepped to a side table, punched a time clock.

"Okay. Woody's already out in the car. We told him to keep a special watch on the library. Not that any of us can do much about a ghost." The man behind the counter picked up a magazine with a cover that I thought Wiggins would find shocking.

Ben bellowed, "Blaming Lorraine Marlow's a crock!" The cords in his neck tightened and his burly shoulders bunched.

The magazine lowered. "Hey, cool off, man."

Ben shook his head and pushed through the door. Out in the night, Ben turned to his left, followed a sidewalk behind the building to a parking lot.

I rode in the passenger seat of his pickup. He drove through sleepy residential streets to a modest neighborhood with one-story bungalow-type homes. I noted the street name. He turned into a graveled drive. He swung heavily from the cab and walked slowly, obviously a weary man, to the front porch.

I didn't follow him. The address was 522 Willow Street. I now knew enough to find out a great deal more about him.

Chapter 3

My first stop was the college's main administration building. Locked doors, of course, posed no obstacle. I dropped into an office and found a campus directory. I perched on the edge of a desk and made a phone call.

"Campus Security." The male voice was alert. It was late to be calling—the round clock on the wall showed twelve minutes after eleven—so I made my voice calm and cheerful. "Sorry to bother you, but I just got off work and wanted to call and leave a thank-you for that nice security officer at the library. I think his name is Ben . . ." I paused expectantly.

"Yes, ma'am. Ben Douglas."

I burbled on. "He found my billfold. I lost it in the parking lot, and he was kind enough to bring it to me. Please tell him"—I hesitated for only an instant—"that Theresa Lisieux sends him her thanks." It was necessary to give a name, and I decided to honor Saint Thérèse of Lisieux, who was always cheerful and happy to be of service no matter how menial the task. In case Wiggins was listening, this clearly indicated that my mind and heart were in the right place. I hung up.

The personnel files were in a chilly room connected to the Human Resources office on the second floor. Four rows of metal filing cabinets looked daunting. I turned on the lights, humming as I figured out the filing system. I was pleased that paper files existed. No doubt the files were also available digitally. I was no expert, but it appeared to me that current earthly residents take unseemly pride in how *everything* is online yet continue to create reams of paper that fill filing cabinets in every office.

I carried Ben Douglas's slim file to a worktable. I verified his address on Willow Street. I read swiftly. Native of Adelaide. Sixty-eight years old. Graduate of Adelaide High School. Entered the Army as a private. Stationed in Da Nang in Vietnam. Lost an arm in a firefight with the Vietcong. Returned to Adelaide. Entered Goddard College. Degree in business. Worked as an insurance claims adjustor. Widower. Retired three years ago, hired as a part-time security guard.

I was walking toward the cabinet to return the folder when a deep voice shouted, "Hands up. Security. Hands up."

Startled, I looked around.

A burly young man with a heavy build and a slender brunette, both in Campus Security uniforms, stood just inside the door, walkie-talkies in one hand, the others near holstered guns. They stood frozen, staring at the folder suspended waist-high in the air.

"Oh my goodness." I looked down at the folder in my hand. I, of course, wasn't visible, so the folder appeared to be stationary some four feet from the floor. I hoped Wiggins would understand that I was between the devil and the deep blue sea. I let go of the folder.

Two sets of eyes followed the green folder's plunge downward. The folder landed with a light splat, opening to let the contents escape.

"That folder. How'd it do that?" The man's voice was perhaps a bit higher in register than normal.

"I don't know." The young woman's voice was a little uneven. "I guess some woman's in here and was holding it and somehow we didn't see her. A woman's voice said, 'Oh my goodness.' She has to be here. Nobody went past us. Hey, Al, you look up and down the rows of cabinets. She's either hiding somewhere or she'll have to come this way." She placed her hand on her holster. "We'll take her into custody. She's trespassing and mucking around with files. I'll be here at the door. No way she can get out."

He nodded and moved fast, his footsteps thudding on the tile floor. It took no more than a minute, and he was back, big face creased in a frown. "Nobody there."

"We heard a woman's voice. Right?" There was a pugnacious edge to her voice.

"Yeah."

"Louis said a woman called from HR." She jerked her head toward the adjoining office. "We came through the door and that folder was in the air and some woman said, 'Oh my goodness.' "

I was mortified. I should have remembered caller ID. My jolly phone call came from a building closed and locked for the night.

"No woman in here." He took a deep breath. "Hey, Betty, what about that folder? It was hanging in the air."

She flicked a glance at the folder, agape on the tiled floor. "Somebody must have left the folder out. Maybe it was on top of a cabinet and something made it fall down." She looked uneasily at the shadowy rows between the cabinets.

"Yeah." He was hearty. "Air current or something. Everything looks all right."

From the way his eyes darted around the room, paused at every shadowy corner, I was reminded of a favorite cartoon. A rangy black cat stared fixedly at a shadowy corner while his owner looked at him uneasily. The caption read: "I'd tell you what I see but it would scare you silly."

The young woman raised a dark eyebrow. "Nobody here but us."

His face squeezed in thought. "Why was the light on?"

She shrugged. "Somebody forgot it."

He thought for a moment. "Nah. Rusty patrols by here on foot. He would've seen the light in the windows, checked it out. Besides, where's the woman who called from here?"

"Somebody was working late."

"Louis checked the name. Nobody named Luhsoo on the staff."

I smothered a laugh.

They both stiffened.

Honestly, what happened next wasn't my fault.

A hand gripped my arm.

Anyone would be startled. "Eeek." I'll admit my voice rose to a squeal.

Al jumped, then swung toward her, glowering. "That's not funny, Betty."

She glared at him. "I didn't make that noise."

"Who the hell squeaked then? A leprechaun?" Heavy irony.

Now it was Wiggins whose sharply indrawn breath could be heard. Hell should not be lightly invoked.

Eyes wide, the security officers looked at each other, turned, ran.

The sound of their running steps faded.

"I would remonstrate." Wiggins's normally cheerful voice was lugubrious. "Precepts One, Three, and Six. However, I made matters worse."

I was stricken with remorse. Dear Wiggins. Always so serious, so well-meaning, so by the book. I broke into a refrain of "Look for the Silver Lining." I loved Judy Garland's version, but my own soprano wasn't half bad. I added a little soft shoe, and the slight shushing sounds added cheer to the surroundings. I hoped. "It's nice to see young people who can move so quickly."

A reluctant chuckle. "Did anyone ever tell you that you are irrepressible?"

"A few times." I kept my tone modest.

Wiggins cleared his throat. "However, it appears this venture is ill-starred. I should not have sent—"

I felt a wave of panic. Did I hear the faint whistle of the Rescue Express? Was I to be yanked off the earth without achieving anything? "Wiggins"—now I was serious—"I must stay. Lorraine needs me."

I sensed an abrupt change in his attitude. Normally confident Wiggins was embarrassed, uncertain.

"I put my own feelings before my duty to the department." His voice was woeful. "Since there isn't any time in Heaven—"

There he went again. For some reason, the concept reassured him.

"—I thought if she stayed and brought happiness . . . well, the world needs happiness, don't you agree?"

Just for an instant I felt the weight of earth's sorrow and anger and despair. "Dear Heaven, yes." The oppressive pressure lifted. "Of course I agree. Happiness matters."

"I always thought so." His tone was plaintive.

"I talked to Lorraine tonight." Without a word from him, I knew Wiggins was listening with every fiber of his being. I smiled. "Lorraine has a lovely voice. She spoke of you."

Lightness and happiness flowed around me in warming waves.

Oh, Wiggins, I understand. Love knows no barriers, not time nor space nor distance nor life nor death.

"She was always kind and good." His deep voice was soft. "She wanted love to flower whenever it could. But during the last few days, peculiar things have happened at the library, and some people—the credulous ones—are saying it must be a ghost, that the Rose Lady has turned mean. I know those with intelligence would not seriously cast blame for odd incidents on a ghost." From his tone, you would have thought such creatures nonexistent. "But there are those who believe the moon landing was a hoax and unicorns inhabit forests. I didn't want dark deeds associated with Lorraine. I wanted to restore her good name." A weary sigh. "But the department has to focus on truly evil acts. That was my mistake."

"Wiggins"—I picked my words carefully—"Heaven teaches us to listen to our hearts. What does your heart tell you?"

"My heart?"

I could scarcely hear the words.

"My heart?" The tone was louder, stronger. "My heart tells me she deserves to be protected. She is the kindest, most beautiful, gentlest creature I've ever known. Lorraine was never selfish or cold or heartless. Yet that is how she will now be remembered by some because of those stories in the student newspaper. I hope she will come home to Heaven, but her spirit will be forever forlorn if she is blamed——"

Running steps sounded in the hallway.

The whistle of the Rescue Express rose in a mournful wail.

"Let me stay, Wiggins. I will prove Lorraine is innocent." Brave words, since I had no clue what dastardly deeds were being attributed to her, but I was intent upon avoiding a swift return on the Express.

"Can you? Will you?" His voice was fading.

The scent of coal smoke lessened, disappeared. The distant clack of wheels indicated I had managed a reprieve.

A covey of security officers burst into the file room.

The rumble of the Rescue Express was scarcely audible, and then the sound was gone. I was still here. Saving a ghost's good name would be a first for me. It seemed odd that Lorraine fled from me. Perhaps I could gain her confidence when she realized I was her champion. Now I must find out what kind of troubles were being blamed on her.

The security officers had left the lights on in the HR office. As they thudded up and down among rows of filing cabinets in the adjoining room, I flipped through a campus directory, found the location of the student newspaper office, blew the officers an unseen kiss, and departed.

∽

The Communications Department was housed in an old frame building atop the highest hill on campus. I landed in the newsroom and smiled, remembering the building's history. Built in the early 1900s, the shabby edifice called Old Ethel had originally been a boarding house, though it was well known that boarders simply came for the night and the owner was a madam named Ethel. After a raid, Ethel left town and the building was unused for years. The college purchased the boarding house and land in the 1930s. The rambling building served as a residence hall until the 1960s, when the Journalism Department took it over. The lower floor housed the *Bugle*. Efforts to change the building's name met stiff resistance from journalism students who delighted in the ramshackle house's bawdy history. The newsroom featured a mural of a buxom woman in a low-cut cardinal red gown. Reporters called her Ethel and included her in ribald exchanges.

Computer monitors glowed eerily in the darkened newsroom. I supposed the terminals required passwords. If need be I could return tomorrow, hover over a reporter's shoulder, and discover a password, but I wanted information now. I also hoped to learn about Joe Cooper, the *Bugle* editor whose actions disappointed the night watchman. I wandered to the end of the newsroom. Enough light slanted through a nearby window to illuminate worn letters on the door to a small office: *Bugle Editor.*

I turned the knob and stepped inside, closing the door behind me. My eyes adjusted to dimness. Though the room was shadowy, I saw a goosenecked desk light on a desk. I started across the small room, stumbled over something lumpy on the floor, recovered my balance, and moved to the desk. Remembering the near hysteria that lighted windows appeared to evoke on the campus, I punched the button at the lamp's base and turned the flexible shaft to focus the beam on a highly untidy desk.

"What a mess." I began to root about. Almost immediately I uncovered a desk nameplate: *Joe Cooper.* I moved papers and uncovered a stack of tabloid-sized *Bugle*s. I picked up several, moved nearer the light, and—

"Okay." The voice was male, a male striving for bluster. "I had two drinks. That was all. Two drinks. Okay, scotch on the rocks, but I'm a big, strapping guy."

I looked across the desk into a shadowy corner of the office. A young man in wrinkled clothes stood by a rumpled sleeping bag.

He rubbed his eyes with balled-up fists, then stared at me. "I'm a big guy. I can handle two drinks. That's why I know I didn't turn on the light. That's why I know I don't see anybody anywhere, even if I heard a woman's voice. That's why I know I'm not slopping through the stuff on my desk. It doesn't tell me why *Bugle*s are hovering above my desk. Hovering *Bugle*s has to be a figment of my imagination. I sound like an English major. But that's what it has to be, a figment." He lunged toward the desk, big hand outstretched.

I zoomed up. Now the papers and I were near the ceiling.

Joe Cooper was a little over six feet tall, husky. His dark hair was mussed, he needed a shave, he had a nose that probably got busted in a football game, his gray sweatshirt had a hole in one sleeve, his Levi's were pale with age, his sneakers grimy and worn. But he looked smart, tough, and utterly determined to grab the papers.

He stumbled into the desk, looked up, clamped his hands to his temples. "Nightmare. I'm having a nightmare. Hovering *Bugle*s. I've been working too hard. I'll go back to my beddy-bye. Such as it is. No wonder I'm having bad dreams. I get stood up last night, tonight my roomie boots me so he can woo his girl, I sack out on my bedroll in the corner of my office and think lousy thoughts about a girl with big dark eyes who acted happy as a mouse in a cheese barrel when I ask her to meet me, maybe get a scoop on gossip at the library, but she never shows." He stood big as a fullback, shoulders hunched, and glared up at the papers. "I'm stupid to still be thinking about her. Hell, Wednesday night's history. She's history. Why should I be mooning around about her tonight?"

He stood between me and the door to the newsroom. If I swooped down to leave, he would grab the papers and probably, from the sound of his voice, crumple them in those big hands.

I was beginning to agree with Wiggins. Maybe this was an ill-starred venture. Immediately, I was stern with myself. That was a defeatist attitude. I was Bailey Ruth Raeburn and I could manage. I would manage.

Joe folded one big hand, gave himself a light punch in the jaw. "Ouch. Okay, I'm awake. Fact is fact. The papers are up there. Come on down, papers." His tone was coaxing. "Come down from the ceiling. This will be a little secret between you and me. Trust me, Ethel, I'll never tell anybody the *Bugle* levitates. You know what? I'll never make fun of anybody who claims Ethel made them do it. Never again."

I laughed. My son, Rob, majored in journalism and now has his own public relations firm. I remembered the insouciance and caustic humor of his friends, who would have delighted in citing Ethel as the source of any mishaps, major or minor.

The big guy stiffened. I might even say he looked haunted.

"Sorry, Joe." I truly was contrite.

His bony face squeezed in concentration.

"I'm not laughing at you. But no one's ever accused me of being a madam."

He looked up. He looked down. He looked left. He looked right. He whirled, peered through the door at the dark newsroom. "Okay, smart-ass. I've heard about ventriloquists. Come on out, wherever you are."

I eased toward the door. Maybe if I moved really fast.

His head whipped around. Perhaps he saw the movement of the papers in his peripheral vision.

I rose higher, papers firmly in hand.

He watched the papers with a peculiar expression. He blinked four times. "They're up there. They can't be up there. This is crazy. Maybe I'm crazy. Maybe I need to think things through. I'll work for a while, finish that feature about the dig on the Mackenzie ranch. Interesting. If you like bones. I got a feeling in my bones that something will break tomorrow on the funny business at the library. Maybe there'll be a body in the library. That'd top today's big news. The *Bugle* will be out right on schedule at two p.m. tomorrow. Even without a body, I'll have a lead story with an update on the investigation. Tomorrow is Friday. Yeah, I got everything straight—except for the papers up by the ceiling."

This was one of those moments that Wiggins simply hasn't encountered. It was time to invoke Precept Six: "Make every effort not to alarm earthly creatures." Even if I could evade Joe's outstretched hands and escape with the *Bugle*s, I shouldn't leave him bewildered and uneasy. I landed behind his desk and swirled into being. I hoped I appeared nonthreatening in a varicolored turtleneck, gray slacks, and gray alligator flats. The socks were in multicolored stripes for a gay note.

He took a deep breath. "Were you crouched behind the desk? Who the hell are you? How'd you make those papers stay up by the ceiling?" He slowly approached the desk, stepped into a circle of light.

I liked his face, long and bony with deep-set eyes, high cheekbones, that crooked nose, and a strong chin. He looked intelligent, abrasive, and alert despite uncombed thick curly black hair, eyes still blinking away sleep, and beard-stubbled cheeks.

"Ethel made me do it." I couldn't resist.

He looked startled, then he laughed. "Okay. Let's start over. I'm Joe Cooper." He held out a blunt-fingered hand.

I was wary, ready to dissolve and swoop away with my prizes, but I grasped his hand and we shook. "Theresa Lisieux." I anglicized Saint Thérèse's baptismal name. "I'm a visitor to Adelaide."

He made a gentlemanly gesture with his hand toward the ratty chair behind the desk. "Sit down and tell me about it."

I gave him what I hoped was a beguiling smile. "You're trained to ask questions and get the whole story. It will be easier on both of us if I keep it brief. I had no intention of causing you any distress tonight. My sole objective was to get copies of this week's *Bugle*. If I recall, the newspaper is free to students and visitors?"

He nodded.

"In that case, perhaps we can wish each other well, and I'll take the papers and go."

He folded his arms. "You got one thing right: I ask questions. Why didn't you drop by and ask for copies in the daytime?"

"I needed them tonight." This was going to be difficult. I tried for another smile, but his stare remained demanding. "I need to know about the odd episodes at the library."

"You got a big bet riding on the answers? I can give it to you quick: A resident spook has turned nasty. What's it to you?"

He spoke so derisively of spooks. . . .

This conversation wasn't productive. I had to distract him and make my escape. "That's very—" I broke off, widened my eyes, came to my feet. "Oh, there's someone out there."

He turned, yanked open the door, and charged into the newsroom. Lights flickered on, illuminating the area.

I disappeared. *Bugle*s in hand, I zoomed out of his office and sped across the newsroom near the ceiling.

Joe looked up and stopped, staring with an expression of utter shock.

I came down for an instant to open the door into the hall, heard his thudding feet. Encumbered by the *Bugle*s, I couldn't simply think where I wanted to go and be there immediately. The physical world can be rather constraining. I didn't want to struggle with the front door. Joe could easily reach me before I managed to open the door. I flowed up the staircase. Though it was dark, I saw the pale oblong of windows at the hall's end. At the windows, I moved quickly to unloose a latch. The window moved grudgingly, but it moved. I pushed it up, thankful for an old building with sash windows, and the *Bugle*s and I were off into the night. Joe Cooper would be bewildered when he found no one upstairs. He might be puzzled by the open window but would assume someone had left it open earlier. I tried not to think about his feelings in regard to airborne *Bugle*s. Perhaps he would decide he'd had a bad dream and avoid two drinks before bedtime in the future.

Now for a spot where I could read in peace and not disturb the occupants. I saw a glimmer of distant lights through the woods.

Of course! I should easily be able to settle into an empty cranny at Lorraine Marlow's old home.

Rose Bower was a showplace of Adelaide, a forty-room limestone mansion fashioned after the great houses of England in the mid-1700s. The estate was on the other side of woods that bordered Goddard College. Rose Bower included fifty acres of woodlands and extensive formal gardens. The great iron gates were closed and locked. Occasional lampposts scarcely penetrated the darkness. A large circular window with stained glass glowed above the arched entrance. How appropriate. Such windows in Gothic architecture are called rose windows.

After a quick look about, I placed my prized handful of *Bugle*s on the sill of a window to the right of the entrance. Once inside, I moved to the window. It was hermetically sealed and wouldn't budge.

Hoping the main door wasn't rigged with an alarm, I drew back the bolt and, after a quick breath, yanked it. The silence remained unbroken, and I breathed a sigh of relief. I stepped out, scooped up the *Bugle*s, and hurried inside. I locked the door.

A golden light from a hanging lamp illuminated stairs that curved from the entry lobby to the second floor. The lower floor was used for entertaining. The upstairs bedrooms were available for important university guests. The second-floor hall was illuminated with wall sconces. Each bedroom door contained a nameplate: *Red Room, Scholar's Room, Retreat Room* . . . Oh, I liked that one. I put the *Bugle*s on the hall floor, wafted inside, flicked on the light.

I don't know who had the greater shock, me upon perceiving

the sturdy lump beneath the bedspread or the occupant who moved uneasily then came bolt upright, staring up at the chandelier.

I turned off the light, regained the hall, and grabbed the *Bugle*s. I zoomed to the ceiling.

The door opened and light spilled into the corridor. A barefoot man in his fifties with a tangled mop of hair peered up and down the hall. Finally, he shrugged, gave a hitch to baggy tartan boxers, and turned into the room. Hopefully he was a visiting poet and would decide crossed wires accounted for the light.

The huge house remained utterly quiet. I didn't have a sense that Rose Bower was packed with guests, but obviously I had to be careful. Rather than blip into more rooms, I decided to depend upon instinct. I firmly believe the inner me is lucky.

I crossed the main hallway and peered at a nameplate: *Master Suite, Mr. and Mrs. Marlow.* A red-velvet swag hung between gold stanchions that stood on either side of the door, marking the suite off-limits. Certainly this wouldn't be occupied. I put the *Bugle*s right outside the door and flowed inside. It took only an instant to turn on the light, open the door, grab the papers, and shut the door.

Matching wing chairs faced a fireplace with incised wood carving and stucco relief that included matching Grecian urns and a garland of roses. Fluted Corinthian pillars framed another portrait of Lorraine, golden hair upswept, classic features in repose. Her loveliness had a remote quality. There was an aura of stateliness and dignity. Was there a hint of sadness in her gaze? A triple-strand pearl necklace matched the ivory of an elegant off-shoulder gown. Facing each other atop the mantel were two quite perfect Staffordshire figurines of dalmatians. I remembered now that two life-size marble dalmatians sat on either side of the drive.

A mahogany four-poster bed was on the far side of the spacious room. Lace flounces hung from the canopy and sides, curtaining the interior. The bed looked small compared to beds at the bed-and-breakfast where I'd stayed when last in Adelaide. The suite was large with a Victorian sofa, several Queen Anne–style chairs in a cream fabric with a vivid rose pattern, two mahogany chests, a dressing table, and a petit point–upholstered stool next to a harp. Whitmani ferns flourished in two blue ceramic vases. I supposed the staff kept ferns in the suite because Lorraine Marlow enjoyed ferns when she was alive.

I turned on a Tiffany lamp on the dressing table. The shade was gorgeous, with a gold and green pattern. I admired cut-glass perfume bottles that glittered like diamonds in the light. A hairbrush and hand mirror with ornate silver handles lay next to a pair of white gloves that looked as if they had been dropped there for only a moment. A hand-painted china tray continued the rose motif with huge blooms of many hues. The tray contained a china thimble, a book of Emily Dickinson poetry, and ticket stubs.

It was as if Lorraine Marlow had walked out of the room a short while ago and would soon return. Apparently Charles Marlow had kept his wife's personal items in place and nothing had been disturbed since her death. I picked up a crystal perfume bottle, lifted the stopper, and sniffed. Shalimar by Guerlain . . . Not that I ever used such expensive perfume, but on a visit to New York Bobby Mac and I had dropped into an exclusive perfume shop, and the scent was unforgettable.

I dabbed a bit behind each ear, gave a yawn, sniffed again before I stoppered the bottle. What a gala week Bobby Mac and I spent. We'd stayed at the Waldorf. I remembered the radiance of tulips when we'd walked hand in hand through Central Park. I smiled and swirled into being. On earth, I enjoy being *on* earth. The room was chilly enough that I chose a pink flannel nightgown. I put the *Bugle*s on the dressing table, looked into the mirror, and picked up the hairbrush. My curls were—

"Where did you come from?" Lorraine's light high voice inquired politely.

I dropped the hairbrush as though it were electrified.

"I knew you were here when the light came on and in a moment my perfume bottle rose in the air. It's a nice scent, isn't it?" The cultivated voice was quite pleasant.

I turned and looked toward the bed. The lace panels had been pulled back, revealing a folded-back sheet and coverlet though Lorraine wasn't visible. Obviously she had retired for the night. I'd made myself at home without a thought for her whereabouts. My face felt hot. She was, as Wiggins said, too gentle to censure me for intruding into her boudoir and pawing over her dressing table. I reached down to retrieve the brush and placed it on the dressing table.

"I don't mean to be inquisitive but tonight on the landing, when you spoke of Paul, I understood you are a spirit, just as I am. Yet now you are here. I see you." A pause, then, admiringly, "You have quite lovely red hair. But please, how can you be here?" The high voice was amazed.

"Haven't you ever appeared?" I was stunned. Half the pleasure of beautiful clothes is admiring them, and I felt sure that Lorraine had always enjoyed the finest apparel. "Oh my dear. You can appear. Picture yourself in your favorite dress."

"Picture myself . . ."

Colors moved and flowed, coalescing into a slender blonde in a padded-shoulder knee-length silk dress with a pattern of ivy against cream. A single strand of pearls graced her slender neck. Tall heels sported an ankle strap. She stood beside the four-poster bed, her lips curving in delight.

If she walked down a street in Adelaide, she would look as distant in time as a flapper in a dropped-waist layered dress.

Lorraine turned and looked into the mirror. Her eyes widened.

I moved to stand beside her. I felt at a disadvantage in a pink flannel nightgown. In an instant, I nodded in approval at my reflection in an A-line dress and sandals. The vibrant shade of aquamarine blue was just right for my complexion, freckles and all.

One thin blonde brow rose as Lorraine saw my image and noted the mid-thigh skirt length.

"Skirts are very short these days." I hoped I didn't sound defensive.

"Oh, I know." She hastened to be agreeable. "Though I have to confess I don't find today's styles appealing. Many women on the staff wear slacks. That was acceptable during the war, when women worked night and day in factories, but now everyone could wear skirts if they wished. As for coeds today . . ." A delicate shudder. She turned toward me, her blue eyes troubled and uncertain. "Why are you here?" There was the slightest emphasis on the noun and I thought I heard a tremor in her voice.

I tried for an appealing smile. "I wanted a place where I could read"—I picked up the slim stack of *Bugles*—"without being disturbed. I didn't know you were here."

"Where else would I go?" Her lovely voice was mournful.

I said gently, "When your work on earth is done . . ."

Her eyes, an arresting shade of blue tempered by gray, brimmed with tears. "I blamed myself."

I scarcely heard the soft words, freighted with sorrow.

"If I hadn't written him . . . I knew he'd understand . . . but I couldn't forgive myself when . . ." She bowed her head, pressed slender hands against her face. Finally, her hands dropped and she walked away from me, her shoulders tight. She stopped near an elegant cloisonné screen, orange and red and green and gold gemstones gleaming in an intricate pattern on porcelain against ornately carved wood.

I followed her. I didn't know why she grieved, what memories caused her anguish, held her to earth. Perhaps I could make her feel better, lift her sorrow. "Wiggins thinks you are wonderful, and he's dreadfully upset that someone is vandalizing the library and hiding behind your legend. I'm here to clear your name. I'll find out who's causing problems at the library. I won't bother you." I had a sudden sense that she felt hounded, and that was my fault. Everyone must have a private place, whether on earth or in Heaven. I'd come to Rose Bower hoping to learn more about Lorraine, but I hadn't intended to intrude where she felt safe.

She turned and gazed at me, her lovely face vulnerable. "He wants to help me?"

"Wiggins wants you to be happy. I promise." I held out my hand. "Friends?"

A slender hand gripped mine, the touch cool and gentle. "Of course I will be your friend. How like Paul to wish the best for me even though I broke his heart. But I can't bear remembering. . . . I've tried so hard not to bring back those days, but now it seems as though it were yesterday and my world turned dark and gray and empty." She withdrew her hand.

Colors dissolved. Lorraine was no longer visible.

"I'll leave." I knew as I spoke that she was no longer here. The room had an empty feel. Yet, just in case, I said quickly, "I won't bother you again." I had no sense she was there to hear me. I had so many questions I wanted to ask. How had she known Wiggins? What made her cry in remembering him? Why did she feel guilty? Why had she remained on earth all these years? And for now, what had happened at the library? Why was she considered the cause of these events? But clearly she didn't want to deal with me about either the past or the present.

Perhaps someday I might learn about Lorraine and Wiggins. For now, I must discover what had occurred at the library, see if I could restore luster to her memory. "I came looking for a place to stay. I'll go now."

I disappeared and once again had to deal with the *Bugle*s. I opened the door cautiously. I stepped into the empty hall, closed the door softly behind me. The *Bugle*s, of course, appeared to float serenely through the air. At the far end of the hall, I saw a nameplate: *Sanctuary*. I took that as an omen, placed the *Bugle*s on the floor, moved inside, made certain no guest was in residence, opened the door, and picked up the papers.

The beautifully appointed room might have been waiting for me. Perhaps it was. I was delighted by a four-poster with floral flounces and curtains at each corner that matched the drapes at the front windows. Violets and ivy, a lovely combination. I admired the lace spread and patted a downy pillow. I took the precaution of wedging a straight chair beneath the doorknob. Anyone trying to enter would alert me in time to remove evidence of my presence. I returned to my pink flannel gown and snuggled into the four-poster with the *Bugle*s.

Chapter 4

The *Bugle*, Page 3, Monday, October 14

History Senior Excited
by Hands-On Project

Bugle editor Joe Cooper

Chair of the History Department Dr. Malcolm Gordon announced Friday that Tulsa senior Michelle Hoyt will be the first student to base a senior paper on private journals.

Dr. Gordon hopes Hoyt will blaze a trail for future Goddard history majors in writing a paper based on original research of previously unexamined material.

In an interview Friday, Hoyt explained she will write a history illuminating the political impact of the late

Susannah Fairlee, a leading Adelaide citizen, based on Fairlee's diaries. Hoyt begins work on Friday.

"My overall objective is a complete exploration of the diaries," Hoyt said. "Mrs. Fairlee retired from the city council two years ago. She began keeping diaries when she was first elected to the council twenty-seven years ago. The diaries that cover her twenty-five years on the city council should provide insight into Adelaide history including bond issues, school expansion, and park development. I intend to scan the last two years, extract any meaningful political observations, and return those two volumes to her daughter, Janet Fairlee Hastings, who wants to keep them as mementos of her mother. I will then concentrate on the diaries that recount her activities on the council. The library will be the repository of the diaries that cover the twenty-five years of her government service."

The diaries were donated by Mrs. Hastings to Goddard Library. Hoyt's study is a cooperative effort between the library and the History Department.

Fairlee passed away September 17 at the age of seventy-three. She was a member of the city council for twenty-five years. Her civic accomplishments include serving as president of the Adelaide Friends of the Library, chairman of the United Way, and on the boards of the Girl Scouts, Habitat for Humanity, and the Adelaide Food Bank. She was active at St. Mildred's Episcopal Church as a Stephen Minister, part of an outreach program by lay persons to individuals who are ill or in trouble, and was a past directress of the Altar Guild.

In the senior paper, Hoyt intends to provide an overview of Adelaide history during Fairlee's lifetime that reflects Fairlee's influence upon Adelaide. Current city council member Ralph Linton said about Fairlee: "Susannah never hesitated to take action when she saw a problem. She established the food bank and often drove to groceries and restaurants seeking leftover foods."

Dr. Gordon described Mrs. Fairlee as a "larger than life" personality and believes that her diaries can provide insight into the power of a single citizen to affect policy.

Hoyt's long-range career aspirations include obtaining a master's degree in history and teaching while writing popular histories. Hoyt said, "David McCullough is my inspiration. Someday I want to write books that bring history alive as he has. This paper will give me a wonderful opportunity both as a historian and as a writer."

Dr. Gordon praised Hoyt's undergraduate work. "She is meticulous, insightful; the kind of student who makes teaching a joy. I foresee a wonderful future for her."

When not reading history, Hoyt relaxes by running 10Ks, reading Charlaine Harris and Harlan Coben, and piecing together intricate puzzles. Partially completed now is a puzzle of the Norman Rockwell March 1, 1941, *Saturday Evening Post* cover of a teenage girl in a sweater set, plaid skirt, bobby socks, and scuffed saddle oxfords. Hoyt said, "Norman Rockwell covers are snapshots in time, and that's how alive and real all history should be."

It didn't take great perception to perceive that *Bugle* Editor Joe Cooper would gladly share a library carrel—or any space—with Michelle Hoyt, preferably after hours. The accompanying photograph suggested why. Michelle was seated at a library table, her hand resting on a stack of red leather diaries. She wasn't conventionally pretty. There was too much character and force in her oval face. Bright dark eyes looked smart and challenging under a tangle of dark curls, but a surprisingly sweet smile suggested good humor and kindness. She didn't look like the kind of girl to stand up a guy with no word.

Now why . . . ? Oh, yes. Joe's lament as he tried to make sense of his night. Maybe she wasn't as nice as she looked. But I shouldn't waste time worrying about the love life of the *Bugle*'s unhappy editor. Obviously this feel-good story had nothing to do with the dark deeds that prompted Wiggins to send me here.

I picked up the Tuesday, October 15, *Bugle*.

Is Unidentified Cupid
Visiting Library?

Bugle editor Joe Cooper

Goddard Library staff and patrons this morning reported the unexplained appearance of single long-stem red roses on desks, in carrels, and among shelves.

Theories to account for the flowers range from a flower-shop promotion to student humor to an old campus legend about Lorraine Marlow, whose portrait hangs on the main landing at the library. The unexpected gift of roses to dating couples has long been attributed to Marlow, who is known as the library's resident ghost.

Annabelle Bailey, Tishomingo senior, found a rose in her carrel. "I was here when the library opened at seven and went straight to my carrel. I wanted to finish a paper due for my nine o'clock. This gorgeous rose, a cream bloom tipped with red, was resting right on top of my stuff. I thought"—Bailey looked regretful—"it was a present from my boyfriend, but when I called him, he said it wasn't from him, and then he got a little worried that some other guy was sending me flowers."

Research Librarian Reginald Vickers reached his office at eight and found several librarians near his desk. "They wanted to know if Thea—that's my wife—had sent me an early Valentine. I checked with Thea and she didn't know anything about the rose. She said"—Vickers said wryly—"if anybody was sending me a single red rose, she wanted to know the details, pronto. After roses were found all over the library, I called her back to reassure her that I didn't have a secret admirer. My guess is that it's a dare of some sort."

(In the interest of full disclosure, a red rose was found this morning on the editor's desk at the *Bugle*.)

Goddard Public Information Director Edward Morgan said apparently only the library and *Bugle* editor's office reported roses. Morgan declined to speculate on the agency behind their distribution or the motivation for the apparent prank. "Roses cause no harm, but Campus Security is concerned that someone apparently gained entry to the library after hours. Anyone with information about the roses is asked to contact the Campus Security office."

Security Officer Ben Douglas insisted every entrance to the library was locked when he made his rounds at eleven p.m. Monday. "Nothing was open and there was no break-in. Staff entrances are opened by electronic keypads. Some of the service entrances require a key. Whoever got in either had a key or knew the code for keypad entrances."

The *Bugle* asked the office of Library Director Kathleen Garza if any staff members used keypad locks to enter the library after hours this week. As of press time, the director's office had not responded.

A telephone survey of local florists revealed no promotional efforts. Jane Nottingham of Roses Are Red Florists said, "Our going rate for a dozen premium red roses is $87.95. I understand they found about two dozen roses, so someone must have a big crush on library staff."

A more ethereal explanation was offered by Security Officer Douglas. Douglas pointed to a portrait of Lorraine Marlow that hangs on the landing of the main staircase at Goddard Library. "Mrs. Marlow was the wife of a wealthy Adelaide banker, Charles Marlow. Her rose garden was famous, and she loved to share her flowers. Their estate included a greenhouse, and roses were available year round, which was very unusual in the 1930s and '40s. In the early days of World War II, she was a volunteer at the Adelaide USO, which welcomed soldiers stationed at a nearby Army post. She soon became known to soldiers as the Rose Lady, and she encouraged young men to send pressed petals to a girl back home. Although she and Mr. Marlow had no children, Mrs. Marlow loved young people and, as a regent of Goddard College, every year hosted a Valentine dance for Goddard students at their home. During the war years, she often shared single roses with young men at the college, urging them to look in their hearts and leave a rose where the girl of their dreams would find it."

Douglas said Mrs. Marlow died a few years after the war in a car accident. According to Douglas, single long-stem roses began to appear on campus not long after her death, often leading to unexpected romances.

When asked how a rose without a salutation or message could connect a couple, Douglas said, "Sometimes the appearance of a rose led a man—or young woman—to seek out someone they'd noticed but felt shy about approaching. Often both a young man and woman received a rose. Mrs. Marlow's been gone more than a half century, but roses still find their way at Goddard."

Morgan smiled pleasantly when asked about the legend of the Rose Lady. "It's a pretty tale and well-known to all of our students. Enterprising young men don't hesitate to take advantage of a romantic illusion. I feel quite sure we have no supernatural visitors at Goddard."

"Oh, yeah?" I might have to make Director Morgan's acquaintance. I waited a moment to see whether Wiggins might be about to chastise me. "I know. Precept Five. But he sounds like a pompous ass."

There was no rumble, avuncular or otherwise.

I picked up the *Bugle* dated Wednesday, October 16.

Latest Library Prank
Worries Authorities

Bugle editor Joe Cooper

A maintenance worker this morning discovered shattered remnants of a gargoyle near the front steps of Goddard Library. Library Director Kathleen Garza said the gargoyle had been chipped loose from its pedestal on the third floor and pushed from its perch. A single red long-stem rose was found on the ledge.

Garza expressed concern at the vandalism. The director said, "The incident apparently occurred sometime after eleven p.m. Security Officer Douglas said there was no debris when he passed the site at shortly after eleven. In light of the roses found strewn about the library Tuesday morning, it appears the incidents may be connected."

Garza declined to speculate about the motivation behind the appearance of roses, now coupled with vandalism. She was emphatic that the college considers student safety its first priority and the destruction of the gargoyle was a serious offense because there could have been an injury had anyone been passing by when the gargoyle plummeted to earth.

Students buzzed about the second unexplained occurrence on campus within the space of two days. John Helton, a junior from Sulphur, quipped that the Rose Lady might be warning guys to "do the right thing." Then he grinned. "Afraid she doesn't realize it's all on Facebook now. Who bothers with roses?"

Campus Security Chief Robert Silas said patrols will be increased.

Wiggins's concern about nefarious events at the library seemed a little overblown. How likely was the falling gargoyle to bean anyone at a late hour of the night? However, I understood the library director's uneasiness. Who had unhindered access to the library, and why was this occurring?

I picked up the last newspaper—Thursday, October 17.

Roses Are Red, Who Stole
the Book and Fled?

Bugle editor Joe Cooper

A grim-faced Kathleen Garza, director of Goddard Library, this morning confirmed the theft overnight of a rare edition of a Lewis and Clark journal. This particular journal, an early reprint of Codex O, was on loan from the American Philosophical Society. Garza said the edition was of interest to students because the original journal was handwritten by Meriwether Lewis.

The leather-bound book was displayed in a glass case in the third-floor reading room adjacent to the rare-books collection. Garza said Archivist Ezra Benson discovered the theft shortly after seven this morning.

Benson said, "I passed the case and saw a rose lying next to a round hole in the top of the case. I looked and realized the journal was gone."

Campus Security Chief Robert Silas contacted Adelaide police. Detective Don Smith said a glass cutter was apparently used. There was no evidence of a break-in at the library.

The library director declined to suggest a value for the missing book, saying only that it was irreplaceable. A search of online sites suggested the book might be worth approximately $120,000.

Once again students and staff found single long-stem roses in various areas of the library.

Director Garza dismissed the roses as inconsequential. "A serious theft has occurred, as well as vandalism. These are not supernatural deeds. If roses were left by the vandal, it was obviously an attempt to disguise what is happening. The library board has authorized a ten thousand dollar reward for information leading to the arrest and conviction of the thief and vandal."

The appearance of the roses initially revived a quaint tale of Goddard's most famous ghost, Lorraine Marlow. After her death in 1948, her widower, Charles Hiram

Marlow, contributed generously to the library in her memory. Their estate, known as Rose Bower, was left by Marlow to Goddard College. The main house, a Tudor revival built in 1927, is used by the college to house distinguished guests, and every year the third-floor ballroom is the site of the annual Goddard Valentine dance.

According to the *History of Goddard College* by the late professor Everett Castle, lovers since the late 1940s have brought tales of hope or woe to Lorraine Marlow's attention. Her portrait hangs on the main landing of the library. Castle wrote that it was common to see young men and women standing beneath the portrait, earnestly sharing their dreams. Castle wrote that young lovers believed Mrs. Marlow led them together by the strategic placement of single long-stem roses on the pillows of particular coeds and male students or in their study areas. The story was well enough known that the arrival of a rose always occasioned enough comment that the identity of the coeds and male students were soon known. Over the years, more often than not, the rose-linked couples soon wed.

So far as the *Bugle* has been able to determine, this past week was the first time in the history of the legend that roses appeared linked to incidents which have resulted in damage or loss to the library.

The Thursday issue was the last in my filched stack. I assumed that meant I had arrived in the Goddard Library Thursday evening. To be sure, I checked the walnut desk in one corner of the guest room. Indeed, the university provided guests with all amenities. The top sheet on the desk calendar read Thursday, October 17. The puzzling events at the library were discovered Tuesday, Wednesday, and Thursday mornings and reported in the afternoon editions of the *Bugle*.

I arrived on the library landing the night of Thursday, October 17, a night when nothing untoward had occurred at the library. Because of my excitement in finding Lorraine, Douglas thought a woman had entered and spoken, but he had decided after a search that all was well.

As I settled into a very comfortable bed, I wondered if the theft of the Lewis and Clark journal was the final bit of chicanery intended. That seemed likely, since nothing untoward had occurred tonight.

I felt sanguine, slipping into sleep, until a vagrant thought occurred: If theft of the valuable journal was the objective, why the roses and smashed gargoyle?

∽

Friday morning, I hovered for a moment in the grand foyer of the library, enjoying the grandeur of the double staircase, vaulted ceiling, and the vivid crimson and gold colors of sunlit stained-glass lancet windows. This grand old building seemed an unlikely setting for drama, though I well knew that good and evil occur equally in a kitchen, a high-rise, or a gothic library.

I had no difficulty finding the director's ground-floor office, a wide, deep room with more lancet windows, framed prints of faraway places on two walls, and a filled bookcase behind a mahogany desk. Kathleen Garza was already at her desk although it was only a quarter past eight. She clicked on her intercom. "Ella, I'm meeting with staff and Campus Security at nine. Hold all calls, no visitors." Kathleen was attractive in an understated Katharine Hepburn way—thick dark hair in a 1940s style, a well-cut pale gray suit enlivened by a garnet necklace.

No visitors? I could circumvent that order.

In an instant I landed in a darkened cloakroom on the east side of the lobby. I made sure the room was empty, remembered the Adelaide police uniform, and appeared. French blue is flattering to redheads, and the royal blue stripe for the trousers is truly stylish. I walked out into the lobby. On some prior efforts in Adelaide, I had assumed the identity of Officer Loy, a tribute to Myrna Loy, who was such a superb Nora to William Powell's Nick Charles in *The Thin Man*. I ran my finger over the engraved letters of my name tag: *Officer M. Loy.* I stopped at the central desk. "Officer Loy. I'm here to see Director Garza about the theft of the rare book."

I was inside her office three minutes later.

She came around the desk to greet me. "I spoke with Detective Smith yesterday. Do you have any news?"

I looked sage. "The investigation is continuing on all fronts, including contacts with rare-book dealers. So far"—I looked regretful—"we've had no success there. Detective Smith said he thinks you have excellent insight and, after considering all the circumstances, may have more useful background information." I gestured toward the chair in front of her desk. "If I might ask a few questions?"

She settled behind her desk, still looking anxious.

I didn't, of course, know what Detective Smith had covered, so

I began cautiously. "In regard to the records from the keypads used to enter the library . . ." I trailed off, looking interested.

She was polite, but dismissive. "Staff use the last four digits of their social security numbers for their entry code. It would certainly take a stupid thief to leave such a clear trail. However, I asked the tech staff for a report yesterday." She swung to her computer, clicked several times. Her thin shoulders stiffened. She turned toward me, eyes wide with surprise. "There was one entry Wednesday night. Actually early Thursday morning. At 1:04 a.m., the code belonging to a student registered. Normally students aren't permitted to enter without a librarian but Michelle Hoyt—"

I managed to keep my face blank.

"—was added to the system Monday at the request of the History Department. I am shocked. The History chair vouched for her." Her face folded in tight angry lines. "We'll see about this. She had no authority to enter the library except during working hours. And certainly it would be an odd coincidence if she used her code the very same night a valuable book was stolen."

I held up my hand. "Before I investigate further with this student, did you ask about entries after hours for Monday and Tuesday nights?"

The director was crisp. "Of course. There are no recorded entries on the keypads for either of those nights." Her thin black brows drew down. "Michelle's entry code was activated Monday. Since it wasn't used Monday or Tuesday nights, does that mean she had nothing to do with the roses or the gargoyle? As for the entry before the theft, possibly someone used her private information, but I will need to see proof of that."

I was puzzled. Why would Michelle Hoyt point an arrow at herself on the night of the theft?

Garza frowned. "It doesn't seem likely the incidents aren't linked."

I was judicious. "Possibly the thief took advantage of the arrival of the roses and the smashed gargoyle to confuse investigators. How do you think an intruder could enter without using the keypad?"

Garza shrugged. "The library is big: three floors with many rooms and closets and restrooms and odd nooks. Just before the library closes at ten, Officer Douglas checks every floor, but anyone determined not to be seen could be in a toilet stall or supply closet or simply evade him in the stacks. It would also be possible for a ground-floor window to be unlocked at some point during the day, and an intruder could enter and leave by that means. However, the record is definite. Michelle Hoyt's code was used the night of the theft. Either she used her code or someone else did." Her pale blue eyes glinted with anger. She looked formidable. "I should never have agreed to permit a student to have access to the library, but Dr. Gordon was insistent. He wanted her to be able to come and go, even though her full workday here was scheduled on Fridays. Actually, she starts this morning. Room 211. She should be there." She glanced at her wristwatch. "We'll see what she has to say for herself."

"Michelle will reassure you." Lorraine's high voice was quite pleasant, but gently chiding. "She's a dear girl who is pinning the dreams of her future on her work here at the library. She would never be involved in a dishonest venture."

Garza stared at me. She could scarcely look more shocked if I'd suddenly jumped to my feet and brandished a sword.

I lifted my husky voice a notch, but it was still an octave below

Lorraine's dulcet tones. I spoke loudly: "Always two sides to every story." I made a shushing motion with my left hand.

Garza's gaze followed my hand.

I let my hand drop, managed a strained smile.

"As for the keypad"—Lorraine's cultivated tone held a hint of disdain—"likely it registered the wrong number. I've heard students talk about electronic mishaps. They happen every day."

Lorraine's voice was utterly distinct from mine. Hers was high, mine was low. Her voice had a bell-like quality with the precise diction of someone who did not grow up in the Oklahoma hills. Mine was deeper, with a hint of laughter and a drawl that was a mixture of Southern forebears and Western pioneers.

Lorraine was kind, but firm. "We must never jump to conclusions, must we?" An unseen hand gripped my elbow. "You'll see about this, won't you?"

Garza's eyes darted around the room.

I wriggled free of Lorraine's grasp, quite possibly resembling a disco dancer with a decided leftward list, and yanked the cell phone from my uniform pocket. I held it up, said loudly, "Sorry, Ms. Garza, sometimes the thing gets stuck on speaker phone and other calls get mixed in, quite a mess actually."

Garza had the wary expression of a woman watching a hooded cobra rising from a basket.

"Certainly I hope your telephone problem is solved"—Lorraine was exasperated—"but technical difficulties are not of great importance at the moment. Please see about Michelle."

Lorraine clearly had no idea she was causing a problem. I yelped into the cell. "Cut it out, Sergeant." I was backpedaling toward the door. "I'm on my way to deal with everything right now. Don't embarrass the police department." I was at the door, and a hand gently fastened on my elbow. I twisted my arm, grabbed a fine-boned wrist. "Straighten out the phone lines, Sergeant." I spoke through gritted teeth, managed a strained smile for the director. "Ms. Garza, my apology for the extraneous chatter."

"Extraneous?" Lorraine sounded puzzled.

"I'll run right upstairs and talk to Ms. Hoyt."

"Oh, good. You'll take care of everything, I know you will." Lorraine was clearly reassured.

Garza retrieved a key ring from her desk drawer, rose. "I will accompany you." She edged from behind her desk, keeping a good distance from me, clearly convinced she was dealing with an un-hinged personality.

"Michelle will no doubt explain everything." Lorraine's voice was fading away.

On the plus side, I sensed that she spoke and left. No doubt she was already in room 211.

I turned toward Garza. I pitched my voice higher than usual. "Hopefully Ms. Hoyt can clear up the matter. Certainly, the use of her code after hours must be explained."

Pale blue eyes stared at me intently. Finally, she gave a short nod, but we didn't exchange a word as we walked down the hall, out into the main rotunda, and up the stairs. On the second floor, she turned to her right.

We passed two closed doors.

At room 211, the director checked her keys, inserted one, and opened the door.

I was right behind Garza. There was a long oak table near the windows. Three boxes sat atop the table. A legal pad and pen lay in front of the oak chair drawn up to the table.

As we started across the room, the lid of one box rose in the air, apparently of its own accord.

Garza stumbled to a stop, stood as rigid as a lamppost, stared at the moving lid.

I was behind the librarian. I shook my head, waved my hands overhead signaling *Stop*.

A red leather-bound book went up in the air, hovered above the box.

Garza backed away from the table, bumping into me. I steadied her with one hand, pointed thumb down with the other.

The book was lowered to the box.

"Odd thing, gravity," I said brightly. "I suppose it was just a tremor. You know, a scarcely felt earthquake, and the book was balanced in some way." I was turning the librarian toward the door. "Obviously, there's nothing here for us to see. Don't worry, Ms. Garza. I'll find Ms. Hoyt."

We were in the hall now.

Garza faced me, but her eyes kept flickering toward the closed door.

I was hearty, displaying an "everything is as it should be" demeanor. "I'll double-check a few things in room 211, then be on my way to Ms. Hoyt's apartment. We'll be in touch."

I turned, opened the door, closed it behind me, leaned against it. "Lorraine—" I no more than spoke the name when I knew no one listened. The box sat undisturbed now on the table. On either side of the room were connecting doors to adjoining rooms. They were closed.

I tried to avoid swear words when on earth. I reached back into my memory and pulled out some old favorites that I used as a substitute. "Fish hooks. Denmark. Halibut."

A rumble of laughter sounded beside me, followed, however, by a clearing of his throat.

I hastened to get the first word in, a ploy I'd found useful when Bobby Mac, face furrowed in despair, came across the room, checkbook in hand. His dictum was always: *Please don't subtract.* That seemed unnecessarily harsh, simply because I'd once transposed some numbers and thought we'd had eight hundred dollars more in our account than was there. On that occasion, I'd looked at him soulfully, and said, as if picking up an earlier discussion, "I know you want to discuss *Finnegans Wake.* Bobby Mac, you are the sweetest man." By the time he'd stopped laughing, the mistakes in the checkbook were safely in my rearview mirror.

"Wiggins, you are just the man I want to see." Ouch. Poor choice of verb.

"See?" His deep voice was dour. "Certainly you know the Precepts frown upon emissaries appearing. If you hadn't been visible"—great emphasis—"that unfortunate scene in the director's office wouldn't have occurred."

"Excuse me, but—" I bit off a tart reply that if Lorraine had kept her mouth shut all would have been well. As Mama always said, "Men won't believe a word against their honeys." A bit of throat clearing of my own. "Lorraine has a knack for knowing the tree from the forest." Admittedly obscure, but proclaimed in a most admiring tone.

"Tree from the forest?" Wiggins could be forgiven for not understanding.

"Definitely. She immediately championed Michelle Hoyt. Of course, Lorraine hasn't been prepped about observing Precepts. That explains her forthrightness"—which was certainly one way of describing the interlude in the director's office—"in speaking out. I rather felt I obscured the situation nicely. I believe no harm was done. Ms. Garza will work things about in her mind until she truly believes the contrasting voices came from my cell phone. In any event, it's obvious now that all this fiddle-faddle about roses and gargoyles was a lead-up to the theft of the book."

"Exactly." He sounded like a man who has pulled himself from a sticky swamp onto dry land. "That's why I'm here. The theft of the book, which apparently was taken by a student, proves Lorraine had nothing to do with the distribution of roses or the destruction of the gargoyle, so—"

I heard the rumble of the Rescue Express, wheels clacking on silver rails, whistle rising like a rush of wind.

"—you can return to Heaven."

I found the relief in his voice disheartening.

"Wiggins, think of Lorraine." I spoke emphatically.

"She's fine. Her reputation will be unsullied when the culprit is revealed. Come now . . ."

The acrid smell of coal smoke was stronger.

"Lorraine is counting on me to prove Michelle Hoyt innocent of theft. If I leave, Lorraine will feel it's her duty to help Michelle. You and I both know Lorraine has the best intentions in the world, but, Wiggins, as I stressed, she isn't aware of the Precepts. To have her doing what she can for Michelle without any department expertise, why, the results could be most distressing. When I have an opportunity, I'll explain to Lorraine that Heaven's work is best done quietly, unremarked by the world." Such sweet sincerity in my voice. "And"—this was the clincher—"you don't want Lorraine to believe we have abandoned her. It means everything to her that you have her best interests at heart. You understand that Lorraine is guided by her heart. She sees a match for Michelle Hoyt and the editor of the *Bugle*, which means Lorraine is convinced of their goodness. We don't want to abandon either Lorraine or Michelle, do we?"

"Oh."

The silence in the small room was filled with tenderness. I felt a prick of tears in my eyes.

"I see." His voice was soft. "You're right, Bailey Ruth. We never want anyone to feel abandoned. However, I must say the evidence against this student appears substantial, although I don't understand this talk about codes, but everything is so newfangled these days. I gather she was supposed to be at her duty station here this morning and she is absent."

"Yes." My tone was suddenly grave. "I find her absence disturbing. I read the article in which she was interviewed about this project. She was thrilled, seeing it as a major step toward her life goal. Would she throw everything away to commit a theft?" I played my best card. "Lorraine doesn't believe Michelle's guilty. I'll find out the truth."

"Lorraine . . ." His voice was growing fainter, the clack of wheels more distant, the smell of smoke was fading. "Lorraine always knows the tree from the forest."

I was alone.

I didn't take time to be pleased. I felt pressed, uncertain, worried. Lorraine believed in Michelle because Lorraine believed in love and lovers. My response was more pragmatic. Michelle Hoyt hadn't achieved a status rare for a senior in college by reckless, dishonest, unreliable behavior. Besides, she wasn't stupid, and to use her own code to surreptitiously enter the library and steal a book was stupid.

Today should have been the beginning of her dream to someday write histories about real people who bumped westward in wagon trains, toiled to lay the crossties and tracks across a wilderness, followed dreams to open shops on new, dusty main streets. Real people with real pain, people whose hearts filled with joy, exulted in doing and daring, grieved at graves left behind.

Where was Michelle?

I'd start at her apartment. Unencumbered with physical matter, I thought and arrived.

Chapter 5

A trim white-haired woman in an orange OSU warm-up jacket and pants stood with arms akimbo in the middle of a small living room. "All right. You have a search warrant. Let's see your ID."

The tall, husky detective's dark hair sprang from a widow's peak above a lined forehead, strong nose, and pointed chin. He was a little over six feet with broad shoulders beneath a nicely fitted black-and-white houndstooth sports coat. His black slacks matched the stripe perfectly. "Yes, ma'am." He reached inside his jacket, pulled out a black leather holder with a plastic card.

She looked at it, then at him. "Detective Don Smith." She returned the holder. "What's the search warrant for?"

"Ma'am, we are responding to a tip that stolen goods may be here." He spread a big hand to encompass the square room with two rattan chairs, a blue sofa that looked lumpy, a desk in one corner. Despite the worn appearance of the furnishings, the room had character. Two posters decorated one wall; one was a replica of a 1939 New York World's Fair poster, the other Dorothea Lange's emotionally wrenching photograph of the migrant mother with two small children. A copy of the most recent *Smithsonian* magazine lay on the coffee table by the sofa.

"Stolen goods?" The manager's tone was incredulous. She made a sound between a snort and a humph. "Nonsense."

He was unruffled. "You are welcome to remain and observe our search. When did you last see Ms. Hoyt?"

"Wednesday afternoon, about five. She was getting out of her car with groceries. I asked her if she was going to have something special for dinner. She's a gourmet cook . . ."

I heard a soft coo of approval not far from me. I would have to point out to Lorraine at some more propitious moment that young women's matrimonial prospects no longer hinge on culinary skills. I made a shushing sound that I hoped Lorraine would heed.

Detective Smith looked over his shoulder. "Hey, Johnny, you hear that noise? Some kind of hiss?"

Officer Johnny Cain poked his head into the living room. I smiled. Johnny was a fine young officer. I had no doubt Johnny Cain remembered the redhead—now he saw her, now he didn't—who made a huge difference for the lovely girl Johnny loved and later married.

"Hiss? No, but look." Johnny pointed at a large black cat staring fixedly at the white-haired woman.

The cat turned and marched toward a bowl on the floor, meowing.

The woman looked worried. "George is hungry. His bowl's empty. Something's wrong here, Detective." She spoke in a no-nonsense staccato with a flat Midwestern accent. "I've been renting apartments to students for twenty-six years. I *know* kids. I don't care if you find the mayor's red negligee—"

The detective pressed his lips together.

Mayor Neva Lumpkin was an oversized blonde with the physical attributes of a Wagnerian soprano. She was supercilious, condescending, and overbearing. I pressed my hand over my mouth to smother a giggle as I pictured her in a red negligee.

"—somebody else put it in here. Michelle Hoyt is as serious a scholar as I've ever had as a renter. She follows all the rules, pays her rent on time, no loud noise—and that's not like some I could name. She's lived here three years and never spent a night away without telling me she would be gone and asking me to feed George. I noticed her car wasn't in its slot when I went out to jog Thursday morning at six. The car should have been there. It wasn't there Thursday morning or this morning."

"Whatever." Smith sounded indifferent. "Lady, we got work to do. We'll talk to you later." He nodded at Johnny, who turned and disappeared from sight. There was the sound of a door opening, likely a closet. Detective Smith moved toward a small desk in the corner of the room.

The cat stood in the doorway to the kitchen, meowed.

"That cat's starving. I'm going to feed him." The manager gave Smith a defiant glare and darted across the room.

Detective Smith looked irritated. He followed her and waited in the doorway to the kitchen. "Make it fast. Don't touch anything but cat food."

A rattle as dry pellets were poured into a bowl. "Here you are, George." A splashing sound. "And nice fresh water."

When she stepped into the living room, Smith said curtly, "Stay by the door." He returned to the desk, pulled open the center drawer.

A knock rattled the partially ajar hall door, pushing it in.

The detective turned. "Stop. Police investigation in progress."

Joe Cooper strode inside. His dark hair was uncombed. He was unshaven. He quickly checked out the room, gave the detective a pugnacious stare. "Joe Cooper. *Bugle*. I got a call, some woman at the library—"

Lorraine obviously had used a telephone in an unused office to lure Joe here.

"—who said Michelle needs help. Where is she?" He looked around.

Deep lines bracketed the detective's mouth. "Ms. Hoyt isn't here. Police investigation under way. Stay where you are." He lifted out the center drawer of the desk, scanned the contents. He replaced the drawer, opened a side drawer.

"Police investigation." Joe's frown was fierce. "What kind? Where's Michelle? What's going on?"

The detective ignored him, closed a bottom drawer, pulled out the upper drawer.

The white-haired woman took a step toward Joe. "They showed up about fifteen minutes ago, had a search warrant. I'm Alice Rogers, the manager. I saw your story on Michelle in the *Bugle*. She said she was going to meet you at the Brown Owl Wednesday night after she ran an errand." There was a question in her voice.

Joe took three quick steps, looked down at her. "When did she say that?"

"About five o'clock."

"She didn't show up."

Ms. Rogers's face squeezed in a worried frown. "I hoped you might know where she is. I haven't seen her since then. Her car hasn't been here since Wednesday afternoon. I don't think she's been home at all."

"Not since Wednesday." Joe took a quick breath, pulled out a cell phone, swiped. "Newsroom." He waited, the muscles hard in his jaw. "Hey, Ted. Joe Cooper. Appreciate a heads-up. Has the *Gazette* picked up anything on car wrecks Wednesday night? Any . . . assaults?" He gave a breath of relief. "Thanks. . . . No. I'll let you know, but a friend's hunting somebody, good to know nothing on the police report Thursday morning." He clicked off the phone, looked at the manager. "Did she say what kind of errand she was going to run?"

"Robbie Upton in 306 was revving up his Harley." The manager was apologetic. "I didn't quite hear what Michelle said. Something about 'never knew I was going to be chief errand runner.' She sounded exasperated, and said, 'I have to hurry. I just have time to put up the groceries and get out there and make it to the Brown Owl by six.'"

"Oh my goodness. Where can Michelle be?" Lorraine's high clear voice quivered with distress.

I whispered, "Hush."

Detective Smith gave the manager a puzzled glance, likely assuming she made the comments but wondering at the difference in the voices. "Maybe she has a good reason not to show up."

A subdued but insistent whisper sounded near me. "We have to do something about Michelle."

"Outside," I breathed. I threw out the only bait I had. "News from Wiggins."

Smith snapped, "Ms. Rogers, if you want to stay in here, I'll ask you to be quiet and stop interfering with our search."

The manager frowned. "I didn't say anything."

Joe's voice had an odd sound. "Her lips didn't move. I don't think she said a word."

Smith was irritated. "That's enough out of you two. She's the only woman in here, right?"

Hoping for the best, I popped out into the hall.

"Bailey Ruth? I don't mean to be a bother." Lorraine's cultivated voice was forlorn.

I said gently, "Wiggins wants us to be unnoticed. Unheard."

"No one is looking for Michelle." Lorraine was distressed. "I'm terribly worried now. I didn't know she was last seen on Wednesday evening. We have to do something."

"I agree." My tone was grave. Michelle wasn't the kind of young woman to walk out and leave a cat with no one to care for him. I didn't like to think what might have happened to her. "We definitely will look for her. First let's see what's happening in the apartment. Let's go back and listen. If you need to talk to me, rattle a window shade." It wasn't exceedingly clever, but for now it would do.

Joe Cooper was talking to the manager. ". . . know who some of her friends are?"

Ms. Rogers shook her head. "Not by name. Maybe someone in the History Department can—"

"Hey, Don." Johnny's voice boomed from the bedroom. "Looks like I found it."

The detective crossed the living room in three strides. Joe Cooper was right behind him. Ms. Rogers followed to the doorway of the bedroom.

Johnny stood in front of an open dresser drawer. He used his cell phone to snap one picture, two, three, four. He put the phone back in his pocket and bent to open an attaché case on the floor. He pulled out a pair of tongs. He already wore plastic gloves, but he used the tongs to lift up a brown leather-bound book. He turned toward Smith with a satisfied expression. "Shoved under some negligees. This matches the description, right?"

Ms. Rogers brushed back a white curl. "Is that the book stolen from the library Wednesday night? I heard about it on Channel Four."

Smith glanced at a card, intoned, "Eight inches long, five inches wide, brown leather covers frayed at the bottom. Slight tear on the upper left back of the cover?"

Johnny carefully turned the book over. "Check." He pulled out a clear plastic bag from the attaché case, gently slipped the book inside the bag. He wrote on a white sticker, placed it on the bag. Turning back to the dresser, he continued his search. "Hey, look at this!" He lifted out a glass cutter. "What do you want to bet the lab finds some traces that match the glass in the display case at the library?" He hummed as he placed the small tool in another evidence bag. That done, he turned back to the drawer. "Looks like that's all that matters. There's a long-stem red rose wrapped in a lace handkerchief. That's all besides silk stuff."

"Ohh." Lorraine's voice was soft and dreamy. "She put the rose in her lingerie drawer. I left the rose on her desk."

Smith jerked his head toward the manager. "You left the rose? How come? You know anything about the roses at the library?"

Rogers glared at him. "I not only didn't leave a rose here, I know nothing about this particular rose or any other roses. Moreover, I did not say anything."

Smith's expression was skeptical. "That was a woman's voice."

"Not mine. Maybe the cat talks. I don't know who's saying stuff, but I can tell you one thing"—the flat Midwestern voice was brusque—"Michelle never took that book. I'm going to file a missing person report. You people need to start looking for her."

Detective Smith raised his cell phone. "We'll look for her, all right. What was she wearing?"

The manager hesitated, obviously put off by his aggressive tone.

Detective Smith was brusque. "You say she should be found. Help us find her."

She took a quick breath. "Light blue blouse, white collar with blue piping, three-quarter-length sleeves, pintucking on the front, white trousers, navy sandals."

"Pintucking?"

"The material tucked to make some vertical and horizontal stripes. She's very stylish."

"What does she drive?"

"Dodge two-door sedan. Green. Maybe a 2006."

"Personal description?"

"Five foot seven, slender, black hair, brown eyes. A face with . . . with character." The last was forceful.

"Thanks." He picked up his cell, spoke fast. "General alarm . . . APB . . . wanted on suspicion grand theft . . ."

I rattled the blind at the window. No one noticed. In the hall I reached out and gently eased the door to Michelle's apartment shut.

The hallway was empty. We could speak without alarming anyone. "I'll pop to the police station, see how the search for her progresses. You keep an eye on Joe Cooper."

∽

I turned on the Tiffany lamp on a side table and looked around Lorraine's spacious bedroom. The gilt chair that sat beside the harp was perfect. In an instant, I lifted the chair—

A soft ripple of laughter. "The chair looks silly moving through the air all by itself."

I turned the chair, wedged the curved back beneath the ornate brass doorknob of the massive oak door to the suite. "I want to make sure no one comes in unexpectedly."

A sigh. "No one has ever come in at night except for you." A little pause. "I'm glad you're here, even if it's under such awful circumstances."

I was struck by the reality of Lorraine's loneliness, years and years and years of loneliness. She took vicarious pleasure from watching young men and women find each other because of her roses. Nightly chats with Ben Douglas offered companionship. I wanted to tell her that Heaven waited, brightness beyond any imagining, warmth and caring and loving hearts. I wanted—

"And we haven't found out a thing about Michelle. Joe's still in his office at the *Bugle*, calling people. And"—she sounded a bit prim—"I'm afraid he swears at them. But he's losing hope." A slight breath. "I am, too." Her voice was small.

I, too, felt worn and weary. All day I'd gone from here to there and everywhere, and I knew Lorraine had done the same. At the police station the search was on for Michelle, an APB with her description, car make, and license number. Joe Cooper utilized every reporter on the *Bugle* and soon everyone who knew her well or only slightly had been contacted. The result was always the same. Michelle drove away from the apartment house at five p.m. Wednesday and had not been seen again.

Darkness clothed Adelaide, and no one had any idea where Michelle could be, including me and Lorraine.

"I went back and forth from her apartment to Joe's office all day and I'm terribly afraid something dreadful has happened to Michelle, since we can't find her." Lorraine was despondent.

"She must be somewhere. We have to keep looking." I was emphatic. "Michelle is alive." If she had left the earth, a victim of violence, Wiggins would know. The Rescue Express would have arrived and I would be gone. An elusive thought flitted in my mind, something to grasp, something . . .

The fruitless day, the pall of gloom emanating from all who knew and cared for Michelle, had dragged me down, made me weary. I needed energy. I needed a boost. I pictured myself in a pale purple blouse and white slacks with a semi-sheer silk jacket in a rainbow of colors. I pirouetted in front of the mirror. I was a new woman. "Lorraine, think of an airy cotton voile blouse in tangerine, a midnight blue, ankle-length pleated skirt, and tangerine sandals." I wondered if she would follow my lead, and then I smiled as she appeared. "You're lovely."

Even with her old-fashioned pageboy, she was striking in the flattering combination.

I smiled at her. "I'll bet you feel better."

She eyed her reflection uncertainly. "I shouldn't be thinking of myself. Not with Michelle missing and the police with that book."

The police with that book . . .

My eyes widened. I took a deep breath. "You've done it."

Now she was alarmed. "I didn't mean—"

"The police have the book. Don't you see what that means?"

Her gentian eyes were wide and apprehensive. "No."

"The police are looking for Michelle, an APB on a charge of theft." I spaced out the words. "She was last seen driving away from her apartment at five p.m. Wednesday. Her entry code was used at 1:04 a.m. Thursday. What's the police theory? She entered the library, used a glass cutter to get into the display case, took the journal. Then what? Did she come back home? If so, she left before Ms. Rogers went out to jog at six a.m."

Lorraine watched me anxiously.

"Michelle didn't show up at the library at eight Friday morning when she was expected. It was going to be her first day to do research on the diaries of . . . somebody's diaries—"

"Susannah Fairlee. Such a wonderful woman." Lorraine spoke as if she knew her.

I suppose I looked puzzled.

"I keep up with everything in Adelaide."

Again I had a sense of loneliness assuaged by other peoples' lives.

"Right. Susannah Fairlee. Somebody called the cops and tipped them that the stolen book was in her apartment. The caller made a mistake."

Lorraine's bewilderment was obvious. "The police found the book there."

"Only because someone knew the book was there and called the police. Don't you see? If Michelle took the book and hasn't been seen since, the conclusion would be that she's eluding capture. Why would she steal the book, run away, and leave the book behind? That makes no sense." Thoughts tumbled like dust devils in a spring wind. "Here's what we know: Michelle set out on an errand at five p.m. Wednesday and hasn't been seen again. Her code was used to enter the library early Thursday morning. The journal was stolen. The police, alerted by a phone call, find the journal in Michelle's apartment Friday morning. Plus a glass cutter."

Lorraine nodded in agreement with every point.

I spread my hands, noted that my polish was really a trifle drab and changed to a sunrise pink. I was on a roll. "At this point, the theft is a failure because the police recovered the book. The only thing the theft accomplished"—and now I spoke slowly, emphatically—"was to land Michelle in huge trouble. She's still missing. I believe she will be found unhurt but unable to account for her disappearance. I believe she will be charged with theft. But here's the critical point. The objective wasn't to steal the book. If that were the point, the book wouldn't have been found in her apartment. But it was. There would have been plenty of evidence to saddle her with the crime, and the book could have been kept and sold if that had been the main idea. Instead, the book was the coup de grâce, nicely placed in her lingerie drawer. The objective was to damage Michelle."

Lorraine fingered a filigree silver necklace that shone brightly against the tangerine blouse. "Why?"

I felt as jolted as if I'd bumped into a wall. Why, indeed? What could motivate anyone to go to such elaborate means to cause trouble for a bright college senior? "Jealousy? We don't know much about Michelle. Perhaps another student had hoped to do the research on the diaries." I didn't sound confident because I didn't feel confident.

"No."

I looked at her in surprise.

Lorraine's smile was engaging. "I keep up with everyone at the library. Kathleen—that's the director—does such a good job. I enjoy attending staff meetings. She has an excellent manner with people. She was very particular about approving Michelle to do the project on Susannah. Dr. Gordon assured her that Michelle was absolutely qualified, and he was emphatic that he hadn't considered any other students and . . ."

I was listening, but once again I was teased by a feeling that I was close, so close to understanding . . . Michelle and the project . . . Michelle missing . . . I gave a whoop. "Michelle didn't show up at the library this morning."

Lorraine spoke gently. "Perhaps it's time that we rested. You may be hungry." Obviously she considered Michelle's nonappearance at the library to be rather minor in comparison to stolen goods in her lingerie drawer. "Possibly we could take a moment and find sustenance. I haven't been hungry in so long. I think being here"— she patted her pleated skirt—"gives me an appetite."

I understood. Being *on* the earth definitely required sustenance. I was terribly hungry, hungry enough for an eight-ounce filet, baked potato with sour cream and chives, and steamed asparagus, but food could wait. I was convinced I understood the reason for Michelle's predicament. "Monday afternoon's *Bugle* announced Michelle would start her research Friday morning. Monday night, the library is strewn with roses. Tuesday night, the gargoyle is pushed from its parapet. Wednesday, Michelle sets out on 'an errand' and isn't seen again. Early Thursday morning, the journal is stolen. Friday morning, the journal is found in her apartment, and"—I clapped my hands together for emphasis—"Michelle did not come to the library to read Susannah Fairlee's diaries." I whirled and gripped Lorraine's arm as I began to disappear. "Quick. To the library."

Chapter 6

The great rotunda was dark. The only illumination came from wall sconces at the tops and bottoms of the stairways. Lorraine's portrait was invisible in the dusky shadows of the central landing. In the distance, the tower bell tolled midnight.

"Ben starts his rounds at eleven." Lorraine's whisper was the tiniest of sounds. "He stops to say hello to me as the tower bell finishes."

How well she knew his schedule. But tonight there was no heavy clump of work boots, no shaft from a flashlight spearing through the darkness.

"I wonder where he is." Lorraine was puzzled.

"He told you he was going to do some things differently. I'll bet he changed his schedule. But I don't expect anyone to come for a while."

Lorraine said hesitantly, "Now let me be sure I understand. You are assuming someone will come to the library to take Susannah Fairlee's diaries?"

"Yes. I think Michelle was framed in the theft of the book to prevent her from working on the diaries. That means something incriminating or dangerous to someone is contained in one of the diaries." If my guess was right, a silent figure would slip into the library tonight, but this time Michelle's code wouldn't be used. I felt a chill, not simply from the somber darkness around us. How had a thief obtained Michelle's code? Where was Michelle? But she must be safe, or Wiggins would have been in touch. I pushed away fear and concentrated on tonight and the diaries. How would the intruder enter without a code? The same way someone got into the library to strew roses and topple the gargoyle, either dropping by during the day and making sure a handy window was unlocked or lurking in the stacks after hours. Tonight I believed our unknown adversary intended to leave no trace that the library had been entered. With Michelle in disgrace, the Fairlee materials might remain unexamined for a long time, and an eventual discovery that a diary was missing would be seen as simply an error in the summary of the boxes' contents.

I expected tonight's foray would occur at a late hour, just as it had the night the rare book was stolen. I felt hopeful. We should be in plenty of time.

"Stay here, Lorraine. I'm going upstairs. If you hear anyone coming other than Ben, come and tell me."

Once inside room 211, I turned on the light. I felt confident I had figured out the timing. The thief wouldn't come when Ben

Douglas was likely to be about. Everything appeared to be as it had been when the director and I were here earlier. Three boxes remained on the oak table.

I opened the box marked *Susannah Fairlee Diaries* and saw slim volumes bound in dark red leather. I picked up the most recent, flipped to the opening page. January first of the current year. I felt pleased when I found a printout of the box's contents, forty-three diaries with this year's date the most recent. Apparently Susannah began her diaries the year she turned thirty. The diaries were packed into the box spine-up in two layers. Working as fast as I could, I emptied the box, checked each diary against its listing. When finished, I was satisfied that every diary was present. I packed them in the proper order. The second box, marked *Susannah Fairlee City Council*, appeared to contain minutes of meetings. I noted that the most recent minutes were dated two years earlier. A list of contents confirmed that twenty-two years of minutes were enclosed. The third box, marked *Susannah Fairlee News Clippings*, was filled to the brim with folders. I opened the one on top and found clippings pasted on white sheets. The most recent was a death notice from the September 14 issue. I read a brief notice: "Adelaide, Jamison, J., died Friday. Graveside services Saturday." I riffled through several sheets. Susannah Fairlee clipped news stories about city council meetings, obituaries, and features on local residents. I assumed she'd either been interested in the people involved or in the topics. I closed the folder, replaced it, shut the lid.

If all went well tonight, I would discover who had implicated Michelle in the theft of the Lewis and Clark journal and I would watch as the intruder took something from the material donated by Susannah Fairlee's family. Once the thief was apprehended—I was a bit fuzzy about how this might be arranged, but I believe in serendipity—it would be an easy matter to skim through the stolen material and find information the intruder was willing to go to any length to keep hidden. Moreover, the intruder must be responsible for Michelle's disappearance, and capture would lead us to Michelle.

I turned off the light and settled in a chair next to the table. No sound broke the silence. Wiggins would be pleased. This entire matter would soon be wrapped up quietly, and neither Lorraine nor I would have appeared tonight, quite a plus from his perspective, although I knew Wiggins would love to see her.

As time slipped away, I enjoyed a little fantasy. If there was time before the Rescue Express appeared, I would invite Lorraine to join me at Lulu's, Adelaide's old café on Main Street, for a delicious breakfast. Lulu's was as wonderful now as when I'd lived here. Lorraine and I would have a chance for a real talk, and she would tell me about Wiggins and I would tactfully urge her to join me on the Express—

Click.

The door swung in. The beam from a slender pencil flashlight flicked around the room, settled on the table and the boxes. The figure behind the beam was scarcely visible, nothing more than a dark shape. The door was softly closed.

I hovered above the table.

The intruder moved quickly to the table, held the light above the boxes. Swiftly a gloved hand lifted the lid of the box with Susannah's diaries. The flashlight was now at the edge of that box.

The other hand, also gloved, picked up the sheet that listed the box's contents, tucked the sheet in a pocket. Then the hand reached again, plucking out a diary.

The door burst open. The overhead light blazed.

I squinted, momentarily blinded by the brightness.

The intruder whipped around, an elbow snagging against the box.

I had a quick back view of a thin form dressed in black with a stocking cap.

Burly Ben Douglas plunged heavily toward his quarry, boots thudding. "Got you now!" he shouted. "Hands up. You're trespassing. The police—"

The crack of a gun cut off Ben's words, the harsh explosion stunning in the small room.

Ben took one more staggering step. His gun clattered to the floor as he clutched at his chest. His big face creased in pain. He moaned, toppled forward to crumple facedown on the wooden floor.

The shooter sprinted toward the door.

I rushed across the room and dropped to my knees beside Ben.

The door banged against the wall and running feet sounded in the hall.

A swift-running rivulet of blood snaked across the floor by Ben's outstretched hand.

The sound of running steps faded. I couldn't follow Ben's assailant. Ben needed help quickly. Blood continued to well, dark red and thick. Panic flooded me. Using all my strength, I managed to half turn him onto one side. His head lolled back. I grabbed the left pinned-back sleeve and pressed the cloth against his chest.

"I'll see to Ben." Lorraine spoke swiftly. "He's hemorrhaging. I was a nurse. Get help." Lorraine abruptly appeared.

I saw her clearly, a young Lorraine with her hair neat beneath a white cap. She wore a long gray cotton crepe dress with a white piqué collar. A Red Cross emblem marked the bib of a white pull-over apron.

"Hurry." She was calm, the calm of experience. "Summon help. I must apply pressure." She pulled the apron over her head, swiftly folded the material into a bulky pad, knelt beside him. "Despite the heavy bleeding, I think the bullet missed the subclavian vein. Hurry. He's lost a considerable amount of blood."

Ben's face was white as goose down. He tried to lift his head. "Miz Lorraine . . ." I heard his weak voice as I carefully unclipped the cell phone from his belt buckle. "I figured somebody'd come tonight. I hid by the main stairs and waited, and I heard footsteps coming up from the end of the hall—" He broke off, coughed.

"No talking." Lorraine's quiet voice was calming, encouraging. "We're getting help for you."

It took only an instant to dial nine-one-one. "Night watchman shot. Goddard Library. Room 211. Losing blood. Needs help immediately. Front door will be open." I placed the cell on the table and flashed downstairs to the door. Thankfully the lock permitted opening from the interior. I used a green trash bin to prop the door open.

On my return, I was startled to see Ben lying there unattended with a thick white pad atop his chest. His face was ashen now. Then I realized his right arm was slightly elevated. Lorraine was present but no longer visible.

"His pulse is very weak."

"They'll come quickly. What can I do?"

"Nothing for the moment. I appeared because I needed the apron. I used the cloth to make a compress. The pressure has stopped the bleeding."

"Miz Lorraine . . ." His eyelids fluttered and he tried again to move.

"Hold still, Ben. We'll get you to the hospital as fast as we can."

Still his words came. "I thought I'd catch the thief."

"Stay still." She spoke softly.

He looked up. "Miz Lorraine . . . I tried . . ."

"Don't worry, Ben. You did your best. I hear the siren. Help is coming."

I heard the siren, too. Doors slammed, heavy footsteps thudded, coming up the stairs and down the hall.

I rushed to the table and the open box. There was a gap at the end of the line of books. The last diary—this year's volume—was missing.

ॐ

The ICU alcove was small, room enough for a bed and IV pole. No one was in attendance at the moment, except for us. Ben hadn't moved since they wheeled him in after surgery, but his breathing, though a little shallow, was regular and even.

"I'll stay here." Lorraine spoke firmly. "I'm concerned about his heart rate. They'll come, of course, if the machine alerts them."

"Do you think he can talk tomorrow? Give a description of his attacker?"

She was silent for a moment. "An officer rode with him in the ambulance. Ben said the person who shot him was dressed all in black: cap, sweater, slacks, shoes. He said maybe five foot seven or eight inches tall, thin. That's all he saw. After the surgery"—her voice was authoritative—"he may have very little recollection of the moment. Why?"

"The police will talk to him again. You don't think he will be able to tell anything else?"

"It's unlikely. You were there. Did you see the person who shot Ben?"

"I glimpsed someone all in black, but I was trying to help Ben. Now I feel dreadful. I was there and I don't know anything at all."

Lorraine asked quickly, "Tall or short? Man or woman? Young or old?"

I closed my eyes, tried to re-create that short abrupt moment with the crack of the gun loud in my mind and Ben stumbling forward and a peripheral view of a dark figure in motion. "Not tall. Not short. Perhaps five foot seven. Trim. Moved fast, so not an old person. I think it was a woman. Though some men are slender. It could have been a man. And, even if Ben does remember, I doubt he saw well either when he turned on the light. Everything happened quickly— the door opened, someone came in with a small pocket flash, went directly to the table, and opened the box. Ben burst in and turned on the overhead light. I looked toward the door. Ben shouted, the intruder shot him. I feel terrible. I was there and Ben got hurt."

Lorraine was quick to speak. "There was nothing you could have done to keep Ben safe."

"Thank Heaven you were there." Ben would not have survived except for Lorraine. "You saved his life by putting pressure on the wound. I didn't know you were a nurse."

"So long ago." Her gentle face was sad. "Ben's injury took me back. Some days we did twenty-five operations, working from dawn until dark and still they carried in the men, some with dreadful wounds, some we weren't able to help. The Marne Valley. I was at a field hospital. We worked with the most seriously wounded when the ambulances came. That's how I met Paul. He was fearless. Word got around about Paul, how he'd go into the trenches even during a bombardment and help carry out the soldiers, how he'd venture out into no-man's-land and bring them back. He was older. He was from Ohio. Cleveland. He used to talk about visiting his family there and how he wanted to take me to Wade Park after the war and we'd go out on the pond in a rowboat. He came to France as a volunteer because his younger brother was in the Army. Joseph was killed at Verdun. Paul and I . . . sometimes we'd eat together, carry our tin plates out to the edge of the camp. There was an old oak tree that had fallen. We'd sit there and have beans and dark bread and coffee in enamel mugs. I suppose it's funny to fall in love over beans and brown bread. Then December came . . . but I can't bear to remember." She spoke with finality.

I knew she'd said all she would say about war and death and Wiggins.

A cloth on the bedside table rose in the air. Water poured from a plastic jug. The cloth gently touched Ben's face.

Ben was in good hands. Expert hands, in fact. As he grew stronger, Lorraine could discover if he remembered anything to help us find his attacker, but it was up to me to start the police off on the right trail.

*

I know my way around the Adelaide police station. In Wiggins's opinion, I am much too familiar with the office of Chief Sam Cobb.

But I believe in going to the source. When crime is afoot, Adelaide's stalwart chief is the man in the know. I was a little surprised the office was dark when I arrived although it was quite early on Saturday morning, not quite half past six. Yet in my experience (which is more than Wiggins would have preferred), Chief Cobb worked early and late during a crime investigation.

I looked forward to seeing the chief, a big man with a thatch of curly, grizzled black hair and a broad face seamed by experience. One look and you knew he was a good man: tough, experienced, determined, nobody's fool, but aware that goodness existed despite all the cruelty and ugliness he had seen.

He and I had an understanding of sorts, not that we often came face-to-face. After all, I had to honor the Precepts. Sort of. Chief Cobb wisely didn't insist upon delving deeply into sources of information. He was willing to accept some Heavenly pointers. Perhaps it was Providential that I had the office to myself for a bit.

I turned on the light. The chief's office was a good-sized room on the second floor of City Hall. His battered oak desk, marred by moisture rings, appeared uncommonly neat, no files strewn about. I went directly to the old-fashioned blackboard on one wall. Several stubs of white chalk lay in the tray.

Chief Cobb disdained the newer fashion of dry-erase whiteboards, saying chalk had been good enough for him when he taught high school math and chalk was good enough for him now. In the past, I'd left important information for the chief on the blackboard. Wiggins might consider such communication not quite in line with the Precepts, but it was a means of being helpful without actually appearing. I gave a little sniff and picked up a hint of coal smoke, so I needed to complete this mission as quickly as possible. If I blazed a trail for Sam Cobb, all would be well. I picked up a piece of chalk and wrote:

1. *Events at Goddard Library, including theft of a rare book Wednesday night, are part of conspiracy to frame Goddard senior Michelle Hoyt.*
2. *Friday night Security Officer Ben Douglas was shot when he confronted an intruder stealing a diary from the Susannah Fairlee papers in room 211.*
3. *Michelle Hoyt was last seen Wednesday evening. She will turn up, likely this morning—*

I was making a leap, but as my mama always told me, "Bailey Ruth, honey, when milk smells sour, don't drink it." Michelle Hoyt would have to be incredibly stupid to have committed a crime in such a clumsy way. Moreover, she certainly didn't call the police to announce the presence of the journal in her apartment. That proved someone else was involved, and I was confident that someone was the figure in black who shot Ben Douglas.

—reporting she was decoyed somewhere Wednesday evening and held against her will.
4. *Intruder entered room 211 of Goddard Library at shortly after one a.m. this morning.*
5. *Security Officer Ben Douglas turned on the overhead light, accosted intruder.*
6. *Intruder, dressed entirely in black, shot Douglas, escaped with Susannah Fairlee diary.*
7. *Earlier episodes at Goddard Library intended—*

The hall door opened.

I turned with a smile, which slowly slipped away.

Sam Cobb didn't enter.

Two strangers stepped into the office.

". . . clear as the nose on your face." The speaker was a shade over five six with thinning blond hair over a round face. He looked cocky in a baggy polo and Bermuda shorts that exposed knobby knees. "That student went on the lam and then she thought better of it. Maybe somebody tipped her that we found the goods in her place." His slightly high voice was strident. "So now she shows up claiming she was kidnapped. Kidnapped, my ass. Smith's going to take her statement. Give her plenty of rope." A snort. "Kidnapped— that's a stupid way to try and cover up she was back in the library last night and shot that guy. Nothing Smith and Weitz can't handle. I don't know why Colleen thinks I got to be here. We got an eight o'clock tee time." He went to the desk. "I can't believe Colleen called me at six a.m. What's she doing here on Saturday? I guess she sleeps with a scanner by her bed and thinks the station can't handle anything without her on board. She should get a life." He pushed a button on the intercom. "Colleen, pick up two Big Mama breakfasts from Lulu's for me and Willard. ASAP."

Colleen was Chief Cobb's exceedingly competent secretary, a matronly woman with bluish gray hair drawn back into a bun. What had happened to the chief?

Her voice over the intercom seemed carefully devoid of expression. "Detectives Smith and Weitz have just—"

"Yeah, yeah, yeah. Smith texted me. Like a fly walking into our web. They've got it under control, right?"

"Chief Cobb always—"

"Spare me, Colleen. Chief Hands-On Cobb. Well, out of sight, out of mind. While he's honeymooning in Galveston—"

I made a soft cooing noise. How lovely. I had hoped that he and Claire Arnold, whose ramshackle old house was the center of intrigue when I was last in Adelaide, might make a match. Perfect for both of them.

"—and Hal's figuring out why grown men don't do wheelies on skateboards, I'm acting chief. Me, Howie Warren. I delegate. Besides, it's Saturday and Willard and me got a date with our sticks. And I didn't sign up to work on Sundays. Smith and Weitz—hey, maybe we should start calling her Wesson"—a pause for a guffaw—"so Smith and Wesson can wrap it up and bring it to me Monday morning on a platter. Now, speaking of platters, be a good girl and trot over to Lulu's." He clicked off the intercom.

Impulse overcomes me occasionally.

Oh, all right—often.

I snapped, "Don't be a sexist pig."

He swung around and glared at Willard. "What'd you say?"

His companion looked startled. "I didn't say anything."

The smaller man snarled, "Stop the funny stuff. I heard that."

Willard was bigger with a fleshy red face and a bulbous nose. At the moment his eyes were shifting around the room. "I did, too. Where's the dame?"

I resisted humming "Ring Around the Rosie" while they prowled around the room. Finally, Howie went to the door, poked his head into the hall. He closed the door and shrugged. "Maybe something came through the air vent." His small pig eyes tightened. "Some broad in the hall being cute."

"Yeah." Willard was hugely relieved. "Making a joke. Nothing to do with us. Anyway, you're on a roll today, Howie. You've solved the Goddard caper in record time. That'll put Price's nose out of joint." A hearty laugh. "Kind of like his leg. Hear he's in traction and will be out for a couple of weeks."

Howie swung around the desk, plopped in Chief Cobb's chair, leaned back looking satisfied. "Poor old Hal. Wonder if he's told Sam I'm the man of the hour? Anyway, soon as we finish breakfast, we're out of here. Bet you fifty I beat you by five." He pulled out a drawer, propped his legs on it. "Neva's gonna be pleased that I wrapped this up ASAP."

Heaven encourages tolerance, but I loathe clichés. At the blackboard, I picked up a chalk stub, wrote: *A SAP.*

"Howie, you're coming out of this smelling like a rose." Willard's smile was just this side of fawning. "You know Neva wants to muscle Cobb out. This may be your chance."

If I'd had more time, I would have added to the blackboard Tallulah Bankhead's classic observation: "There is less here than meets the eye." However, I now had a more pressing duty. Michelle Hoyt needed help.

∽

I was familiar with the interrogation room at the police station from my previous visit to Adelaide. The windowless room was unchanged: dingy tan walls, scuffed linoleum floor, a desk with a goosenecked lamp that could be twisted to focus on a wooden chair about five feet away.

Michelle Hoyt sat in the chair. She was dressed in the blue blouse and white slacks she'd worn when the apartment manager last saw her on Wednesday. She looked disheveled and exhausted. Her dark hair needed a brush. She wore no makeup. Her face was tired and strained, her blouse and slacks wrinkled. On the floor next to her feet was a black leather shoulder bag.

Behind the table sat a uniformed officer, a stocky woman with a smooth round face beneath a fringe of black bangs. Her hair was cut short. Her fingers rested near a keypad attached to a laptop computer. Lounging next to her, feet stuck out straight in front of him, was Detective Don Smith, his handsome face sardonic. Standing at the end of the table, arms folded, was a trim woman in a gray polyester jacket and gray short skirt. Her broad face was expressionless beneath an untidy mop of billowy brown hair. Oh my, how I yearned to take her to a makeover. That hair, tamed a bit, could be flattering. Dowdiness was not a requisite for officialdom. Perhaps a pleated patterned long silk jacket, a vivid marine blue blouse, and black trousers.

The woman adjusted the cone of light until it struck Michelle full in the face.

Michelle lifted a hand to shade her eyes. She looked upset and exhausted. "I don't understand why you brought me in here. Why are you beaming that light at me? Who are you?"

Smith answered. "I'm Detective Don Smith." He inclined his head. "Detective Judy Weitz. You want to report a crime?" He spoke in a flat tone.

Michelle sat straighter. She lifted a shaky hand to brush back a strand of hair. "Yes." Her voice was shaky. "I got a phone call—"

"How?" The stocky woman's voice was sharp.

Michelle squinted against the bright light. "On my cell. I was driving to my apartment. It was about a quarter to five Wednesday. The call came from the History Department. A woman—"

"Name?"

Michelle gave a tired head shake. "I don't remember. Simpson, maybe. I don't know. You can ask at the department. She told me Dr. Gordon wanted me to pick up an important folder that he needed for a talk that night. The address was 928 Montague Street. She told me how to get there. I just had time to take my groceries home and then I drove there. It took me a while to find the house. Montague is out near the country club, and there are lots of woods and this house was tucked behind a whole lot of trees. I pulled into the drive, and it curved around. The house is a two-story brick. She'd told me to come to the kitchen door and come in. I parked in front of the garage, a double garage separate from the house. I was in a hurry, so when I got out of the car, I left my purse on the seat and my keys in the ignition. I was just going to be there a couple of minutes. I went up the back steps and there was a note on the door. It said, *Come in. Go to the right and down steps to basement, folder on desk.* I stepped into the kitchen and saw a light coming from an open door, and I thought that must be the way down to the basement. I walked across the room and saw the steps leading down. I hurried down the stairs. I was almost to the bottom when the door slammed behind me. I thought maybe somebody'd come into the kitchen and there was a draft. Anyway, I went on down the stairs. That's when I thought something was odd. It was a basement room with a pool table and a sofa and I didn't see a desk. I went around the room, but there wasn't a folder anywhere. I went back up the stairs and the door to the kitchen was locked. I knocked and banged and yelled. No one came." For an instant her voice was uneven. "I couldn't imagine what had happened. I thought there'd been some kind of mistake, but nobody ever came. Not then or that night or the next day. Or the next. I tried to get out. I looked for something to break down the door but there wasn't anything. I looked everywhere in that room for some kind of tool. There wasn't anything. There's a padlocked door that goes somewhere and a little half bath, but there wasn't anything in there but soap. I got really scared. You see"—she swallowed and again pushed back a strand of dark hair and stared at them with hollow eyes—"I thought some crazy person had caught me and was keeping me for some reason, because when I looked around there was a microwave and a little refrigerator and it had food, sandwich stuff and bread and frozen meals, enough for two days. And the cot"—she shuddered—"was made up into a bed. At night, when I couldn't stay awake any longer, I put some of the balls from the pool table on the top step, and I thought if somebody came in, they would fall and I'd have a chance to get out. But nobody came. The balls were always there the next morning. Last night I ate the last frozen dinner. I decided either somebody was coming to get me today or something was going to happen." She took a shaky breath. "I got up early this morning. I went up the stairs, moved the balls to one side. I had one of the pool cues and I thought I could jab it at somebody. I didn't have any hope I could get out. I'd checked the door lots of times. I turned the knob, and this time the door was unlocked." There was a memory of fear in the sharp planes of her face. "I eased the door open a little bit at a time. I didn't hear anything in the kitchen. Nothing. The kitchen was dark. It wasn't light outside yet. I tiptoed across the kitchen to the back door and opened it, and I was outside. And there was my car in the driveway. I couldn't believe it. I ran and got in and locked the doors, and there was my purse and my keys were in it and I came straight here."

Detective Smith cleared his throat. "That's quite a story."

"It isn't a story. That's what happened to me, and I want you to find out who kept me a prisoner. It was awful." Her voice was ragged.

Smith picked up his cell. "Check out 928 Montague Street. ASAP."

When I was an English teacher, I stressed the poverty of mind indicated by constant use of clichés. Chief Cobb's exchanges with Detective Sergeant Hal Price, who was the only man I'd ever thought as handsome as my own Bobby Mac, were intelligent even if sometimes profane. Sam was on his honeymoon and Hal was in the hospital and somebody named Howie indicated he didn't intend to be in the office until Monday and expected these detectives to wrap everything up. Howie had already made up his mind that Michelle Hoyt was a thief, and likely he would be delighted to finger her for the shooting of Ben Douglas.

I had planned to drop by Sam's office, indicate Michelle was being framed, and be on my way. Instead . . . I sniffed. Not a hint of coal smoke. Wiggins understood. I was Michelle's only hope.

Smith pushed up from his chair. There was something ominous in the way he stood, leaning forward.

Michelle stood, too. "It's against the law to hold people against their will, right?"

"If what you *claim* is true, yes. Tell us what happened again." There was a taunting tone to his voice.

"Why should I?" she demanded. "I've reported a crime. It's up to you to find out what happened." She glared at him. "I'm tired. I've been scared. I've missed classes. I haven't been home and I've got to see about my cat." She picked up her shoulder bag and started toward the door.

Smith moved to intercept her. "Not so fast, Ms. Hoyt. We're holding you for questioning."

She jolted to a stop, stared up at him. "Questioning?" Her voice rose. "Why?"

"On a charge of theft. And aggravated assault with a firearm. Anything you say from this point on may be used against you in a court of law. You have a right to an attorney. Do you wish to waive that right?"

I leaned close to Michelle's ear, said very softly, "No."

She swung toward the sound of my voice.

Smith frowned. "Ms. Hoyt, what's your answer?"

I tried not to be heard, but I suppose even my whisper was loud in that small room. "Call Joe Cooper."

"Hey." The detective was irritated. "What'd you say?"

Michelle's face hardened. "I didn't say anything. But I've got a lot to say. I was the victim of a crime, and now you are accusing me of stealing something and assaulting someone. Who am I supposed to have assaulted?"

"Where's the gun?"

Her hand rose to her throat. "Gun?"

"The night watchman at the library is hospitalized with a chest wound. Why did you shoot him?"

"I didn't shoot anyone. I wasn't at the library last night. I was locked up in that house on Montague Street."

"Let's start with Wednesday night. You came into the library at shortly after one a.m." Smith pointed toward the chair. "Sit down. Tell us about it."

She stood rigid, eyes huge, hands clenched. "I won't sit down. You have no right to accuse me. I've never entered the library at night. Not Wednesday night. Not last night. Not any night. I didn't steal anything. I don't have a gun. I don't even know how to shoot a gun. Who was shot? Where?"

I liked this girl. She reminded me of a cat Bobby Mac and I once had. Big Girl was a brown tabby who never saw a dog she wouldn't confront. Big Girl was scrappy, tough, and clever. When she was an old, old cat, too feeble to chase harassing blue jays, she ambled slowly into the yard, rolled over on her back, waited unmoving as blue jays swooped down at her. Finally a blue jay dived too close and, in one swift, lethal roll, Big Girl caught him.

Smith was brusque. "All right. You got one phone call. Then we'll book you on suspicion of aggravated bodily assault with a firearm, and you can sit in a cell until you're ready to give us some answers. You can lawyer up all you want to, but you won't lie your way out of this. Make your call."

Michelle's hand shook as she drew out her cell phone. "I don't know a lawyer. I don't have any money—"

"I guess I'll call Joe Cooper." I tried to imitate her voice. She had a nice voice, low and contained, as if she measured out words carefully.

Michelle drew in a sharp breath, lifted the cell. She tapped, found a number, held the phone close to her ear. "Joe—Michelle Hoyt . . ." She almost managed a smile. "I'm all right, but I was trapped in a house on Montague Street from Wednesday night until this morning. I came directly to the police station to tell them, and they're holding me and they say I stole something and shot somebody and it's all crazy." She listened. Her eyes widened. "I didn't take that journal. . . . My code used? . . . Oh my God, what am I going to do? . . . Yes. Please come." She clicked off the phone.

Smith looked at her with a slight curl of his mouth. "Big surprise, huh?" He jerked a thumb at the uniformed officer. "Escort the lady to a cell."

As the lock clicked and the officer moved down the hall, Michelle looked around the small cell with a single bed and toilet. She walked stiffly across the cement floor, sank down on one end of the bed. "This can't be happening to me." She spoke aloud, her voice quivering. Her oval face looked bewildered and frightened. "Nothing makes sense."

I hoped Wiggins understood. Precept Four was all very well and good—"Become visible only when absolutely necessary"—but Michelle needed a boost. I stood with my back to the wall next to the bed. Colors swirling and forming—well, I can see how that might be unnerving. By the time she sensed my presence and turned, I was there. I'd chosen a vivid rayon top with vertical swaths in bright coral, aquamarine, and violet, with pale blue trousers and cream sandals. Drop earrings and a long necklace of silver rings interspersed with beaten silver coins added a note of cheer. I smoothed my red curls and smiled at her. "Don't be distressed. I'm here for just a moment"—I couldn't stay long, because surveillance cameras would already have revealed me—"to reassure you that there are those of us who believe in you, and we will make sure you are exonerated."

Michelle's dark eyes were huge. One hand clutched at her throat.

Running footsteps sounded in the corridor.

I gave her another smile. "George is fine. I'll be back." And I was gone.

Chapter 7

Leaves scudded on the path beside me. The downtown park that faces the police station was quiet. A jogger disappeared around a cluster of pines. A woman sauntered past with an elderly cocker spaniel who stopped to snuffle every few yards. When she and the dog were twenty feet distant, I appeared.

I felt festive and dressed accordingly in a light green tunic with cobalt blue embroidery on the front, the sleeves, and around the hem. Cropped slacks, also in blue, matching green sandals, a green canvas purse, and I was good to go. After all, I am a redhead and I know what makes redheads look their best. This isn't vanity. Looking our best gives confidence, and even Wiggins would agree that Heavenly emissaries must exude confidence. If there is some thought—not on my part—that I am too attuned to fashion, I simply mention that peacocks are admired for a reason.

I crossed the street, noting there were plenty of parking spaces in front of the police station. I spotted Michelle's car, a green Dodge sedan. Certainly, she must have been shocked to find her car and purse this morning. I thought it possible her car had been used by the intruder in black Wednesday night on the foray to the library, then left in the drive on Montague Street because there was no further need of either the car or the purse, with its useful personal information. Michelle had been entangled in a devilishly clever trap, her code used to enter the library Wednesday night and the rare book placed in her apartment. Michelle's nemesis had craftily linked the crime to her.

Now a night watchman had been shot, and the police, of course, considered Michelle a suspect. I felt a ripple of shock. Last night's intruder had not arrived intending to shoot anyone. Instead, the intruder had planned an undetected visit and removal of a diary. But when capture was imminent, the intruder didn't hesitate, and Ben was gunned down. The intruder would now, of course, want to associate the crime with the book theft and see Michelle accused.

I abruptly disappeared. I had intended to indulge myself with breakfast at Lulu's and consider how I could free Michelle, but that would have to wait. Instead I felt an urgency to talk to Michelle.

Michelle stood by the bars of her cell, staring into the long hall-way, her face forlorn. Obviously, she felt abandoned. Anger bubbled within me at the figure in black who was disrupting Michelle's life, entangling her in every way possible, using her entry code the night the journal was stolen, placing the journal in her apartment, tipping off the police. Worse might lie ahead. . . .

"Michelle," I whispered, "did you open the trunk of your car when you came out of the house on Montague this morning?"

She stood rigid. She gripped iron bars. She looked around the very bare cell. The planes of her face sharpened. "No one is here. Only me. I'm alone."

"I was here. I told you I'd come back."

Michelle edged along the bars, her gaze swinging all over the small cell, which was obviously inhabited only by her. "Do you have red hair?" The words were a bit jerky.

"Yes." The same tone I used when a slow pupil successfully diagramed *The cat chased the dog.* "Heaven prefers that emissaries remain unseen." I didn't have time to explain the Precepts. Or Heaven. Or the department.

She made a sound between a laugh and a sob. "I'd say you're definitely unseen. At least by me." She pressed trembling fingers to each temple. "I started out on Wednesday to run an errand. That's all I did. A simple irritating errand, and somebody tricks me into a basement, locks me up, I finally get out, and the police put me in a cell, and I'm hearing voices."

"Just my voice," I emphasized. I wanted to reassure her. I was confident I sounded pleasant, a low, rather husky tone. Bobby Mac once rather poetically compared my voice to Lauren Bacall's. Now that was a compliment.

"Okay. Only your voice. Maybe I'm not totally nuts. Yet. Only one voice. Maybe I don't need to worry unless it's a bunch of voices. Even one voice bothers me."

"Michelle, I have to hurry—"

"Don't let me hold you." She made flapping gestures with her hands, as if shooing geese away.

"Your car." Seconds were fleeting. "Did you check the car, look under the seats or in the trunk?"

"No." It was a whisper of sound. "I got into the car as fast as I could and came straight here."

Of course she did. Ben Douglas's assailant would count on that response. She was in dire straits as it was, but the evidence to be used against her could be much worse. Ben's assailant had the gun used to shoot him. If the police found that gun in Michelle's car, she could never explain how it came to be there.

"Stay calm. I'll be in touch." She didn't look reassured as I left.

Upstairs, I checked out the main office. Two uniformed officers sat at desks near a bank of filing cabinets. I scanned the desks and two tables and didn't find what I sought. I flowed into the squad room, which was broken up into four quadrants with work stations. Only one was occupied. A uniformed officer sat at a computer, engrossed as he typed.

I heard voices toward the back. In an adjoining small, windowless room, I found Detectives Smith and Weitz. Wearing plastic gloves, Weitz stood at a table, emptying Michelle's purse. Smith filmed her actions using a small camera mounted on a tripod.

". . . change purse, notebook, three pens, compact, lipstick, car keys . . ."

Michelle's belongings were being catalogued and a record made of the emptying of the purse, footage to prove the contents of the bag, the time and date of search duly noted. I scanned the objects on the table, spotted a set of car keys on a pink ceramic fob. I wanted those keys before the police arranged for a search of her car and before her purse was placed in a receptacle for a prisoner's belongings.

". . . cell phone, vial of cologne . . ."

I studied the exact location of Weitz, Smith, the keys on the table, and the purse. I moved to the doorway, slammed the door shut, and turned off the light, plunging the room into total darkness.

"Hey, Don, what's going on?" Weitz snapped.

Hand outstretched, I moved around the perimeter of the room until I found the tripod. I tipped it over and gave Smith a shove. He stumbled, swore. I immediately moved to the table. Hovering, I reached down, my fingers flying over the objects Weitz had removed from the purse. I connected with the car keys, grabbed them, then my fingers closed on the bag. I hadn't counted on Weitz instinctively clutching the purse. I yanked hard, and the denim bag was in my hand.

Weitz yelped.

A clanging bang suggested Smith was tangled in the tripod. I heard a grunt and a thud as he scrambled to get up.

I swept the purse across the table. Michelle's possessions clattered onto the floor. The confusion should hide the absence of the keys at least for a little while. I tossed the bag in a corner. I opened the hall door wide enough to slip out, closed it again, but that shaft of light was enough for Det. Smith. He stormed out into the hall, looking each way. Fortunately, he looked at eye level. I pressed against the ceiling, held my hand with the keys on the side of the light fixture opposite him.

When he swung back into the room, turning on the light, I sped to the end of the corridor, opened a door, and entered an empty office. I smiled hugely. Windows. This building was constructed in the 1950s, and the windows, though closed since central heat and air had been installed, were old-fashioned. I flicked the catch, lifted the bottom pane, placed the keys on the outside ledge, and closed the window. I left the window unlocked. Rather on the order of *what goes up must come down*, in this case what went out must be brought back.

Outside, I hovered near the sill and surveyed the scene below. A good Oklahoma breeze scuffed dust in a graveled parking lot and rustled leaves in a big cottonwood on the other side of a chain-link fence. Keys in hand, I zoomed to the top of the cottonwood, slowly floated down until I was next to the large trunk. A quick glance up and down the street to be sure no one was near. I appeared. I thrust Michelle's keys into my green canvas bag and strolled up the sidewalk, no more remarkable than any other citizen abroad early on a Saturday morning.

When I reached Michelle's car, I didn't hesitate. I unlocked the door, slid behind the wheel, and drove to the other side of the park. Only a few cars were in a small lot near a playground.

I started my search in the trunk. I lifted up a lawn chair shoved against a wheel well. A gym bag lay on its side. I unzipped it. There, nestled next to a swimsuit, was a gun. I swiftly slipped the gun into my purse and closed the trunk. Once behind the wheel, I started the car, but I didn't know where I should go. I was determined to drive somewhere and find safe storage for the gun. The gun, of course, must be the weapon used to shoot Ben Douglas. Its intended discovery by the police was to be the coup de grâce in the web surrounding Michelle.

I drove sedately. This was no time to be picked up—

A siren sounded. In the rearview mirror, red lights flashed atop a cruiser that was closing rapidly. Even though Michelle had driven straight to the police station from Montague Street, very likely the alert for her car was still operative. For an instant, I felt a quiver of despair. What could I possibly do? I almost jammed my foot on the accelerator, but perhaps Saint Christopher was riding with me. It isn't only physicians who must heed the dictum *Do no harm*. A wild chase could endanger a great many people enjoying outings on a Saturday morning. I couldn't outrun the police. But there might be another way. . . .

I slowed, put on the turn signal, and lowered both windows. I pulled up to the curb.

The police car snugged in behind the Dodge. As the officer opened his door, I disappeared. I was interested to see that I, my clothes, and accessories were gone. Only the small black pistol lay on the front passenger seat. In a swoop, I grabbed the pistol and was out the window by the curb. I held the gun against the car door, out of the approaching officer's sight.

He stopped a foot or so from the car, bent to look inside. "Hey." He turned and looked in every direction. He opened the front and rear doors, eased his head inside.

Immediately the gun and I rose, twenty feet, thirty, fifty. As he withdrew his head from the car, I was above a thick tangle of woods. I settled high in a tree and studied the terrain. Off to my left, smoke curled into the sky from the cement plant, a large white building with two big chimneys. Dark water gleamed in the river between the woods and the plant. In the early sunlight, the rusted railings of an abandoned railway bridge gleamed orange. Keeping close to the treetops, I reached the river, dropped low, skimmed just above the water. In only a moment, I reached the railroad trestle. I zoomed higher and wedged the gun securely into the V of the middle trestle. There the gun was and there the gun would stay. For now.

❦

In the squad room, Officers Smith and Weitz hunched at neighboring desks. From the flush in her cheeks and the set of his shoulders, it was clear that they had exchanged sharp words.

I looked over her shoulder as her fingers flew over the keyboard:

> . . . after Det. Smith entangled himself in the tripod and disrupted the recording of items in Prisoner M. Hoyt's purse, I again catalogued Prisoner Hoyt's belongings. When I finished the list, I realized Hoyt's car keys were missing. Det. Smith insisted no keys could have been in the purse since we searched thoroughly and there absolutely were no keys present in the room. However, I saw the keys and distinctly recall a key chain with a pink porcelain fob. I described the key chain to Det. Smith.

She slid a venomous glance at him, continued to type:

> Det. Smith claimed he was vindicated when Patrolman Sykes reported the prisoner's car was stopped on Wheeler. I spoke with Officer Sykes, inquired about keys. Keys were in the ignition. He confirmed the key chain had a pink porcelain fob.

She paused and her face crinkled in puzzlement.

Smith's chair creaked. "Hey, Weitz." His voice was conciliatory. "How come you knew those keys had this pink thingamajig before we got Sykes's report?"

They looked at each other.

Smith broke an uneasy silence. "Somebody shoved me into the tripod. You were on the other side of the table. Everything on the table got knocked on the floor. I didn't do that. The door opened, then the door closed. You didn't open it. I didn't open it. I blundered over to the door and yanked it open. I went into the hall. There was nobody there."

She studied him, apparently decided a truce had been called, because she too spoke in a conciliatory tone. "The keys were there before the light went off. When you turned the light back on, I picked up everything from the floor. No keys."

Smith rubbed knuckles along his chin. "The keys were in the car."

"Yeah." Weitz stared at him. "The keys and no driver."

"I don't get it."

Weitz's eyes narrowed. "Sykes searched the car, found nothing of interest."

Smith frowned. "How did the car get where it got? I mean, she came here to report a crime. Figures she drove here, right? We interrogated her. She's in a cell."

Weitz's thin shoulders lifted and fell. "Makes no sense. If anybody was with her, you'd think they'd have come in to find out what was going on. But somebody drove that car over to Wheeler."

I left them gnawing at their puzzle. They say puzzles are healthy for the brain.

⌀

Upstairs in the chief's office, I turned on the light. The computer monitor glowed. I opened the center drawer of his desk. The chief had not changed his habits. I found a list of scratched-out words.

At the bottom of the list, not scratched out, was *puppy7*. The list wasn't entitled *Password*, but I figured that's what it had to be. And it was. I settled in his chair, my hands hovering over the keyboard. After a moment's thought, I e-mailed Detectives Weitz and Smith:

Re: Library theft, subsequent shooting of night watchman.

New evidence confirms Michelle Hoyt's report of abduction. She is no longer a suspect in the theft of the rare book or the shooting of the night watchman. Her immediate release is authorized. ASAP, conduct a search of the basement area of the home at 928 Montague Street where she was held. Fingerprint and take into evidence the frozen food packages. Respond to this directive with e-mail reports. I will not be in the office but will be picking up e-mails throughout the weekend. Acting Chief.

I leaned back in the chief's chair, pleased with myself, though, of course, modesty prevented me from erupting with an Oklahoma *yee-hah.*

✺

I sat at the counter at Lulu's facing the mirrored wall. Behind me were several tables and five red leather booths. Lulu's was jammed, mostly men gathering with cronies for the Saturday morning equivalent of a coffee klatch, deep voices rumbling, occasional bursts of hearty laughter.

It would take at least a half hour for Michelle to be released.

Likely Joe Cooper would have arrived by then. I expected she would at once wish to return to her apartment. I was glad I had arranged for her freedom, but I needed to come up with a clever plan for Michelle and Joe and for me. I needed a sustaining breakfast and time to think. I ordered a rasher of bacon, cheese grits, two eggs over easy, and two biscuits with cream gravy—an Oklahoma breakfast for sure. I felt I'd earned every morsel. I took a reviving swallow of coffee strong enough to kick a horse.

A harrumph to my right froze my mug in midair. I slid a sideways glance.

Wiggins sat on the next stool, burly in a blue work shirt and khaki trousers. It was odd not to see him in his stiff white shirt, suspenders, heavy black wool trousers, and laced high-top black leather shoes. Obviously he understood that emissaries must appear in ordinary clothing. I smoothed one of my embroidered sleeves and felt liberated as a fashionista. He had not, however, changed his thick muttonchop whiskers and walrus mustache.

Wiggins ordered a short stack and link sausage. As the waitress turned away, he gave me a somewhat abashed smile.

"Wig—"

He raised a reddish eyebrow.

Remembering how Mama always said, "Bailey Ruth, honey, dance with a toss of your head when you don't know the steps," I started again. "I'm glad to see you." With only the tiniest emphasis on the infinitive.

He had the grace to blush. After all, how many times had he repeated the refrain *Do not appear*?

Another harrumph. "When in Rome . . . Possibly I have been

too rigid about the matter. When on earth, it may occasionally be necessary to experience the moment. Briefly."

I almost teased him at his about-face, but an inner cherub gave me a psychic kick: *He's only here because he wants to know about Lorraine.* Heaven knows I understand that love prompts many about-faces in life (and beyond). "Lorraine saved Ben Douglas's life. She told me about the field hospital."

His brown eyes were suddenly somber. He stared toward the front plate glass window of Lulu's, but his vision wasn't here. "Thinking of Lorraine kept me going. Desolation. That is what I remember, desolation. Trees twisted and blackened, leaves all blown away, cratered ground, trenches with men standing in cold water, rot and pain and suffering and shells whistling. I'd think of Lorraine and the way the sun touched her hair."

"She wrote you."

Head back, chin up, he looked determined, vigorous, confident. "She wrote that a young captain whom she'd met once or twice in Paris came by the hospital and had only a few minutes to spare. He told her he'd fallen in love with her the first time he saw her and if she'd promise to marry him, he knew he'd make it back from the front. What would a girl do, especially a girl like Lorraine who knew how easy it was to die at the front? Why, just what Lorraine did. She promised, and then she had to write me. Tears smudged the words. She said"—and his voice was hushed—" 'Dear Paul, we never spoke of love, but I must tell you how much I love you, since I now know we can never be together.' We'd never put it into words; we both knew we loved each other." Wiggins's grin was robust. "I didn't blame him." His tone was forgiving. "Anyone who saw Lorraine would love her. Anyway, I was going to get to the hospital the next day, tell her she could be engaged to him until the war was over, and then the best man would win."

He looked at me, his gaze earnest. "Don't you think that was fair enough? I didn't have a doubt in my mind that I would win out. I guess"—and he sounded a little bemused—"I always had the feeling I would win, no matter what I did. That last evening during the shelling, I heard there was a boy hurt in the trench near some woods, and I knew I had to get to him fast, anyone bleeding that bad. I ran and swerved and reached the trench and jumped down and then a shell hit us." He tugged on one end of his mustache. "I fought leaving the earth. I wanted to stay. Lorraine and I . . . But then I understood. My time there was over. I had a new station, a new purpose. And"—there was a twinkle in his brown eyes—"running the Department of Good Intentions gave me a bit of a window on the world. I confess I took advantage of it to keep an eye on Lorraine. That captain? Charles Hiram Marlow. I was glad when she married Charles. He was a good man. He cherished her. When she died, I thought she stayed on earth to be near him." Wiggins was perplexed. "But when Charles died, she remained in Adelaide. There must be some other reason." He sighed. "She still resists coming to Heaven. I don't understand why."

I didn't want to make him any sadder, but I felt he was right. Lorraine was determined not to leave Adelaide.

The waitress served our plates. Oh my, what lovely grits. As they say in Oklahoma, I was in hog heaven, which is not as grand as Heaven but quite nice on an earthly scale.

Wiggins speared a link sausage, waggled it at me. "Not that we should make appearing a habit, but I know how fond you are of Lulu's, and I wanted to say"—his spaniel brown eyes were admiring—"your assumption that the troubles at the library re-volve around the theft of Susannah Fairlee's diary may be correct and should be investigated. Unfortunately, the acting chief erased the information you left on the blackboard in Chief Cobb's office. The official conclusion is that Michelle Hoyt committed all the crimes at the library. I trust your instinct—and Lorraine's—that such is not the case."

I had no doubt Lorraine's championing of Michelle weighed a lot heavier on the scale than mine.

"Therefore, it would be premature to consider your assignment at an end. Find out the truth of the matter and help these young lovers." His face softened.

I knew he recalled other young lovers from long ago.

"Bring the guilty party to justice." He looked concerned. "This is a daunting task, since you have no means of gaining support from the proper authorities." His brown eyes bored into mine. "I am confident you will not fail."

A twenty-one-gun salute could not have thrilled me more than Wiggins's confidence in me.

"I had hoped to obtain information that would resolve the mat-ter." He shook his head. "I have it on good authority"—Wiggins, of course, had access to Heavenly files not open to such as I—"that Susannah Fairlee was struck down."

I sat stone still. "Struck down?"

His face was grave. "In early evening as she gardened."

Like rapidly fluttered still photographs, I remembered the black-clad figure opening the box of Susannah Fairlee's papers, grabbing a diary, the overhead light blazing, the thief wheeling and firing at Ben Douglas. Oh yes, there might be a very good reason to steal that diary, which must contain knowledge dangerous enough to a killer that it needed to be obtained no matter the cost.

"Who killed Susannah?"

"She was struck down from behind and didn't see her assailant."

I understood. God knows every human heart, but Wiggins and those who serve the department aren't privy to all knowledge.

I'd scarcely taken in the implications of Susannah's murder when I realized the seat beside me was empty. Wiggins was gone. A bill lay atop his check and mine on the counter. Always the gentleman, he was paying for my breakfast.

Struck down...

I recalled a sentence in Joe Cooper's story about Michelle Hoyt in the *Bugle*: *Fairlee passed away September 17 at the age of seventy-three.* If Susannah's death had been a homicide, he would have included that fact. Obviously, her death must have appeared to be an accident.

I sipped coffee and considered what difference it made if Susannah Fairlee was murdered. Nothing out of the ordinary occurred at Goddard Library until the story appeared in the *Bugle* that Susannah's diaries had been given to the library and they would be read. After the story, odd events occurred at the library, Michelle was decoyed and held, a rare journal was stolen and planted in her apartment. The result? Michelle did not begin her research into Susannah's diaries Friday morning. By the time, if ever, that Michelle was cleared or anyone got around to thinking about the Fairlee project, the last diary would be long gone. Since the contents list was also taken, the diary's disappearance might not be noted.

The intruder skipped Thursday night to let a quiet evening reassure the authorities that illicit activities at the library had ended with the theft of the rare book. The intruder knew Michelle was safely out of the way and wouldn't be at the library Friday morning, so the last act could wait. But Ben Douglas thought there had been an unauthorized entry into the library Thursday evening because he heard me exclaim on the landing. He searched the library, found nothing out of the way. But he didn't assume the disturbances at the library were over, so he varied his routine Friday night and was alert for a late-night visitor. He was shot for his vigilance.

Someone was desperate to prevent anyone from reading Susannah Fairlee's current diary, desperate enough to break and enter, kidnap, steal, and shoot an elderly guard. In her diary, if Susannah was like most people, she confided her thoughts and concerns and uncertainties and fears.

Now Wiggins informed me that Susannah Fairlee did not know who struck her down.

⌒⌒

Chief Cobb's office was dim. I turned on all the lights. I like light, though earth's lights, even at their brightest, can't compare to the glow of Heaven. The light in Heaven . . . Oh yes, Precept Seven: "Information about Heaven is not yours to impart. Simply smile and say, 'Time will tell.'"

I looked at the blackboard and pressed my lips together. The erasure of my comments had been sloppily done, and now the board was a smear of chalk with occasional letters remaining. There was no point in re-creating the text or adding to it, since Chief Cobb was gone.

My eyes flicked around the silent office, empty except for me. The chief's bumptious substitute was taking the weekend off. I smiled as I strolled to the chief's desk, settled in his chair, and turned to the computer. It took a little while, but I found a file for Susannah Fairlee. I remembered the brash ME Jacob Brandt. He had submitted the autopsy report to Chief Cobb, since all unexplained deaths are investigated.

Brandt's e-mail was brisk:

> Autopsy file attached. No need to worry your pretty head. Short version: cause of death drowning. Takes bad luck to drown in a goldfish pond. Maybe she felt dizzy, in her seventies. Anyway, she apparently fell forward, cracked her head against one of the decorative boulders, slid into the water facedown, and that's all she wrote. Time of death estimated (you know the parameters, 30 to 45 minutes either way) at six thirty p.m.

I started to tap into the chief's e-mail directory, then noticed an old-fashioned Rolodex on the desk. In an instant, I had Jacob Brandt's cell number. I picked up the chief's phone, dialed.

"Yo, Sam. Thought you and your lady were lapping up piña coladas on the beach in the moonlight." There was more than a hint of envy in his tone. "Or does the Galvez run more to tea and cookies at bedtime? Went there once with my grandmother. Old and stately—the hotel, not Gram; she's a pistol—but maybe you can see the Gulf from your windows."

I made my voice chummy. "We can almost hear the surf from here. But the chief's always in touch. I'm Officer Luhsoo"—I mumbled—"and he's got me working on a file that may turn out to be a cold case. You did the autopsy on Susannah Fairlee in mid-September. We got a squeal"—I hoped my lingo was not too 1940s, but people, bless them, are very uncritical, especially young men when addressed by a woman's husky voice—"that somebody bashed Fairlee, put her in the water. The chief said you are bright, very bright, and if anybody could figure out how it was done, it would be you."

I remembered the brash, tousle-haired, wiry ME clearly: young, irreverent, but very bright eyes and a quick mind.

"Never knew Sam thought so highly of me." The tone was flip, but there was an undercurrent of pleasure in his voice. "Okay. Let me think back to the scene. No preconceptions. Floodlights rigged when I came. Body of white female lying next to a goldfish pond. Livid bruise right temporal lobe, evident drowning victim, confirmed by autopsy. Cops on-site figured she either tripped and took a header into a decorative boulder or felt faint, ditto. Could it have happened another way? Sure. Her garden trowel was right there by this clump of orange flowers. Say she was kneeling, doing whatever the hell gardeners do, and her attacker comes up behind her with a brick—tippy-toe very likely, though it was soft grass, no reason to make noise if he tried to be quiet. Yeah, I can see it in my mind: brick in a gloved hand, bend forward, full-force swing, catch the right temple. Sure as hell she'd be stunned. A shove against the decorative boulder leaving an artistic blood smear, then face in the water, knee on the back, over pretty quick. Take the brick and toss it in a lake somewhere. Better tell Sam it will be hell to prove."

"Many thanks. We'll let you know what happens."

I hung up, turned back to the computer. In an instant I had the website for the Hotel Galvez. I studied the telephone number long enough to commit it to memory, then I clicked and pulled up the *Gazette* story about Susannah Fairlee's "accident."

Civic Leader Dies in Pond

Susannah Fairlee, 73, longtime Adelaide civic leader, was found dead in her garden yesterday evening by next-door neighbor Judith Eastman, 327 Arnold Street. Police Detective Sergeant Hal Price said the death appears to be accidental, pending an autopsy.

Officers arriving at the scene found Mrs. Fairlee unresponsive, partially submerged in a goldfish pond. Police said Mrs. Eastman discovered Mrs. Fairlee facedown in the water at a quarter to eight and pulled her to the bank, then called 911.

A tearful Mrs. Eastman told authorities she felt dreadful that she hadn't checked on her neighbor sooner. "I knew something was wrong when her kitchen light didn't come on around seven, because her car was in the drive and that meant she was home and should have been fixing her supper. I called before I went over, but finally it got real dark and still there wasn't any light, so I got my flashlight and walked over. I saw her legs on the bank and I knew something was awfully wrong. I ran to the pond and pulled and pulled until I got her out of the water, but she was cold as ice. I was too late, and her head was all bruised so bad."

Mrs. Fairlee was known for her . . .

I was familiar with Susannah's background, thanks to Joe Cooper's story on Michelle, with Susannah's public service on the city council and the many other organizations with which she served. According to the *Bugle* story, Michelle intended to scan the last two diaries, covering the period of time after Susannah's retirement, and return those to her daughter, then begin an exhaustive study of the diaries pertaining to Susannah's years when she was on the city council.

I believed that particular piece of information was the trip wire that resulted in the theft at the library, Ben Douglas's injury, and Michelle Hoyt's peril. Did I know enough to call Chief Cobb? Slowly I shook my head. Not yet.

Michelle's peril . . .

Chapter 8

Joe Cooper leaned against the pale blue kitchen wall. "That's the damndest story I ever heard." Absently he reached out to stroke the long-legged black cat standing on the counter.

Michelle whirled from the stove top, a spatula in hand. Scrambled eggs began to thicken. "I didn't make it up." Her voice wobbled.

Joe looked surprised. "I got that. I'm just saying it's nutty. Somebody"—his face squeezed in concentration—"went to a hell of a lot of trouble to make you a fall guy. There has to be a reason. So, who hates you?"

She finished swirling the eggs, scooped them onto a platter with bacon. She carried the platter to a small wooden table.

Joe followed, slid into a chair opposite her, looked at her inquiringly. His bony face was attractive with a stubble of beard. He'd obviously been caught by surprise when Michelle called him from the police station and had taken only enough time to pull on a threadbare sweatshirt, faded jeans, and sneakers.

She pushed the platter toward him, retrieved toast as it popped up in the toaster on one side of the table.

Joe served himself generously, handed the platter to her.

She took several pieces of bacon, a small portion of eggs, then said quietly, "Nobody hates me. That makes everything even scarier." Her young face was exhausted, vulnerable. She buttered a slice of toast.

He took a moment to eat, then said, oh so casually, "You're not in love with some guy and there's another girl?" He watched her closely.

His query brought a wry smile to her face. "The last guy I dated dumped me for an oilman's daughter, but nobody ever said Bobby didn't have his eye on a cushy future." She piled bacon and eggs on a piece of toast and began to eat.

Joe held a piece of bacon in one big hand. "Tough, huh?"

She finished half the toast, looked as amused as an exhausted, scared woman could. "I always knew he was short-term but he was fun. I wasn't interested in him really. Now Bobby and Susie Lots-of-Bucks are a twosome, I'm on my own, and we are all fine with that." The smile slipped away. "Neither of them have any reason to want to get me in trouble, and frankly Bobby doesn't have the brains to figure out the kind of mess I'm in. Long on looks, short on thought."

"There has to be a reason." Joe was emphatic. "Either somebody hates you or you have something somebody wants or you pose some kind of big-time problem."

Michelle looked bewildered. "There's no Heathcliff in my past."

Joe picked up his last piece of bacon, ate it in two bites. "Okay. Let's say it's not personal. Somehow, someway you are a threat to someone."

She shook her head. "I don't have a ruby hidden in my sock. Nobody handed me a letter at midnight with a key to a bank vault. I don't have the goods on anybody. In short"—she finished the toast and wiped a smear of butter from her chin—"no one has any reason to frame me for anything. Joe"—her voice was shaky—"what am I going to do?"

It was time for me to approach them.

In the hall outside Michelle's door, I was halfway visible in a French blue uniform when I stopped. The colors faded. Not so fast. I couldn't appear as Officer Loy. The light might not have been strong in the *Bugle* office, but Joe Cooper had studied me carefully, and I'd told him I was Theresa Lisieux. Moreover, attempting to reassure Michelle, I'd briefly appeared in her cell and later spoken to her.

I wanted Joe's help and I had to warn Michelle. Was I stymied? Then I grinned. As Mama often told me, "Bailey Ruth, honey, when all else fails, try the truth." Possibly said with a slight edge, though Mama was kind and patient even when sorely tried by one of her redheaded brood.

I gave a decided nod. Colors curved and curled. I didn't have a mirror, but knew I was elegant in a paisley lily top with thin solid bands at the modest V-neck and flared three-quarter-length sleeves, ash gray twill trousers, and sleek gray leather flats with a silver buckle. A paisley purse completed my ensemble. I smoothed my hair and knocked.

The door opened. Joe Cooper looked big and immovable. Instant recognition flared in his startled gaze.

I'd been wise not to appear as Officer Loy. I hurried to speak, because recognition had been followed by cold, questioning appraisal. Maybe the first law for reporters was: *Coincidences stink like boiled cabbage.* "We met in your office." My bland tone oozed sincerity. "I'm here because Michelle is being falsely accused and I can help her."

Michelle stood at his elbow. "You . . ." Her eyes were wide and staring.

Joe turned toward her, jerked a thumb at me. "You know her?"

"Not exactly . . ."

I glanced at the breakfast table. The plates had been cleared. They'd finished their breakfast while I'd considered my entrance. I took a step forward.

Joe hesitated, moved aside.

I beamed at them and swept into the small living room. As though invited, I sank into one of the rattan chairs. "I know you are trying to make sense out of what's happened. Let me help." I gestured toward the blue sofa. "Do sit down."

Joe stood his ground. "Lady—"

"Theresa Lisieux."

Michelle drew in a quick, sharp breath. She was trembling slightly.

I smiled modestly. "Not that I deserve her name, but she was always willing to serve, and that's what I hope to do."

Joe glanced at me, then at Michelle. "Okay, so I'm the big dumb guy who's out of the loop. Michelle looks like she's seen a ghost, and I get a vibe that Theresa Lisieux isn't exactly your name. Spell it out for me." His tone was slightly belligerent.

Michelle sank down on the sofa, clasped her hands tightly together. "Saint Theresa, the Little Flower. My mom's favorite saint. 'Perfection consists in doing His will, in being that which He wants us to be.'" She looked at me intently. "Did Mom send you? She's in Nepal right now, tracking down falcons."

Joe stood beside the sofa. His glare was intense and his stance pugnacious with his thumbs hooked in the pockets of his jeans.

I almost heard a Heavenly chorus. When we listen, we hear what we need to know. "Your mom wants you to be safe. I'm delighted to be of service." If Michelle now assumed I was there on behalf of her mother, the conclusion was hers. And, as I well knew, mothers offer daily prayers for children's well-being, so perhaps I *was* here on her mother's behalf. "Now," I spoke crisply, "here's the situation." I marshaled the important points. "Joe wrote a story that appeared in last Monday's *Bugle* about your project to study the diaries of Susannah Fairlee. That story triggered everything that happened the rest of the week: the roses in the library, the vandalism of the gargoyle, your kidnapping, the theft of the rare book, and, finally, last night, the shooting of Ben Douglas. Everything except the shooting was carefully planned to hide the fact that the true objective was to take Susannah Fairlee's last diary."

"Why?" Joe looked skeptical.

"Susannah Fairlee was murdered." I repeated the ME's scenario.

Joe Cooper raised a skeptical eyebrow. "You think somebody came creeping up on an old woman in her garden, slammed her with a blunt instrument, pushed her into a boulder, then held her down in water? Why the hell? Was she rich? Did she know stuff she shouldn't know? Why?"

"That's what I intend to find out."

Joe folded his arms. "Her death was certified an accident, right?"

I wasn't quailed. "She was murdered. I not only have that on good authority, I know that Susannah Fairlee's last diary was stolen from the library, and when the night watchman tried to stop the thief, he was shot. Only Susannah's death by murder explains the necessity of obtaining that diary."

Michelle's eyes were wide and staring. "You think someone went to the effort of kidnapping me and blaming me for a theft to keep me from reading that diary?"

"Exactly." I looked at Joe. "Process it. Susannah was murdered. Susannah kept diaries. Susannah's diaries were to be used for a history project. The murderer knows there could be something incriminating in a diary. If you murdered her, what would you do?"

Joe frowned. "I'd figure out a way to get that diary. I'd make it a certainty the researcher wouldn't get into those boxes anytime soon. If ever. Yeah. I can see it."

Michelle shivered, wrapped her arms tightly across her front. "Murder." Michelle's voice was faint. "It has to be something like that. Why else would anyone go to such immense effort to smear me? And"—there was remembered fear in her eyes—"I was scared at that house on Montague. I didn't feel right when I stepped into the kitchen. I thought I'd move fast, get the folder, get out of there. I ran across the kitchen and started down the stairs, and then the door slammed shut and I was trapped."

Joe's gaze was distant. He was obviously thinking hard. "We've got two ways to go after the murderer. Maybe Michelle knows something, anything that can give us a lead. The other way is to figure out who wanted Susannah Fairlee dead."

"Exactly. There is a great deal we can do." I turned toward Michelle. "Let's go back to the phone call that decoyed you to Montague Street. Can you find the number on your cell?"

Michelle popped up to retrieve her leather purse from a small table by the front door. She returned to the sofa. She checked the cell, spoke the number aloud.

Joe pulled out a small pad and wrote down the number. "University number. I'll call. . . . Hello. Joe Cooper at the *Bugle*. I'm speaking to? . . . Henry Roberts. Henry, were you at this number around five o'clock Wednesday? . . . I spoke to a woman calling from this number. Could you suggest who might have used this phone? . . . This phone is in which office? . . . Right. Would the office be locked after you left? . . . Thanks." He tapped End. "History Department. Henry's a work-study student, was there Wednesday afternoon correcting multiple-choice exams for a professor. This desk is one of several near Dr. Gordon's office that's used by work-study students. He left around four. The office wasn't locked."

Michelle waved a hand in dismissal. "Anybody could call from there. I know where it is. There are some big ferns in pots that screen the room with the work-study desks."

I looked at Michelle. "I want you to remember Wednesday afternoon." I didn't miss the quick flicker of her eyes toward Joe. She remembered Wednesday afternoon and her eagerness to be done with her errands and her excitement that she was going to meet Joe at the Brown Owl. "Your cell rings. You answer."

Michelle twined a strand of dark hair around one finger, hunched in thought.

"A voice said, 'Michelle.' There was a cough, and a kind of husky voice said, 'Sorry about my cold. Calling for Dr. Gordon.' Then I thought she—I guess it could have been a man—said, 'Dr. Gordon's speaking at the student center at six and he wants you to pick up a folder for him. Go to the back door at 928 Montague Street. The door's unlocked. The folder is inside. A tab on it reads: *The Origin of the Phoenician Alphabet*. Take the folder to Dr. Gordon. He'll be waiting in the foyer at the student center.' She—or he—hung up. I was irritated. I mean, I didn't sign on to be somebody's errand boy, but you do what the boss tells you to do. I jumped in my car and drove over there. It's an old-fashioned two-story brick house, kind of rambling. You can't see it very well through the trees. Lots of sycamores and weeping willows. A long driveway is screened on one side by evergreens. There was no car in the driveway. I didn't think about that. I went up to the back door and started to knock and saw a note taped to the doorjamb. The note—it was printed, thick block letters on a piece of lined paper—said to go inside and go down to the basement, the door was open, and get the folder from the desk. I stepped inside, called out, 'Hello.' "

For an instant her face was shadowed by remembered fear.

"It was awfully quiet. I had an uncomfortable feeling." She touched her cheek with shaky fingers. "That's not right. I was more than uncomfortable. I was scared. I didn't like the way the air felt. I didn't like the way it was deathly quiet in there. I saw light shining from the doorway to the basement. I didn't want to go into the basement, but I felt like I had to. I decided to hurry and get the folder and get out of there. I started down the stairs. The door slammed shut."

"Did you see anyone?"

"The kitchen was empty. I didn't see anyone. I didn't hear anything until the door slammed."

"What did the house smell like?"

She looked surprised, then thoughtful. "That's odd when I think about it. I was in the kitchen and it didn't have any smell at all. It was stuffy. No air moving. No scent of anything cooking." She brushed back a tangle of hair, looked forlorn. "I don't know anything that will help."

Joe leaned toward her. "You've already helped. We know the call came from the History Department. That gives us a place to start. The caller also had to be at the house when you came. Maybe somebody saw a car, maybe somebody saw a pedestrian, maybe somebody saw something. The caller was in those two places at those specific times. But we've got more than that. How did the murderer know you could be held there and nobody would find you? There has to be a link between the murderer and that house."

I looked at him with respect. "Exactly. Here's what we'll do." I gave them their instructions.

⟡

I hummed as I settled into Chief Cobb's chair and turned to the computer. I nodded in satisfaction as I read the report from Detectives Weitz and Smith:

> To: Acting Chief
>
> From: Detectives Weitz and Smith
>
> Search of basement at 928 Montague Street indicated recent use. Sheets on cot wrinkled. Damp towels in half bath. Taken into evidence. Emptied frozen food containers stacked on counter by sink. All containers show fingerprints matching those of Michelle Hoyt. No

other prints found on containers. This may be seen as evidence corroborating her claim of abduction, since there should have been smudged fingerprints on the boxes from handling by store employees. Also taken into evidence.

Hoyt's prints were found in the bath, on several chairs, some pool table balls, on a pool cue, on the doorknobs on either side of the basement door, and on the kitchen door. Her prints were not found otherwise in the kitchen area.

The house is the residence of Professor Wendell Hughes and his wife, Abigail. Hughes teaches romance languages. According to next-door neighbor Edith Mallory, Hughes is currently in Andalusia, Spain, on a year's sabbatical with his wife, and the house is not occupied. Mrs. Mallory has a key to the house and checks every week or so. She last visited the house about ten days ago and found everything in order. Mrs. Mallory said the drive is not visible to her through the hedges between the houses. She had no occasion to look at the drive in the past few days and therefore cannot say if a car was parked there from 5 p.m. Wednesday afternoon until Saturday morning.

Further examination revealed a hole in a back window pane that had been made by a glass cutter. The hole was large enough to make it possible for an intruder to reach inside, unlock the window, and gain access to the house. There was no damage apparent inside the house.

I replied:

To: Detectives Weitz and Smith
From: Acting Chief

Excellent work.

Inform Goddard Library Director Kathleen Garza that Ms. Hoyt is not a suspect in the theft of the rare book, that she was held captive from Wednesday night to this morning, that the book was stolen Wednesday night and placed at her residence to incriminate her and prevent her from reading the diaries of Susannah Fairlee, and that this plot was exposed by the shooting of Security Officer Ben Douglas Friday night in the room where the Fairlee material was housed. The connection to Hoyt's abduction is reinforced by the discovery of a window pane at the house on Montague Street with a hole made by a glass cutter, which was the instrument used to effect the theft of the rare book.

The investigation now centers on the murder of Susannah Fairlee Sept. 17. Pursuant to a crime tip, the ME confirms that the trauma Fairlee suffered supports the theory that Fairlee was struck on the head and, while stunned from the blow, was held down in the water by her assailant until she drowned. The library intruder who shot Douglas removed Fairlee's most recent diary from the collection.

Inform Dr. Gordon of the History Department that Ms. Hoyt has been exonerated and released.

Canvass Fairlee's neighborhood for information about anyone seen in the vicinity at dusk Sept. 17. Jog neighbors'
memories by reminding them Sept. 17 was the evening when
police and emergency vehicles arrived at the Fairlee residence after her body was discovered by next-door neighbor
Mrs. Eastman. If no one, familiar or unknown, was observed
near the Fairlee residence, create a map to determine how
an assailant could approach without being seen.

Like a politician spinning a story, I was making progress in
placing Michelle in a favorable light publicly. For the moment. My
glow of self approval vanished quickly. Michelle was home free
this weekend, but she would be yanked back to jail Monday faster
than a flea hops unless I figured out who killed Susannah Fairlee
and connected her murder to the events at Goddard Library.

Essential to determine Susannah Fairlee's contacts the
last week of her life. Use additional officers if required.
Submit e-mail report by six p.m.

Acting Chief

Detectives Weitz and Smith would do their best and maybe their
efforts would give me a lead. I looked at the round-faced clock on
the wall. It was shortly after ten a.m. on Saturday. In less than forty-
eight hours, Howie Warren would amble back into the chief's office,
ready to hold a news conference laying out the case against Michelle.
So far he apparently was too lazy and absorbed in his free time to
check on the progress of the case. Of course, when he left to play

golf, he knew Michelle was in custody and the case was a fait accompli, so he assumed the focus would continue to be on Michelle.

Before that news conference occurred, I needed to discover the truth about Susannah Fairlee and why she had to die.

Who was Susannah Fairlee?

I don't know about big cities, but obituaries are personal in a small town. I remembered how touched I was to read what our daughter, Dil, wrote about her father and me: Mama and Daddy were always the first to the party and the last to leave. Mama never met a person she didn't find fascinating, and Daddy was willing to mortgage the house when he drilled a wildcat well. Mama's temper was as red as her hair. You didn't tell her you couldn't. She knew you could. Daddy's laugh was as robust as his favorite Benny Goodman, "Stompin' at the Savoy."

I called up Susannah's obituary in the *Gazette*. I studied her photo. Susannah was likely in her sixties when the picture was taken. Her broad face was sunny and cheerful, her gaze direct, her smile genuine. She looked competent, interesting, lively, a woman who had been places and done things.

Susannah Martin Fairlee

June 25, 1941–September 17, 2014

Susannah Martin Fairlee passed away unexpectedly at her home September 17. She was the daughter of the late Captain Edmond Jones Martin and the late Regina Evans Martin. Susannah was born in Honolulu. She was the youngest of four daughters. Her father, an Army pilot, was killed during the bombing of Hickam Field on December 7, 1941. Her mother brought the family to Adelaide and was a teacher here for thirty-two years.

Susannah played tennis at Adelaide High School and at the University of Oklahoma. She received a degree in business in 1963. She returned to Adelaide where she worked in the family floral business. In 1964, she married Jonathan Fairlee, who owned Fairlee Furniture Mart. She and Jonathan were the parents of a daughter, Janet, and son, Michael. In 1972, Susannah ran for a seat on the city council and won. On the council, she twice supported a bond issue for new schools. She was the leading force in the transformation of the old railroad station into a city theater venue. She was a founder of Kate's Corner, a nonprofit that serves meals to the poor. She worked tirelessly to encourage creation of parks throughout Adelaide. She opposed tax relief to attract corporations, believing that corporations should choose Adelaide because of its stellar workforce and locale. She retired two years ago from the city council.

A lifelong tennis player, she was Missouri Valley Champion in every age group in which she played. She was a lifelong communicant at St. Mildred's Episcopal Church and twice served as directress of the Altar Guild. She was a Stephen Minister for five years up to the time of her death. Susannah's favorite Bible verse was Philippians 4:8: "Finally, brethren, whatever is true, whatever is honorable, whatever is pure, whatever is of good repute, if there is any excellence and if anything worthy of your praise, let your mind dwell on these things."

Susannah was preceded in death by her parents and her husband, Jonathan. She is survived by her daughter, Janet Hastings, son-in-law Richard, and beloved grandchildren Mark, Brittany, and Catherine, of Anchorage, Alaska, and son, Lieutenant Colonel Michael Fairlee, daughter-in-law Marie, and beloved grandson, James, of Fort Bliss, Texas.

In addition to tennis Susannah loved barbecue, antiques stores, summer twilight, Edna St. Vincent Millay's poetry, faded photographs, cold beer, Jay Leno, train whistles in the night, the sound of laughter, and her good friends, former business partner Harriet Beal, bridge partner Ann Curry, and tennis partner Pamela Wilson.

Mom, we love you.

In lieu of flowers, please consider a memorial gift to St. Mildred's Episcopal Church, the Salvation Army, Habitat for Humanity, or your favorite charity.

A woman well loved. But somewhere in a life marked by humor and caring, Susannah Fairlee had encountered the person who caused her death, put Michelle in jeopardy of prison, and coolly shot Ben Douglas.

Chapter 9

Ben Douglas moved restively. Fever flushed his face. A damp cloth gently wiped his forehead and cheeks, apparently moving under its own volition. "They're doing everything they can." Lorraine sounded weary. "Antibiotics in the IV and two shots. But his pulse is weak. I'm very afraid."

I knew where Lorraine stood because of the cloth. I reached out and gently patted a thin shoulder. "If God opens the gates of larger life, Ben will find joy."

Her reply was whiplash fast, her tone fierce. "Next week is his granddaughter's birthday. He's very proud of her. She's coming all the way from El Paso to see him. He has presents waiting for her in his living room. Several times he's been awake for a bit, and he keeps saying her name."

The pull of this world against the welcome of the next.

"Would it help if I told you that Wig—that Paul loves his train station, that he finds happiness in sending the Rescue Express to help people on their journeys here, just as he did in life, would that make it easier—"

"You want me to let go? But Ben shouldn't have been hurt." Her voice was uneven. "Ben misses his wife so much. Oh, I wish I knew what was best."

"Paul"—it still seemed odd to speak of Wiggins by his first name, and I hoped he understood I intended no disrespect—"said when the shell burst, he didn't want to leave the earth. He tried to stay because he loved you, but his time here was done. He had a new purpose." I took a quick breath. "He said he was glad you married Charles."

"Charles." Lorraine's voice was soft. "We were happy. He never knew about Paul. I couldn't tell him. He might have blamed himself."

"Blame?"

A gurgling sound and Ben Douglas's body jerked.

Sudden strident beeps filled the small space.

The curtain was pulled aside and a nurse hurried in. She rushed to the bedside. Suddenly a voice over the intercom announced, *"Code Blue ICU 5, Code Blue ICU 5."*

The bed was soon surrounded by figures in scrubs intent upon the still figure of Ben Douglas.

I couldn't help Ben. That was in the hands of those working fast to save him. But I could do my best to discover who had put him in peril.

⁂

I have fond memories of St. Mildred's. My life was entwined with the church: regular attendance, weddings, christenings, funerals, the Altar Guild, and, of course, my first arrival as an emissary was on a dark evening in the backyard of the rectory to find the rector's wife standing over the body of a murder victim.

I took a moment to drop by the chapel and light a candle for Ben. I added Lorraine to my prayer. She had spoken about blame. Who would be blamed for what? I tucked that puzzle at the back of my mind to consider when we again met. I went from the chapel to the office of the church secretary, blessedly empty on a Saturday. It took only a moment to find the name of the current directress of the Altar Guild and to dial her number.

I was relieved when a cheerful voice answered. In a world of answering machines and cell phones, ringing a landline often leads to a recorded message. If Emma Carson had caller ID, she had already identified the call as coming from St. Mildred's. I introduced myself as Margaret Scott (in honor of Margaret of Scotland, who was among the first to organize women to care for altar vestments), a friend of Susannah's daughter. I must remember that I was Margaret Scott to Susannah's friends and Theresa Lisieux with Joe and Michelle. And then there was Officer Loy. . . . "I'm in town quite briefly. I'm creating a memory book about Susannah to give to Janet on Mother's Day as a surprise. I'm hoping you can give me the phone numbers and addresses of Susannah's dear friends Harriet Beal, Ann Curry, and Pamela Wilson."

⁊

A bell sang as I pushed open the door of Now and Again. Cheerful '40s band music—Glenn Miller's "In the Mood"—was a fitting backdrop for an eclectic collection of movie posters from the last century, World War II memorabilia, stacks of *Saturday Evening*

*Post*s, vinyl records, vintage paperbacks, garden statuary—including spaniels, deer, and a squirrel in a top hat—and a shelf of kachina dolls. The counter was a couple of boards balanced on top of a cardboard Stutz Bearcat.

I stepped inside and sniffed appreciatively at the aroma of robust coffee and—I didn't think my senses deceived me—burnt-sugar cake. Mama made the best burnt-sugar cake I ever tasted. I remembered perching on a stool with a big wooden spoon and stirring melting sugar in a heavy iron skillet as it turned brown. *Mmmmm.*

A hearty laugh sounded. A heavyset henna-haired woman with a kerchief around her head and a cake plate in one hand was standing in a doorway behind the cardboard car. "You know how to get yourself a serving, young lady. Make yourself at home over there." She gestured casually toward a couple of wooden tables with bright red wooden chairs.

I still thrill to being twenty-seven again. "Thank you. I'd love a piece of cake."

She served us each a mug of steaming black coffee and a generous slice of cake. I knew the recipe was authentic when I tasted the burnt-sugar frosting. I introduced myself as Margaret Scott, an old friend of Janet Fairlee Hastings.

Harriet Beal was eager to share memories of her years in business with Susannah. "She was a rock. Like we say in Oklahoma, a straight arrow. Even insisted"—Harriet gave me a wicked smile—"on labeling stuff that wasn't old as 'in the tradition of . . .' She got herself a rep. If she said a piece was authentic, everybody took her at her word." Her smile slid away. "Miss her." Her voice was gruff.

"This will be meaningful to Janet. She was really busy with the kids' sporting stuff this fall, and she felt like she neglected her mom and that something was worrying Susannah."

Harriet's thickly mascaraed eyes widened. "Janet can rest easy. Susannah was talking about Janet just the week before she died. Susannah said Janet always tried hard to do everything right and Michael had excelled at everything he did. He's retiring from the military and coming home to Adelaide. That would have been special for Susannah. Susannah didn't have any problems."

"You can't think of anything recently when Susannah seemed worried or upset?"

Harriet took a last bite of cake. "Nothing that concerned her personally."

I was grasping at any straw. "Anything at all. Any indication of stress or concern about anybody?"

"As I said, nothing to do with her personally. We were out to dinner the week before Susannah died. She was awfully quiet. I thought I knew why." Her expression was earnest. "Some people go out of their way to help others. Susannah was like that. She was a Stephen Minister. The only reason I knew was because once I wanted her to be here at the store for me on a Tuesday afternoon, and she said she couldn't help out on a Tuesday. She had a Stephen-care recipient. Of course, she didn't say a word about who it was or anything like that. But Tuesday night at dinner, she wasn't her usual self. I said, 'Hard afternoon?' She knew I meant her Stephen visit. She said, 'I wish I could give her peace.' Then she shook her head, started talking about going to Anchorage for Thanksgiving."

Ann Curry was one of those women who were as beautiful at sixty as they were at sixteen. Short-cut silver hair framed classic features with camellia-fresh skin and blue eyes as guileless as a child's. I knew her sort. Utterly charming and as cutthroat at the bridge table as any riverboat gambler. She shared insights about her friend—"honorable . . . kind . . . beneath that kindly exterior quite immovable on important matters"—and listened attentively as I concluded. "Susannah distressed?" Something flickered in her eyes. "We played bridge the week before she died. Top of her game that day. Doubled and won."

She had not directly answered my question. I shot her a quick look, knew I was dealing with a reticent woman who was careful in what she said and to whom. My demeanor changed. "I hadn't intended to reveal this, but there is suspicion that Susannah's death was not accidental. I'm an investigator. The family, of course, wants the truth known, and that's why I approached you as an old friend putting together a memory book." I spoke crisply, shedding the attitude of a charming young woman. I was sure Susannah's family would indeed be on board if they knew the circumstances. "If anything struck you as unusual or different in Susannah's behavior, please tell me."

Ann smoothed back a strand of silver hair. She studied me, finally nodded. "I saw Susannah on campus the day she died. I teach violin. I'd finished my eleven o'clock class and was on my way to lunch. Gorgeous day. Mid-September. Not a cloud in the sky. I looked across the oval and saw her coming out of the Administration Building. I was surprised. It wasn't a matter of town versus gown, but when Susannah was on the city council, she jealously protected Adelaide's independence from undue influence by the college. She had friends on the faculty, but it wouldn't be commonplace to see her on campus. I was pleased. I thought I'd catch her and see if she wanted to go to a tea shop with me. I hurried. She didn't see me as she came down the steps. I saw her face as she turned away. I didn't call out." She stopped.

I waited.

"She had a look I'd only seen once before. A woman we both knew had an abusive husband. I saw Susannah the day she went to his office to tell him that Gail was moving out and coming to Susannah's home, and if he threatened her or refused a divorce, Susannah would see him in jail." Ann sighed. "I almost followed Susannah. I felt something must be seriously awry. But the way she was moving—head down, shoulders tight—made me think this wasn't a good time to talk to her. That night I kept thinking about it and I was worried. I wondered if there was something wrong at the college, something I should know about. I decided I'd call her the next day. I was getting ready to go to bed when the call came that Susannah had died."

༄

Pamela Wilson's narrow, tanned face was pleasantly ugly, her nose a little too long, her chin a little too sharp, but there was bright intelligence in her dark eyes and a no-nonsense jut to her jaw. ". . . excellent forehand. A little weak on her backhand."

"You learn a lot about someone when you play tennis with them." I made it a statement, not a question. Some of my happiest memories were of hot summer days on the local courts and icy orange sodas when we cooled down in the clubhouse. "What did the game tell you about Susannah?"

"She played the game right. She was like a terrier. She never gave up." Her face softened. "A little foolhardy sometimes in rushing the net. Fearless. But she'd give a big whoop of laughter when someone got a shot past her. Always pleasant. Not something you can say about everybody you play with. The only time she turned crusty was when somebody consistently called good balls out."

"How did Susannah feel about an opponent who made questionable line calls?"

A short bark of laughter. "Next time she was at the net, Susannah'd slam the ball right on the line and give the woman a hard stare. The calls got better after that." Another bark of laughter.

I finished my cup of black tea and resisted taking another lace cookie. My, they were good. I closed my notebook, then asked, seemingly as an afterthought, "Pam"—we were comfortably on a first-name basis now—"Janet had a feeling something was troubling her mother not long before she died. Did Susannah say anything to you?"

Pam looked suddenly sad. "I keep going over and over the last time I talked to her." She pressed her lips together for an instant before she continued. "We played singles every Wednesday morning. Played every week for years unless one of us was sick or out of town. She didn't show up." Remembered astonishment lifted her voice. "I mean, thank God, it was just us. Singles. Not doubles. But she didn't come or call. I kept calling but her cell was turned off. Finally I caught her that afternoon." Tears glistened in Pam's eyes. "I reamed her out. She said was she was sorry, something had come up that she had to deal with, but she sounded like she wasn't really hearing me. I could tell her mind was a million miles away. God, isn't it awful how every little molehill can be a mountain? I built a mountain out of her not showing up. I got mad and hung up on her." Tears rolled down her thin cheeks. "Hell of a way to say good-bye."

"Do you recall—"

"I'll never forget." The words came in short bursts. "The day she died." Pam used the back of one hand to brush tears from her cheeks. "I should have known something was terribly wrong. She was always thoughtful. But I can't imagine what upset her to the point she'd forget our game. She wasn't sick. Hale and hearty, that was Susannah. She got along with her neighbors. I won't say everybody loved Susannah. She could be sharp. She had no patience with phonies. She spoke up when something didn't sit right with her. But the last time I saw her, our usual game, I'd swear she was on top of the world. She was proud as can be of Janet and her family and talking about going to Anchorage for Thanksgiving. Nothing wrong there. I was the one Father Bill called that night after he'd contacted Janet with the bad news. I immediately called Janet and told her I'd see to everything until she and the family could come—"

If Pam talked to Janet in Anchorage the night her mother was murdered, I need not include Janet in my suspect list. Not that I had a suspect list yet.

"—and I got in touch with the funeral home and started calling friends."

I left Pam looking somber, remembering the night her friend died.

෴

I sat unseen on a stone bench at one side of the Administration Building and tried to picture an older woman hurrying down the steps on what was to be the last day of her life. Angry. Upset.

Harriet Beal recalled an untroubled Susannah except for a sad afternoon when she visited her Stephen-care recipient. But Harriet knew of nothing that might have made Susannah angry.

Yet Ann Curry saw a furious Susannah leave the Goddard Administration Building the day Susannah died. The expression on Susannah's face was such that Ann made no attempt to speak with her.

Susannah did not have a close connection to the college. Why had she visited the Administration Building? Who did she see, if anyone?

Pam Wilson spoke to Susannah the afternoon of the day she died. Susannah told Pam she'd missed their tennis game because something came up.

Something led Susannah to visit the Administration Building on the day she was struck down in her garden.

If her killer was Goddard staff or a faculty member, everything about the series of crimes made sense. A person familiar with the campus was likely to read the Goddard *Bugle* and learn about Susannah's diaries in the library, be aware of the old legend about lovers and roses, and be adept at entering and leaving the library undetected.

The fact that Michelle's ID number was used the night the rare book was stolen indicated sophisticated knowledge of keypad locks on campus. The *Bugle* also likely reported on the sabbatical plans of Professor Wendell Hughes, whose home was used as a place to imprison Michelle.

I looked at the broad, shallow front steps leading from the sidewalk to the closed doors of the Administration Building. Ann Curry said the weather was lovely that day. I imagined it was much like this afternoon, a sunny fall day. The leaves then would have been tipped with red and gold; now they blazed with autumn color beneath a cloudless sky. The building had towers at the corners. Ivy clung to the walls. An idyllic setting in academia, but Susannah came out of that building with her face grim. I felt certain that Susannah had confronted someone there.

I didn't know what an empty building could tell me, but I decided to look around. Inside, my eyes adjusted to dimness. It was an old building with well-worn wooden floors. The lobby had an aura of faded elegance with a French provincial sofa flanked by two large Elizabethan chairs. A tapestry on the back wall depicted an old-fashioned wooden oil derrick. The Goddard family had owned town lots, ranches, and banks, but much of their fortune came from the early oil field not far from Adelaide. To my left was a frosted door with the legend *Office of the President.* To my right were two doors with the legends *Office of the Vice President* and *Office of the Treasurer.*

Hallways ran to the left and right of the central stairway, and I imagined support staff had offices there. At the base of the stairs was a directory. I studied the offices listed. On the second floor were the Bursar's Office, the Dean of Students Office, and Student Affairs. On the third floor, the Hall of Regents and four named rooms which likely were used for social functions.

Susannah Fairlee left the Administration Building obviously agitated. Which office did she visit?

✍

I arrived in the *Bugle*'s empty newsroom and heard Joe's voice in the editor's office. I reappeared in the paisley lily top, ash gray twill trousers, and gray leather flats I'd worn earlier. I hiked the paisley purse over my shoulder and moved to the office doorway. Joe sat on the edge of his desk, holding a legal pad. Michelle perched cross-legged on a ratty-looking beanbag chair

Joe stopped in midsentence. "How'd you get in? The front door's locked."

I am so accustomed to unhindered access I hadn't thought to check the door. I gave a negligent wave of my hand. *Mmm, perhaps the nails should be rosier to accent the moss green in my blouse.*

Michelle's eyes were riveted on my fingers.

As Mama always said, "When you put your foot in it, do a dance step."

I beamed at Michelle and spread my hand for a closer view. "You have a good eye. The hue depends upon where you stand. It's the very latest thing in nail polish." Did I get a whiff of coal smoke? I finished covering my tracks, hoping to avoid a departure on rising silver tracks. "Perhaps the door only seemed locked. These things happen." Wiggins should give me some points for mental agility.

"They do. When you're around." Joe's voice was dour.

Michelle continued to stare at my hand.

It was time for a high kick. Or a Hail Mary throw, whichever simile you like best. "I only have a moment. What have you found out about 928 Montague Street?"

Joe rubbed a bristly cheek. "Somebody's clever as hell. I took one side of the street, Michelle the other."

Michelle's dark curls appeared a bit windblown. She looked not only weary but hopeless. She turned both hands up in a gesture of defeat. "Nobody saw anything, nobody heard anything. It makes sense. Shrubbery and woods hide the house from the street. Nobody saw my car. Nobody saw any other car turn in."

Joe was truculent. "Anybody who reads the *Bugle* knows Hughes is on sabbatical. We had a story in mid-September and another one a couple of weeks ago. We did an e-mail interview with him about his classes there and what he hopes to bring back to campus next fall."

Michelle's face brightened. "Faculty or staff, that's what it has to be. Who else would know about the keypad codes at the library?" Her face drooped. "There's a lot of faculty and staff."

I glanced around Joe's office, noted a whiteboard with possible story ideas listed, the printing precise and easily read. I moved swiftly to the whiteboard, picked up a purple marker. I wrote *Susannah Fairlee* on one side, *Administration Building* on the other, and below them, I wrote *Library*. I drew a line from *Susannah Fairlee* to *Administration Building* to *Library*.

They listened intently as I described Susannah's departure from the Administration Building on the day she died.

Joe didn't need prompting. "Now we have a place to start."

I left them peering at the college website. They would round up every scrap of information about those who worked in the Administration Building.

I had to find the person or event that brought Susannah there the day she died.

⁊

By late afternoon, I understood Chief Cobb's reliance on M&M'S. I munched on a handful filched from the half-filled sack nestling in his lower-left desk drawer. But I needed more than a sugary punch. I needed inspiration. I'd made so many calls from the chief's phone, my fingers ached from holding the receiver. I had a quick memory of the lines I'd drawn on the whiteboard in Joe Cooper's office from *Susannah Fairlee* to *Administration Building* to *Library*. I understood the connection between Susannah and the Library. That's where her diaries were placed. But Susannah and the Administration Building? I pushed back from the chief's desk, stood, and began to pace. She wasn't a Goddard student, so she had no reason to visit the Bursar's Office. She wasn't a faculty member. I'd used the chief's computer to access all stories that included Susannah, and none connected her to anyone on the campus.

For once I wouldn't have minded a whiff of coal smoke. Perhaps it was time for me to scuttle Heavenward, a failure.

It was almost as if I heard Mama's voice. "Bailey Ruth, honey, if the front door slams in your face, go around back."

I glanced at the clock. I had an hour before I could expect a report from Detectives Weitz and Smith.

⁊

I wondered if Joe and Michelle would notice if I appeared in a different outfit. Possibly I should restrain my delight in fashion. I mean, the paisley was lovely, but I was feeling more in silk georgette mood. I appeared in the now-even-dimmer newsroom as shadows lengthened outside. I took a step and loved the swirl of a multicolor ankle-length silk georgette dress, regretfully shook my head. Joe's gaze was too sharp. By the time I reached the doorway, I was wearing paisley again. Tomorrow would be another day. That added a feeling of urgency to my thoughts. Tomorrow would be one day away from Howie's return to the chief's office.

And I was stumped.

I stepped into the office. Joe had somehow found time to shave, and his polo and chinos looked fresh. His angular face was too bony to be conventionally handsome, but he had a masculine appeal I was quite sure Michelle appreciated.

Each, in fact, was keenly aware of the other's every move.

Joe thumped his fist on his desk. Papers slid every which way. "The kid saw Fairlee's pic and ID'd her immediately. She has no reason to make it up."

Michelle, whose glossy dark hair was obviously fresh from a shampoo, looked exasperated. "I'm not saying she made it up, but I don't see how it helps."

I was ready to grasp at any straw.

"Tell me."

They both stiffened and jerked toward the doorway.

I smiled.

Michelle almost managed a smile in return.

Joe lowered his head like a buffalo irritated by gnats. "The front door's locked." He said it flatly.

I can't help teasing men. They are so serious. "Doors," I murmured, "are made to be opened." I ignored his glare. "Who saw Susannah?"

Michelle was trying not to laugh at Joe's response.

I admired how she had bounced back from an ordeal that would leave anyone shaken. She didn't know her reprieve was temporary. My challenge now was to keep her from being arrested on Monday.

Joe looked triumphant. "Ellen Kelly. Nineteen. Junior from Adelaide. Lives at home. Works in the Bursar's Office. She was running an errand that Wednesday. She remembers because she saw the story in the *Gazette* the next day about Susannah Fairlee's death and she recognized her picture as a woman she'd seen coming out of the Dean of Students office." His gaze at Michelle was combative. "Why'd she notice Fairlee?"

Michelle was crisp. "That's what makes me wonder how reliable her observation was. She claimed Fairlee looked upset, and she wondered if she was there because a kid was in trouble. That sounds like after-the-fact embellishment to me."

Joe leaned back in his chair, folded his arms, glowered. "The only way to get results is to get people's attention. Like a slap to the side of the head."

"Telling her you're investigating a murder and did she see this woman in the Ad Building on September seventeenth pretty well invites exaggeration."

They were going to be one of those couples—think Hepburn and Tracy—that spark like flint striking steel.

"Peace, children."

Joe yanked a thumb at Michelle. "She wants to ask questions like a historian, which is fine, but right now we have to get results. I know how to get people talking."

Michelle turned a graceful hand. "Joe's probably right, and"—she gave a small sigh—"Ellen's the only person we found who remembers seeing Susannah."

"Let me get it straight. You two spent the afternoon contacting people who work in the Ad Building?"

Joe's eyes narrowed. "We haven't talked to that many, actually. I figure whoever put together the snare for Michelle has to be pretty important, somebody with a lot to lose and somebody who knows the ins and outs of Goddard. Not a kid. So we spent the afternoon finding out about work-study students and student employees in the Ad Building. I figured none of them can be the perp. We hit the jackpot with Ellen Kelly."

Michelle flashed a smile at him. "He got a JPEG of Susannah. We were able to send the photo as we talked to people."

Joe looked satisfied. "The JPEG clinched the deal with Ellen."

Michelle nodded. "Sending the photo was smart. I'm not saying Ellen didn't see her. I'm saying"—and now she sounded discouraged—"we don't know why Susannah went to the Dean of Students Office. For all we know, she was lost and stepped inside to ask directions."

"Oh, come on, Michelle." Joe snorted in exasperation

She was contrite. "I'm sorry. You've done a great job. But I feel like we've looked awfully hard and this doesn't help much."

"We definitely have her pegged going into the Dean of Students Office. It's a place to start." He burrowed among the papers on the desk, pulled out a sheet. "I did a story about the honor code a couple of weeks ago. I talked to Marian Pierce, who works in the Bursar's Office. I called her, said sorry to bother her at home but I was setting up some stories for next week, we were doing a feature on work-study students, we'd picked the Dean of Students Office, could she give me their names and the names of all the staff and I'd be getting in touch with people." He looked cocky. "I got the roster for that office: Eleanor Sheridan, dean of students; Jeanne Brace-well, assistant dean; Jill Bruner and Laura Salazar, secretaries; Sabina Diaz; receptionist; Daisy Butler and George Graham, work-study students." Joe glanced toward the clock. It was almost five thirty. "We'll order in a couple of pizzas and call the list."

"Not yet." I wasn't there the day Susannah Fairlee stalked down the steps of the Administration Building, but I felt sure I knew the outcome of that visit: a stealthy approach across her yard, a stunning blow, life lost in inches of water. I held up my hand. Really, a very attractive shade of rose on the nails. "No calls to anyone in the dean's office."

"Why not?" Joe hunched his big shoulders and looked combative.

I gave him a steely stare. "If Susannah went there and threatened someone, the last thing we want to do is alert that person. Instead, we'll find out everything we can about Susannah and that office." I was counting on Detectives Weitz and Smith. "You've done a great job finding out who works there. I want you and Michelle to get some background on each one and we'll talk to them Monday. When you finish the bios, print them out, leave them on your desk." I ignored Joe's cold stare. To allay his suspicion that I entered and left Old Ethel too easily, I said, "I'll look at them when we get together again. When you're done, take the rest of the weekend off. Have a beer at the Brown Owl. Thrash out the plot lines of *True Blood*." I wanted the bios. I didn't want them poking into what might turn out to be the equivalent of a rattlesnake's lair. The less Joe and Michelle knew, the safer they'd be. "In any event, give me your cell numbers"—I jotted them on a card—"and stick together." That final order improved Joe's mood.

I started to disappear, realized I wasn't quite on that basis with them. Fortunately Joe was frowning at his list. However, Michelle was watching me with huge, questioning eyes.

I patted her shoulder and ignored the rigidity of her muscles. "Lights at night make things waver, don't they? Blink and you'll be fine." I opened the door, beamed at them. "Have a good evening." And closed the door gently behind me as I left.

Chapter 10

I was careful to remain visible until I was around the corner from Old Ethel. The bells in the library tower tolled the half hour. This time last night, Ben Douglas likely heard the deep peals as he planned his stakeout in the library. Today Ben was fighting for his life.

The ICU unit was familiar now: nurses in thick-soled sneakers moving quietly, checking monitors, administering medicine, fighting to save those at risk. I was relieved to find Ben still in his cubicle behind the drawn green curtain. A monitor glowed green. Lines snaked out from the IV pole. If a nurse glanced within, he would appear to be alone, though I guessed that one slightly elevated hand was held by another, smaller hand.

I kept my voice to a whisper. "How is he?"

"Guarded prognosis." Lorraine's soft voice was even.

I knew her modulated tone had taken great effort. Nurses must maintain their composure even when their hearts are breaking.

"There's danger of clots. They had to inject a blood thinner in the abdominal artery." A sigh. "Occasionally his eyes open and he tries to move. He's still caught in that moment before he was shot. I tell him I'm here and he's safe and we're going to make him well. Once, I think he said, '. . . stay with me?' I promised I wouldn't leave."

"Are they doing everything they can?"

"Yes. The nurse comes every few minutes to check on him. He could go either way."

"I wish I could help."

"Find out who hurt Ben." Her tone was fierce.

"I'm trying."

Beyond the green curtain there were muted sounds, wheels of a gurney, low voices, beeps, tings.

Lorraine sighed. "I sat by so many men."

I had a vision of a crowded ward in that long-ago military hospital, scarcely room to squeeze a straight wooden chair between them, young men in every kind of condition: bandaged eyes, missing limbs, some moving restively, some not moving at all.

"I'd promise I wouldn't leave. I was always tired. When ambulances came with the wounded, we all helped, and then I'd have a night shift. So often"—and now her voice was forlorn as she recalled a young woman near a battlefield—"I'd fall asleep holding a hand. When I'd wake, there was no life left, only a hand limp in mine. Such young hands."

I heard tears in her voice.

Now it was my turn to be fierce. "Sometimes they lived. Thanks to you and the others who made them well."

"I wasn't able to make Paul well."

What could I say? That he was happy? That he loved her still? I didn't know the right words, so I remained silent.

"Tell me"—clearly she made an effort to be brisk—"what you've learned."

I realized that Lorraine knew only that Michelle Hoyt was missing, a stolen book had been found in her apartment, and Ben had been shot in the room where Susannah Fairlee's diaries were stored. I had much to tell her.

"Susannah Fairlee was murdered. Michelle was decoyed to an empty house and held captive until this morning to prevent her from reading Susannah's diaries. A gun, likely the one used to shoot Ben, was planted in Michelle's car. I found the gun in her trunk and I've hidden it. Michelle was taken into custody for the rare-book theft." I described my efforts at Chief Cobb's office. "I sent down word that she was cleared. She's safe until Monday. I discovered Susannah Fairlee went to the Dean of Students Office the day she was murdered. I haven't found any connection between Susannah and the dean's office. Why did she go to that office? Why did she look grim as she came out of the building? Michelle and Joe are gathering information on everyone in the dean's office."

"Joe's helping Michelle?" Lorraine's voice was soft. "You can always count on the roses."

I smiled. Roses or chemistry or propinquity. But then, a rose by any other name . . . "I'd say they are definitely interested in each other. Now if only I can figure out who killed Susannah, Michelle will be safe. I'm hoping Detectives Weitz and Smith have some leads."

⌘

Chief Cobb's office was dusky, but I used only the desk lamp. Light shining from the windows might catch the attention of someone entering or leaving City Hall. I clicked to read the e-mail from Detectives Weitz and Smith.

To: Acting Chief

From: Detectives Weitz and Smith

Neighbors were contacted on both sides of Arnold Street concerning anyone observed in the area between 6 and 7 p.m. Sept. 17. Next-door neighbor Judith Eastman, 327 Arnold Street, didn't see anyone on Mrs. Fairlee's driveway during that time. Mrs. Eastman said she last saw Mrs. Fairlee Wednesday morning. The Sandler family lives across the street. Teenagers Adam and Will Sandler played basketball in their driveway from six o'clock until dark. According to the boys, the only cars that came on the block were people who lived there returning home. They were paying attention because a new family with a teenage daughter had moved into the house east of the Fairlee address and they were hoping the girl—Linda —would come outside but she didn't.

The Fairlee house is midblock in a modest residential area of bungalows built in the 1930s. Unlike newer areas of town, alleys run behind the houses in this development. Officer Weitz explored the alley behind the Fairlee house. Most houses have fences separating the back-yards from the alley, but the Fairlee house is unfenced. Across the alley and three houses west of the Fairlee yard is a home belonging to Brady Stanwell, a retired machin-ist. Stanwell recalled the night in question because police rigged lights in Fairlee's backyard. He was smoking a cigar in the back garden after dinner. He said he came outside about a quarter after six. While he was smoking the cigar, a woman on a bicycle passed. He estimated the time at approximately twenty past six. He had only a glimpse of the figure. He said he was sure it was a woman and was aggravated when pressed, said he knew a woman when he saw a woman but it was getting dark and he didn't know how big she was or what she looked like, only that she had on a bike helmet and a black top and slacks. He went inside a little later to watch baseball.

No one else reports seeing the bike rider.

Officer Johnny Cain contacted by phone everyone men-tioned in Susannah Fairlee's obituary. In his report, Cain . . .

I nodded in approval, but I stared glumly at the printout. Not even another mouthful of M&M'S lifted my spirit. So far as both Johnny and I had been able to determine, Susannah Fairlee's life had followed its usual course until Ann Curry saw her visibly up-set on campus the day she died. I was impressed by the amount of information he'd gathered on a Saturday, but I didn't find a link to the Dean of Students Office.

Johnny spoke to Susannah's daughter and son, next-door neighbor Judith Eastman, friends listed in her obituary, the rector of St. Mildred's (I smiled as I thought of Father Bill and Kathleen and their red-haired daughter, Bayroo), the Altar Guild directress Emma Carson, Kate's Corner manager Dwight Baker.

I understood the plaintive conclusion that it was difficult to determine what may or may not have occurred the last week of Susannah's life because she lived alone.

As an addendum to Johnny's report, Weitz observed tartly, "For all we know, she entertained Martians after midnight." Detective Smith added, "Judith Eastman next door has a key to the Fairlee house. Apparently the son is retiring from the military next spring and plans to move back to Adelaide and live there. Eastman offered to take us over there to look around but we didn't have a search warrant."

I tore a sheet from a fresh legal pad in the chief's center desk drawer and made up a calendar of Susannah's regular activities based on Johnny's report:

Mondays—Served lunch at Kate's Corner

Tuesdays—Weekly appointment with Stephen-care recipient

Wednesdays—Tennis with Pamela Wilson

Thursdays—Bible study at the church, taught by Father Bill

Fridays—Bridge

Saturdays—Errand day

Sundays—Nine fifteen service. On Altar Guild duty
Sunday before her death.

I slowly reread the report, wrote down important signposts:

1. *Susannah's last Monday—Dwight Baker at Kate's Corner*
   said Susannah was in good spirits. "Talking about going
   to Alaska for Thanksgiving. She was fine. Just as always.
   Cheerful, outgoing, kind."
2. *Susannah's last Wednesday—Ann Curry saw Susannah*
   leave the Administration Building obviously upset.

Monday at noon Susannah Fairlee served food at Kate's Corner and in no way appeared troubled. Shortly before noon on
Wednesday she was in a place she was not known to visit, and
Ann Curry thought she was too upset to welcome a greeting.
What happened between Monday and Wednesday? I glanced
again at Susannah's usual schedule. On Tuesdays she regularly
visited a care recipient as a Stephen Minister. What was her demeanor that day?

I turned back to the computer.

To: Detectives Weitz and Smith
From: Acting Chief

Excellent report. Check e-mail tomorrow in case further
developments arise.

Acting Chief

I was well aware that further developments must arise or feathers would hit the fan Monday morning when Acting Chief Howie Warren returned to find Michelle freed and an investigation begun into a death that had been officially termed an accident.

On Main Street, I lurked behind the trunk of an oak tree and appeared, then I strolled to Lulu's and stepped inside, welcoming the familiar, comfortable surroundings. I sat at the counter. I chose meat loaf, mashed potatoes, and green beans. As I took a last bite, I made up my mind. Susannah's care recipient was first on my list.

Outside, I walked across the street into the park and disappeared. At St. Mildred's, I took a moment to hover above the backyard of the rectory. Outdoor lighting illuminated the sandy volleyball court in the early dusk. Squeals and shouts sounded as young teenagers jumped. A gangly, big-handed teen slammed the ball, driving it over the net and into the sand. Bayroo clapped her hands to her red head. "I missed it!" Bayroo's glorious red-gold curls were in disarray, but her eager freckled face was as dear as I remembered. It seemed like only yesterday when I helped her mom avoid the difficulty of a body on the back porch of the rectory. I felt a little twist deep inside as I remembered how near we'd come to mortal peril for Bayroo, but all was well that ended well.

"Not your fault," her earnest friend Lucinda called out. "I got in your way."

I wished I could spend more time watching the middle school group enjoying a picnic and game on a beautiful fall night. Cars filled the church parking lot.

But it was time for business. In the church secretary's office, I closed the window blinds and turned on the light. It took a little while in the files to find the folders for the Stephen Ministry. I was pleased that Susannah's folder had not been removed, though a dark pencil on the outside had marked: *Deceased*.

I took the folder and sat down. The folder contained more information about Susannah, most of which I knew, than about her care recipient, who was identified only as JoLee Jamison, resident, Adelaide Hospice House. I puzzled for a moment. Had I seen that name somewhere recently? I squeezed my eyes in concentration. Possibly. But I could not dredge up where.

෴

In a parking lot shaded by sycamores, I landed between a delivery van and a pickup truck. No one was visible in the swath of parking lot open to me. A massive German shepherd watched me from the back of the pickup. I appeared. I straightened my name badge reading *Officer M. Loy* and admired the crispness of my uniform trousers. The black shoes had a high gloss. There was nothing shabby about Heavenly garb, whether there or here.

I strode briskly around the side of the truck.

"Cool." The high voice was admiring. "Are you some special kind of cop?"

I looked past the truck's tailgate into the interested gaze of a little boy about five years old.

"You were up high and now you're on the ground." He sounded delighted.

I hadn't noticed him because of the big shaggy dog. I heard a heavy sigh. I knew its origin. My head turned back and forth. It is hard to be convincing when you may be staring five feet to the left of your audience. "Wiggins, it's essential I speak with JoLee Jamison. You know that means I have to *be* here."

No answer. I supposed he was loath to add to my observer's unusual experience.

The little boy pointed up. "Don't you see him? He's floating up there. I want to float." Of course the little boy saw Wiggins. I wasn't surprised. Children see and know more than adults ever realize. I'd reappeared as an adult, so I lacked that special sense.

"Bailey Ruth." Wiggins's tone was commanding. If I didn't manage a satisfactory resolution to this encounter, I would soon hear the clack of the Rescue Express's wheels. It was time to draw on real-life skills honed in city politics. I moved close to the tailgate, murmured conspiratorially to the stocky little guy, "I'll bet you know how to keep a secret."

He stood a little straighter, puffed out his chest. "Yes, ma'am."

"What's your name?"

"Bucky. What's yours?"

"Officer Loy. Let me give you the lowdown, Bucky." I drew on my most recent adventure in Adelaide. "I'm on the trail of a guy who's wanted for making up fake treasure maps. Man to man, I need for you to keep your lip buttoned. Can't have people knowing police can come and go, can we? Can I count on you? Not a word to anyone until next summer." Summer was an eon away to a child.

"Cool." His gaze flicked to my right. "I want to float."

"Only very special people float. Maybe next time. Now I want you to close your eyes—"

Bucky squeezed his eyes shut and for good measure placed grubby small hands over them. All I could see was a mop of curly blond hair, a freckled face, and a rounded chin.

I jerked my thumb toward the one-story building for Wiggins. "—and count to ten."

Bucky's treble voice started slowly, "One and two and . . ."

I walked swiftly away and turned toward the front walk and was soon out of his sight. Weeping willows lined the walk, shading several wooden benches. I sank into one and prepared to plead my case.

I sniffed. No coal smoke. Yet.

Wiggins thumped heavily onto the seat beside me.

For a moment there was profound silence. Oh, dear.

Wiggins sighed. "If only I could tell her . . ."

He wasn't thinking about me or the Precepts or a little boy who likely would always remember a sunny October evening in the bed of a red pickup.

I felt the warmth of his hand through my uniform sleeve. "I know you are doing your best for Michelle. You've come to this place hoping to learn more . . ." His voice trailed off. "I'm afraid I haven't focused on the mission. It seems clear Michelle's plight arose from her connection to Susannah Fairlee's diaries. I understand that. But all this going hither and yon . . . Possibly you will connect everything. I can't let my personal feelings interfere, so continue your quest, but please see to Lorraine when you can. Ben Douglas came home to Heaven tonight."

Wiggins spoke kindly, knowing Ben Douglas's earthly duties were done, but this would likely not offer solace to Lorraine. She would be caught up in the sadness of Ben's plans to welcome his granddaughter and anger at the black-clad figure who shot him down.

"Lorraine needs . . . Oh, she needs love, and your heart over-flows."

The warmth of his touch was gone. I was alone on the bench. Lorraine . . . Yes, I would do what I could to comfort Lorraine, but first I'd take a moment to see JoLee Jamison. I might learn if Susannah Fairlee, on that last Tuesday visit, had been upset or distressed, though, of course, it would be Susannah's aim to offer support to a dying woman, not add to her burden.

In a spic-and-span tiled lobby with several chairs and potted ferns, a white-haired volunteer in a blue smock sat at a desk. She looked up, her eyes widening a little at the sight of a uniform.

I gave her a reassuring smile. "I'm Officer Loy of the Adelaide Police Department. If possible, I would like to speak with your director."

"It's after hours. Our resident manager, Betty Cook, is in. Could she help you?"

"Yes. Of course." I doubted I could simply ask to talk to JoLee Jamison.

"If you'll wait a moment . . ." She rose, gave me another curious glance, then walked swiftly to a closed door. She knocked once, opened the door. "Betty, there's a policewoman here to see you." An indistinguishable murmur. The volunteer turned to me and nodded.

I walked across the tiled floor and entered a bright square office with yellow walls. A plaid upholstered sofa faced a maple desk. A cut glass vase held a mass of bronze chrysanthemums. Family pictures in assorted frames—wooden, porcelain, and metal—ranged on either side of the desk.

The resident manager came around her desk. "Betty Cook." Her voice was firm, a match for a square face beneath tight, iron gray curls. She wore a no-nonsense white blouse, dark blue slacks, and sturdy running shoes. Dark brown eyes appraised me carefully. "You wanted to see me?" There was no warm fuzzy feeling in the room.

This woman would not easily part with information. I tried to appear genial, agreeable, and nonthreatening. "I'm Officer M. Loy. I'm seeking information about Susannah Fairlee, a Stephen Minister who visited here September sixteenth to see JoLee Jamison."

She shook her head. "You are misinformed."

We were still standing.

I said, perhaps more sharply than I should have, "My informant was sure that Mrs. Fairlee came here every Tuesday."

"Mrs. Fairlee came on Tuesdays." The gruff voice was somber. "Not Tuesday, September sixteenth. JoLee passed away the previous Friday." Betty Cook glanced toward a small figurine on her desk and for a moment her blunt face softened. She turned a hand. "We have some crafts. JoLee painted a Madonna for me. She made one for Mrs. Fairlee, too."

I looked at the soft hues and pictured a weak hand using a brush to add color to a cheap ceramic figurine. "I see." Now I remembered the death notice in the folder included in Susannah's papers, the announcement of graveside services for J. Jamison. I suppose my shock was obvious. I'd counted on talking to JoLee Jamison. I knew of no one else who could offer insight into Susannah's mood on the day before she died.

"You didn't know?" The manager mistook my response. "Sorry

to upset you. Got to all of us. JoLee was so young." She gestured toward the sofa. "Please sit down."

When I settled on the sofa, she sank into a brown leather chair behind the desk. I hadn't until this moment thought about the age of Susannah's care recipient. I had assumed, wrongly, that Susannah visited an elderly person. "I didn't know." A young woman. How young? I took a chance. "Was she a student at Goddard?"

The manager hesitated, then shrugged. "We don't discuss residents. Privacy laws. But JoLee's gone and she didn't have any family. I can't tell you much, but I know she was at Goddard until she got sick last winter. Dr. Forbes, our director, got a call in July from the rector at St. Mildred's looking for a place for JoLee. Her roommate tried to take care of JoLee as long as she could, but she was in school and had to work, and JoLee needed care. Terminal leukemia. No family to speak of. Her mom died a few years ago and her dad apparently dumped them when JoLee was little. There was an aunt in California but she couldn't help. Anyway, JoLee came here. There was no one her age, of course. She was only twenty. I don't know who asked the church, but Susannah Fairlee started visiting JoLee a few weeks after she moved in. JoLee often spent her days in a chair looking out the window." She squinted at me. "Nobody sitting around waiting to die is singing a happy song. But most of the people here are old. Some are scared, some worry about leaving their families, some are resigned. Some are easy with it. Like they're on a ship and they see the shore coming up and they're ready to land. JoLee was different. It was like she carried a big weight. She sat and stared out the window and looked miserable. It was only after Susannah started coming that I sensed a kind of relief in JoLee's manner. Perhaps Susannah reminded her of someone she'd known and trusted. I don't know. But Susannah was a great comfort to JoLee. When I called Susannah to tell her JoLee was gone, Susannah said, 'Now she's at peace.' Then Susannah said, and her voice was sad, 'It seems wrong to be healthy, looking ahead to good days, when someone so much younger is dying. I wish I could have helped her more.' She thanked me for calling. You can imagine our shock when Susannah died the next week. I don't suppose she ever saw JoLee's letter."

"Letter?"

Betty Cook picked up the small figurine of Mary. "Maybe JoLee knew she was almost done. I don't know why else she'd write a letter. Maybe she just wanted to say thank you to Mrs. Fairlee. JoLee was a nice girl. Very polite and always thanked everyone. Anyway, one of the aides boxed up her things on Saturday. Usually there's family, someone to take the personal effects. Not for JoLee. I thought I should look through, make a decision about what to do with the contents." She pulled open the center drawer, rummaged, found a sheet. "The contents." Her voice was determinedly flat. "Inexpensive laptop. Cell phone. Four blouses. Three pairs of slacks. Lingerie. Two pairs of ballerina flats. A book of poetry by Billy Collins, one page dog-eared at the poem 'I Ask You.' An agate marble, orange with a sea blue swirl shaped like a crescent moon."

The resident manager had studied the box's contents and seen a lifetime in those meager possessions.

The flat voice continued. "Two pairs of earrings, three necklaces. A poster of Daniel Radcliffe. A ticket stub to a June first, 2012, Flaming Lips concert in Dallas. A Kodak print of a woman standing on a front porch with inscription and date on the back:

Mama 2007. A New Testament. An unstamped, sealed letter addressed to Susannah Fairlee." Betty folded the sheet, returned it to the drawer, pushed the drawer shut. She looked at me and there was a combative edge to her jaw. "Maybe some would say the box should have gone to her aunt out in California, but JoLee never talked about her and the aunt never came or called. JoLee's former roommate was here every weekend. She and Mrs. Fairlee were the only visitors except for Father Bill from St. Mildred's. I decided to give the things to her roommate."

"What about the letter?"

"It was in the box. I figured her roommate would mail it if she thought she should." Her brows drew down in a frown. "I didn't think later that maybe it would hurt her feelings that JoLee hadn't written her. But kids don't usually write. I know they kept up on Facebook. Anyway, I called and she came and got the box. Looked like she'd cried her eyes out."

"Do you remember her name?"

"Of course. Jessica Fitzhugh."

✑

I was in the parking lot and almost ready to disappear when I stopped. Was it possible? . . . I opened my purse, rummaged about. Ah, a cell phone. Heaven provides. I returned to the bench I had shared with Wiggins. Thanks to the resident manager, I had Jessica Fitzhugh's cell phone number. I left a message, asking her to call me, identifying myself as a friend of JoLee's. But on a weekend, catching a college student might be tough. I dropped the cell into my purse.

Now to try and offer comfort to Lorraine. When I reached the parking lot, I was relieved that the red pickup was gone. I stepped into the shadows of a weeping willow and disappeared.

∽

No lights shone in Lorraine's suite at Rose Bower. "Lorraine?" I called softly, then turned on the Tiffany lamp. I had hoped she would be here. As she had once said to me, "Where else would I be?" But not tonight.

I thought of her portrait on the landing at Goddard Library. When I stood on the landing, I listened to the bell tolling eight o'clock. The library had just closed. One by one, lights went dark in the great rotunda and soon there were only the lights at the top and bottom of the stairs as there had been the night I arrived.

"Lorraine?"

I had no sense of her presence.

I decided to linger and take time to review what I had learned from Detectives Smith and Weitz, aided by Johnny Cain. I paced on the landing. Smith and Weitz had checked with the neighbors and no one saw anyone approach the Fairlee house. That didn't mean that someone hadn't come, simply that if the killer approached from the front, no one had noticed. The back-alley neighbor saw a woman on a bicycle. In my brief glance when Ben was shot, I'd thought his attacker was a woman. I had an impression of athleticism and—perhaps—a slender figure. Not someone large or powerful.

I felt stymied. The police had interviewed every possible source. I still didn't know why Susannah was upset when she went to the campus that Wednesday morning.

Wednesday morning . . .

I pressed my fingertips to my temples. Detectives Smith and Weitz had spoken with Susannah's neighbors, including her next-door neighbor. Judith Eastman told them she last saw Susannah Wednesday morning. When did Mrs. Eastman see Susannah Wednesday morning? Before or after Susannah's visit to the campus? That mattered.

Tomorrow I would talk with Mrs. Eastman.

For now . . . again I spoke softly. "Lorraine?"

I wasn't surprised that no one answered. Lorraine wasn't here. I hadn't found her at Rose Bower or here.

There was another possibility.

Chapter 11

A single light in a tall lamp gave some illumination to a small square living room with an old-fashioned wooden rocker, a shabby brown sofa, and an easy chair. Two gaily wrapped packages rested next to an open photo album on the coffee table in front of the sofa. I expected the gifts were intended for Ben Douglas's granddaughter. On a card table in one corner was a partially completed puzzle of a New Mexico landscape. The small pieces in irregular shapes and barely differentiated shades of gold, tan, cream, rose, and sienna would require infinite patience. An accordion with yellowed keys was propped against a bookcase. I wondered if Ben had played the accordion with one hand? Perhaps it was a family heirloom. A gas stove sat in the fireplace. Brown drapes were closed.

A page was lifted and turned in the photo album on the coffee table.

I hovered near and looked down at old-fashioned black-and-white photos taped to creamy paper. As a young man, Ben Douglas had thick springy black hair, a genial face, a firm nose, and a blunt chin. In this photo there was a bitter twist to his mouth and he stood a little sideways, as if to hide the emptiness of a shirt sleeve.

I didn't want to startle Lorraine. I spoke softly. "I thought you might be here."

Another page was turned. "Ben slipped away about seven."

"I'm sorry." I settled beside her on the sofa.

"I knew Ben a long time. Oh, he didn't know me, not for a while. He came back from Vietnam without his arm. He'd been quite an athlete in high school. He got a job with Campus Security and kept to himself, didn't talk much with anyone. He started talking to me—to the portrait—at night, how he wasn't good for much, didn't have two hands to work with. He'd planned on being a mechanic. He was lost and lonely. He talked about things I didn't understand, pistons and carburetors and brake rotors and upper ball joints. One night he was talking about how maybe he'd take his rifle out, go hunting, not come back. Even with only one arm, he could shoot himself and then he would be done with it all. That's when I spoke up. I told him to stop that nonsense, that he was an upstanding fellow and he could make of his life what he wanted it to be. He stood on the landing and stared up at the painting and then he turned and ran down the stairs. I didn't think he'd come back." She sounded amused. "But the next night he walked up the stairs real slow and looked up. 'What good's a man with one arm?' I said anyone who could be a mechanic was smart enough to be anything he wanted to be and I'd bet he was smart with figures and I wanted him to march right into the college admissions office and enroll in the business school. The next night he came and he told me he was starting school in the fall. He kept his night job, but I still worried. He didn't have anything to do with other students. They were younger. They hadn't been to war. I often visited his classes. One day I noticed a girl who looked at him, and there was something in her eyes. It was close to Valentine's Day Ben's senior year. I knew it was time for roses. I was"—there was quiet pride in her voice—"rather clever about it."

It was good to hear remembered happiness in her tone. "What did you do?"

"The night before that class, I taped a rose beneath her desk and his. The next day I waited until just before the ending bell, then carefully pulled away the tape. I lifted one rose and dropped it on Ben's notebook, did the same with Chloe's rose. Of course they were both startled. Each one picked up the rose and held it up and everyone in the class saw and looked from one to the other, and one of the girls called out, 'Why, Ben, how did you manage? Look, everyone, Ben's given a rose to Chloe!'

"Chloe's face turned pink and she looked at Ben so eagerly. Anyone could tell she was thrilled. I was proud of Ben. He would never have embarrassed her in front of the class. He took a deep breath and said, 'I hope I can always give roses to Chloe.'" Lorraine's warm laughter added gaiety to the small empty room.

"And they lived happily ever after?"

"They had a wonderful life together. Chloe died six years ago." Several album pages turned.

I looked at a wedding photograph of Ben and Chloe, Ben facing forward and standing proudly, Chloe with one arm slipped through his, the other holding a bouquet of roses.

The page lay open for a moment, then slowly the album was closed. I spoke gently. "He's with Chloe now."

The bow on the larger gift box was moved a bit straighter. "I wish he could have seen his granddaughter one more time. But finality is finality." A pause. "As I know perhaps better than most." Once again her tone was brittle. "I accept what I must, but I will not rest until Ben's murderer is brought to justice. Tell me what you've discovered."

She listened without comment until I finished.

She said quietly, "You can be sure that Susannah was struck down since Paul told you, but I see no way to prove that fact to the authorities."

"I told the police that her most recent diary was stolen and the thief shot Ben to prevent capture."

"True. Nonetheless, you offer deductions, not proof."

I wasn't offended. As Lorraine indicated, reality was reality.

She continued, her tone thoughtful. "Moreover, Detectives Weitz and Smith will report Monday morning to Acting Chief Warren, who didn't authorize Michelle Hoyt's release. Warren will be shocked to find that she was not only released, but Ben Douglas is dead and no one is in jail either for his murder, the incidents at the library, or the theft of the rare book. Warren will denounce your e-mails from the 'acting chief' as fake. He will probably claim Michelle or Joe somehow got into the chief's computer. He will immediately order Michelle's arrest. As for Susannah Fairlee, he will dismiss the possibility of murder, pointing out that her death was deemed an accident and the assertion of murder is based on uncorroborated information from an unknown informant. Further, it is an imaginative leap—"

How nice for Lorraine to consider me imaginative.

"—to link Susannah's death to a visit to the office of the dean of students."

Here I felt on firmer ground. "Ann Curry knew Susannah well. Ann insisted that Susannah was deeply disturbed, too upset to be approached. That very night Susannah was murdered. The incidents at the library suggest intimate knowledge of the college. The only link between Susannah and Goddard appears to be that visit to the dean's office."

Lorraine looked thoughtful. "Is it a coincidence that the young woman in hospice was a former student?"

"I don't know yet. Tomorrow I will try to find out more about JoLee."

Lorraine shook her head. "The connections seem vague."

"There is one definite connection to the campus—Susannah's visit to the Administration Building. There is a possible connection through JoLee Jamison, who was a student last year."

Lorraine wasn't convinced. "I'm afraid your theories are as gossamer as a spiderweb and as easily destroyed."

"Well put." If not very encouraging. "I understand the difficulty. Between now"—I looked at an old-fashioned clock on the mantel above the gas stove. It was a quarter to nine on Saturday night—"and nine o'clock Monday morning, I must discover who killed Susannah Fairlee and why, and arrange for the capture of the murderer."

There was a slight ripple of laughter. "And possibly, on the side, you can arrange for world peace?"

I tried not to sound defensive. "I know it sounds impossible, but as Mama always said, 'When the yarn is all balled up, keep picking 'til you find the right thread, and then tug.'"

"All right, Bailey Ruth. Keep picking. Can I help?"

"*Certainement.*" I hoped Wiggins was admiring my French. I still harbor hope he might send me to Paris on a mission. "It's time to go to Old Ethel."

⌒

"What an interesting office." Lorraine's cultivated voice sounded sincere.

Joe Cooper's office could as well be described as eclectic, frowsy, challenging, and a nose-thumber. The desk was still inches deep in papers. Hanging on one wall was a poster of US Marshal and famed gunfighter Bill Tilghman wearing a top hat and staring out with a "don't give me any guff" gaze, a Georgia O'Keeffe print, and a map of the proposed route for the Keystone Pipeline with *YES* stamped in red. A quote from William Saroyan, *The writer who is a real writer is a rebel who never stops,* was scrawled in blue chalk on a dingy wall between two windows.

As Lorraine read the quote aloud, I grabbed a green folder perched on top of Joe's in-box. A sticky note on the outside read in a masculine scrawl: *For Theresa Lisieux.* I suspected he asked Michelle how to spell the name. I flipped the folder open. "Here are the bios I asked Joe and Michelle to put together. Let's take the folder to Rose Bower and get to work."

It was easy to transport the folder as we zipped high into the night sky. I waited, the folder hovering above the porch floor while Lorraine entered. She opened the front door, carefully locked it behind me as I came inside. Once in her suite, I high-fived her, then realized she couldn't see me. I appeared. Since the night was rather cool, I chose an orchid velour top, black leggings, and black huaraches.

Lorraine was silent and unseen. Did she think the leggings too formfitting? Possibly she wasn't familiar with leggings. Would it be rude to offer fashion advice? "Make yourself comfortable, Lorraine." I had a brilliant thought. I walked across the bedroom to a closet. I opened the door. It didn't surprise me to find that Charles had kept her dresses. I stepped inside, picked out a blouse and skirt.

In an instant, Lorraine stood in the middle of the room in a white blouse and white-and-green pleated skirt that touched just below the knee. A black belt and flats completed the ensemble. She looked like she'd stepped out of a *Vogue* issue circa 1948, but definitely *Vogue*. She smoothed the skirt, smiled. "I remember shopping in Neiman Marcus. We had tea that afternoon before we drove home. Charles"—her voice was gentle—"told me I reminded him of a field of shamrocks."

I had a pretty good idea what my husband would say of my outfit tonight. "Great legs." Bobby Mac always went straight to the point.

I settled on the loveseat, patted the space next to me. "Let's see what Joe and Michelle found." I opened the folder. In today's digital world, information is easily accessed, but Joe and Michelle had not only rounded up facts, they'd supplied color photos.

Dean of Students Eleanor Sheridan

Dr. Eleanor Jane Sheridan, 33. Named dean November 2012. Assistant dean, 2009–12. Student counselor, 2006–09. Graduate assistant in psychology, 2002–05, University of Oklahoma. Native of Cushing. BA in psychology, University of Central Oklahoma, 2001; MA, UCO, 2002; PhD, OU, 2005. College activities: student government, intramural softball, river rafting club. M. 2001 to Ham-lin Woody, divorced 2003. No children.

Trash talk re Sheridan: Meg Ryan lookalike. Cool digs, an A-frame cabin in the woods near the country club, 110 Laramie Lane. Dates R. R. Colbert, 44, assistant professor of history. Sheridan big on PR (personal responsibility) talks to students with drug, alcohol, or honor code violations. Beat out Assistant Dean Bracewell for the top spot with lots of gracious jockeying and murmurs about youth speaking to youth. Translation: Bracewell is an old hag (ten years older than Sheridan).

I studied a montage of photos of a delicate-featured woman with a pixie haircut and a confident smile, Sheridan clapping at a student musical, Sheridan seated behind her desk, a gowned Sheridan in an academic procession, Sheridan on a tennis court.

"Do you know anything about her?"

Lorraine shook her head. "I never had occasion to visit that office."

I picked up the next sheet.

Assistant Dean of Students Jeanne Bracewell

Dr. Jeanne Bracewell, 42. Native of Bartlesville. Assistant dean, 2002–13. Assistant professor, Rose State College, 1997–2001. Graduate assistant in psychology, University of Oklahoma, 1991–96. BA in psychology with a minor in Spanish, University of Tulsa, 1992; MA, OU, 1993; PhD, OU, 1996.

College activities: president, Anthropology Club; member, Student Council. Part-time jobs: Sonic, Braum's, and student health club. Collects china thimbles. Single. Volunteers as a mentor at a local grade school. Two-bedroom frame house in an older neighborhood, 703 Choctaw Road.

Trash talk: Students call her Old Ironsides. If she ever laughed, it isn't recorded. Insists on dotting every i, crossing every t. Leads aerobics workouts at Goddard fitness center.

Lorraine picked up a sheet of photos. "Rather stern looking."

Jeanne Bracewell was blunt-faced and stocky. In a formal business portrait, her dark hair was streaked with gray and she stared straight ahead. She wore old-fashioned wire-rim glasses, a modicum of makeup, and a tailored gray suit with a black blouse. One shot showed her in a white tee and gray leotards, another sitting at a child-size table holding out a Dr. Seuss book to a thin-faced little boy about seven.

Lorraine cleared her throat. "I fail to see how this material is helpful."

"Susannah spoke to someone in that office." I rushed ahead, this time reading out loud, because Lorraine looked restive. "Two secretaries. Jill Bruner is twenty-four, married, and went on maternity leave at the end of September."

Lorraine was firm. "We can exclude her. Young women having babies do not creep across a lawn and murder anyone."

I agreed that anyone nine months pregnant was unlikely to be an assailant. "The second secretary is Laura Salazar, fifty-three.

Worked in the office for twenty-three years. Married to Robert Salazar, director of the physical plant, mother of six—"

Lorraine tapped the sheet. "Exclude her."

"I'm glad you hold motherhood in esteem, but fecundity does not correlate with character."

She smiled. "I never thought it did. However, position within an office does correlate with power. If you are correct that an angry and upset Susannah went to the office to confront someone, it suggests she intended to speak with someone in authority, not a work-study student or receptionist or secretary. Authority resides in the dean or assistant dean."

Lorraine was likely right. Tomorrow I would find out everything possible about Dean Sheridan and Assistant Dean Bracewell.

⁂

I loved the pealing of the bells as the early service ended. Lorraine had been reluctant for us to be visible, but I persuaded her. My Kelly green (admittedly flattering for redheads) belted sheath with matching faux alligator sling-back heels immediately lifted my spirit. We sat toward the back of the church, so we were among the first to walk out. Father Bill, of course, immediately recognized us as visitors. I noted that he gave me a quick, puzzled glance, as if perhaps we'd met before, but now I appear much younger than my Altar Guild portrait that hangs in the hallway outside the parish hall. "Welcome. We're so glad you came to St. Mildred's." I thanked him and murmured something vague about visiting in town.

As we came outside, I squinted a little at the bright sunshine and looked back longingly. "It would be fun to go to coffee hour."

Lorraine's smile was kind, but she shook her head. "Too many people have seen my portrait in the library."

She had a point. Moreover, my portrait was included among those of past directresses of the Altar Guild, which hung in the hall outside the parish hall. Wiggins likely was pleased that we'd attended Communion, but he would draw a line across the entrance to the parish hall.

We reached a small garden established in memory of Susan Flynn. I still thrilled to remember when Susan Flynn first greeted the grandson she didn't know she had. We stood near a trellis, out of sight of the church. Parishioners by now were either at the coffee hour or in their cars. I almost started to tell Lorraine about my visit to Adelaide and a little boy left on the front porch of Susan's home on a snowy night before Christmas. But one look at Lorraine's face and I knew she was struggling with her grief at Ben's death. I said quickly, " 'Neither sorrow, nor crying.' "

She managed a smile though her eyes were shiny. "Ben is fine, but I will miss him."

"Remember the roses you gave to Ben and Chloe. Trust me"— I didn't see this as a violation of Precept Seven—"he and Chloe now walk among the loveliest roses imaginable. And you made an excellent choice to give roses to Joe and Michelle." Joe and Michelle . . .

Lorraine was undoubtedly empathetic. A graceful hand touched my arm. "You're worried about them?"

"Michelle likely will be patient, wait for me to get back in touch."

Lorraine smiled as I described my activity as Theresa Lisieux. "You are never at a loss, are you?"

"I wish that were true." The day ahead loomed over me like towering, unscalable granite crags, and I was no mountain goat. But as Mama always told me, "If anyone can do it, so can you, Bailey Ruth." Still, I felt as if time were squirting through my fingers like little greased pigs, and I had places to go and people to see, yet I was worried about Joe and Michelle. More specifically, I was worried about Joe. "I'm afraid Joe will get restive today and try to talk to people in the Dean of Students Office, and that could be very dangerous for both of them."

"I'll see to Joe and Michelle." Lorraine's face was transformed by a kind and loving smile. "Perhaps fresh roses . . ." She was gone.

Now it was time for me to prove Mama was right. I had only hours left to find the truth about Susannah Fairlee's death. I glanced toward the wall that marked the boundary of the cemetery next to St. Mildred's. I needed for luck to be a lady. I gave a last appreciative pat to my gorgeous sheath dress before I disappeared. In my era, wearing your best on Sundays was expected. I understand today's wish to emphasize inner glory rather than outer, but I still take pleasure in presenting my best finery, both outer and, hopefully, inner.

In an instant, I was in the cemetery at the Pritchard mausoleum, which houses Hannah and Maurice, great benefactors of Adelaide. I think highly of both, but the objective of my visit was the marble greyhound on Maurice's tomb and the Abyssinian feline on Hannah's. As every Adelaidian knows, a gentle caress to each and lucky days follow. The stone was cool to my touch. I hummed "I Feel Lucky."

I was still humming when I reached the Goddard College Administration Building. Built in 1912, the Gothic Revival structure

was marked by arches, dormer windows, buttresses, and a crenelated wall along the roof. I stood in the entryway to the second-floor
office of the dean of students. The room had a feeling of age: high
ceiling, paneled walls, a wooden floor. No-nonsense straight chairs
sat against the hallway wall facing a wooden counter perhaps four
feet in height. Beyond the counter were three metal desks in a row
facing a bank of filing cabinets. Heavy red velvet drapes framed
tall windows.

At either end of the corridor fronting the counter were two
closed doors. To my right an ornate mahogany nameplate proclaimed:

Dean of Students Dr. Eleanor Sheridan

The nameplate to my left was much less ornate: navy letters on
a white metal background:

Assistant Dean Dr. Jeanne Bracewell

I turned to my right, entered Sheridan's office. The office was
large, with room for a magnificent desk in a Southwestern style
with rope edges. The caramel-colored alder wood evoked a dusty
sun-drenched landscape. A rearing horse was carved on the front.
Shelves filled the wall behind the desk. Several shelves held books.
Two shelves held carved wooden horses. The desktop was bare of
papers. A tooled leather box sat next to a framed lithograph of a
ghost town. I opened the box to find a sterling silver Montblanc pen
coated with a translucent blue-gray lacquer and note cards with a
Goddard crest and the legend *Office of the Dean of Students.*

I opened the center drawer of the desk. A tray with separate compartments held paper clips, rubber bands, an eraser, rubber stamps and a pad, keys on a ring, and fruit throat lozenges. The interior of the drawer contained a campus directory, a student manual, a list of campus department phone numbers, and an academic calendar. I opened all the drawers, saw files and folders.

I had a swift memory of my own desk when I was a secretary at the Chamber. There were always personal bits and pieces in my drawer, phone numbers scrawled on the backs of envelopes, ticket stubs, photos of the kids in addition to the ones on my desktop, plus I always had a Kodak shot of our current cat, grocery coupons I intended to use but never did, a half-eaten Baby Ruth, a partially filled book of Green Stamps, and the latest *Time* magazine.

The paucity of personal items in Dr. Sheridan's desk intrigued me. Was she über-organized, or did her purse serve as her personal catchall?

Two Mexican-style chairs with armrests, textile backs, and leather seats faced the desk. There was room for a sand-colored leather sofa and a mahogany coffee table near windows that looked out on the campus.

Filing cabinets lined the wall just to the right of the door. I looked through each drawer except a bottom drawer that was locked. At the end of an hour, I was overwhelmed. The dean's office oversaw student activities, Greek life, residential services, intramural recreation, student leadership, campus security, the student health center and student counseling center, food services, major events coordination, student judicial affairs, a diversity program, student conduct, and served as liaison with Adelaide community leaders.

I found no reference to Susannah Fairlee.

I paid particular attention to files about student disciplinary matters, but there was no file for JoLee Jamison. I riffled through several folders. My eyes widened at some of the amazing messes in which hapless students found themselves, everything from the awful—date rape—to the absurd—wasn't a Peeping Tom; was trying to see if his girlfriend was in the apartment next door—to the pitiful—ran out of money and stole a banana from the grocery.

By comparison, Jeanne Bracewell's office decor was utilitarian—plain gray metal desk, metal filing cabinets, wooden straight chairs. There were more personal touches: a photograph of an elderly woman sitting on sofa holding a mass of fleecy knitting and photos of Bracewell and another woman in a canoe. Papers were stacked neatly atop the desk. The in-box was empty, the out-box full. Her center desk drawer was a welter of pens, pencils, a roll of Tums, two packages of Juicy Fruit gum, an old-fashioned appointment book. I wondered if she also kept a calendar on her iPhone.

I grabbed the book, thumbed back to September 17, and found neat notations: *9 a.m. Interview student floor manager Hesketh House. 10 a.m. Review cafeteria pricing policies re complaint from Student Council.* The rest of the hour slots were empty so she had no other appointments that day.

I replaced the appointment book, continued to poke about. An empty glasses case. A prescription for a muscle relaxant. Several menus from local restaurants. A list of local social services. A folded head scarf. A pocket flashlight. A screwdriver. An Oklahoma road map. I closed the drawer. The side drawers held files. The bottom right drawer was locked. I supposed both she and the dean kept personal material in respective locked drawers, the dean's in a filing cabinet, Bracewell's in a desk drawer.

Vintage movie posters decorated two walls, Deborah Kerr and Cary Grant embracing in *An Affair to Remember*, sultry Elizabeth Taylor in a white slip in *Cat on a Hot Tin Roof*, somber Humphrey Bogart and Ingrid Bergman cheek to cheek in *Casablanca*.

The assistant dean's files were in standard-issue gray metal cabinets similar to those in the main office area behind the counter. I checked through these files swiftly and found nothing remarkable.

I looked around the room. My gaze stopped at the *Casablanca* poster. Years fell away and I was a teenager hearing Rick's tough voice: "Of all the gin joints, in all the towns, in all the world, she walks into mine. . . ." Ilsa came to Casablanca. Call it fate. Call it destiny. But she came and the world was different because of her. Susannah came through the door into the main office of the dean of students and the course of lives changed for her, for Joe, for Michelle, for Ben.

I hadn't found the reason yet for Susannah's visit. I had to keep looking.

⁓

I like bungalows—modest homes, some with stucco exteriors, often with wooden siding. I looked around the Sunday-peaceful neighborhood. Small, well-kept yards, several with white picket fences. Older model cars were parked in single driveways. Bikes were propped against wooden garages. I stood near Susannah Fairlee's bungalow at 325 Arnold. Stuccoed columns supported the roof's canoe brackets. Shallow wooden steps, painted red, led up to an entry porch. An elevated porch to the left was protected by an over-hang. The house had been there a long time, likely built in the 1920s. Even though the bungalow now had an uninhabited air, the yard evidenced years of love and care lavished by a devoted gar-dener. Pansies bloomed in the front bed. A wisteria-laden fence screened the side yard. Sycamores loomed on either side of the drive.

I moved into the shade of a sycamore, looked carefully in all directions, mindful of windows and cars, including pickup trucks. Certain that no one was observing this spot, I appeared in a swirl of French blue. In a moment I was on the front porch of Judith Eastman's shingle-style, one-story bungalow at 327 Arnold Street. A Chinese red door was a vivid counterpoint to the soft gray of the bungalow's granite facade. A blue pottery vase to the right of a doormat held red salvia and its blooms rivaled the door.

I pushed the bell.

A tall, willowy woman with frizzy gray hair and sharp features opened the door. She wore a pink apron over her Sunday dress, a voluminous purple silk. Her expression changed from inquiry to concern.

I spoke quickly. "Mrs. Eastman, I'm sorry to bother you on Sun-day." I smelled chicken frying, the Adelaide dinner of choice on Sundays after church. "I won't take up much of your time. Officers Smith and Weitz appreciated your help. I have one more question if you can give me a moment." I doubted that she knew officers usually worked in pairs.

Belying her somewhat severe appearance, she responded pleas-antly. "Come right in. The family won't be here for a little while.

The chicken's frying." She led the way to a small living room with potted ferns, comfortable furniture, and an oak cabinet with art glass. The door was ajar, revealing various pieces of china. I felt a wave of nostalgia. Very likely she'd opened it to select a china bowl for the mashed potatoes and a platter for the chicken. Sunday dinner always brought out the best.

She sat in an easy chair and gestured me to the sofa. For an instant, her face was somber. "I feel kind of shaky when I think about Susannah. The idea that someone hit her seems crazy and makes me wonder about the neighborhood. I've lived here thirty years and never had a bit of trouble except for that boy two doors down who was always trying to hit squirrels with his BB gun, but he's all grown up now and a lawyer in Houston."

"Please don't worry, Mrs. Eastman." I spoke with confidence. "The neighborhood is safe. Mrs. Fairlee posed a danger to someone who carefully planned her murder and has no connection to the neighborhood. We are making progress"—I hoped—"in solving the crime. In the report from Detectives Smith and Weitz, you told them you saw Mrs. Fairlee that Wednesday morning. Can you describe that moment?"

Mrs. Eastman's pale blue eyes held sadness. "She waved at me. It was just after eleven. Susannah always had a bright smile. She looked happy. I wondered if she was expecting a package from her daughter. About once a month Janet sends"—a pause—"sent some little delicacy from Alaska. Susannah would have me over and we'd have spiced tea and a treat."

"Package?" I wasn't connecting the dots.

Mrs. Eastman nodded. "In the mail. We almost always saw each other if we were both home. I love to get letters and Susannah did, too." Mrs. Eastman described walking down their front walks to the postboxes.

It was a slap-to-the-side-of-the-head moment. A happy Susannah walked to the mailbox. Not long after she picked up her letters, a distraught, unapproachable Susannah left the Administration Building.

A ringer sounded. Mrs. Eastman's head turned.

I stood. "That's all I needed to know. Thank you for your time."

Her mind was clearly in her kitchen as she closed the front door after me. I walked sedately to the weeping willow, moved into its shadow, disappeared.

The air was musty in Susannah Fairlee's front hall. The house had the air of emptiness that comes when a home is no longer inhabited even though everything was in order. In the wood-paneled front hallway, a silver tray sat on a tiled side table. Just past was a painted umbrella stand, white pottery with an orchid bouquet. The knobs of several umbrellas—red, green, and black silk—poked out.

I hurried to the tray. There were two stacks of envelopes along with several magazines. I expected most were sympathy cards to the family and perhaps Janet had left them on the tray planning to reread them. I checked the dates, put aside all mail that came after September 17. There were only a handful of earlier letters. I skimmed the contents, returned them to the tray.

If I was right, Susannah received a letter the morning of September 17 that had led her to the campus. I tried to imagine Susannah carrying her mail, walking into the main hall. Did she read her mail in the living room?

I gazed about the small room with rosy cherry paneling, formal overstuffed furniture, and marble-topped tables crowded with family photos. There were no current touches of occupancy, a sweater dropped across a settee, an open magazine on a table, a coffee cup and saucer. Obviously the room had been tidied to welcome friends after Susannah's service and left in order, awaiting the arrival of Susannah's son after his retirement.

The pigeonhole front desk in one corner was similarly neat. I opened several drawers, found a collection of correspondence, all the postmarks earlier than what I sought. Most were family letters. I smiled. I had always saved letters from family, too.

I grew less and less hopeful as I went from room to room, opening drawers, checking boxes. If Susannah was upset by a letter that morning, it wouldn't have been relegated to a box of mementos. . . .

I stood in the middle of the cheerful kitchen: yellow walls, ruffled white curtains at the windows, a maple breakfast table and chairs. I tried to imagine Susannah Fairlee opening her mailbox, drawing out advertising circulars and perhaps a magazine or two and a letter. She carried the mail inside, opened the letter. Soon she would rush from the house and drive to the campus. Susannah was in good spirits before she retrieved her mail. I believed she received a letter that upset her.

What would I do after I read an upsetting letter, one that galvanized me into action?

I began a second search. In Susannah's bedroom I crossed to the chest. On top sat a navy leather purse. I carried the purse to the bed, opened the clasp, and let the contents spill onto the white

Martha Washington's Choice bedspread. I noticed there was no billfold. Susannah's daughter likely retrieved the billfold. There were credit card accounts to close. Tumbling out with lipstick, powder, mirror, comb, and Kleenex was a small red address book and a lavender envelope addressed to Susannah Fairlee, postmarked September 13.

Chapter 12

I sat on the edge of the bed and held two sheets filled front and back with uneven, wobbly handwriting. No paragraphs, just words, some running into the next words.

Dear Susannah,

I didn't mean to tell you about her. That day you found me crying, you said if I wanted to share the burden, it might help me feel better. I don't know if I can ever feel better. You told me you wanted to help and it might make me happier if I let go of what troubled me. So I told you how much I hated her. I didn't tell you why, just that she had ruined my life. You said hating hurt me, not her. You said if I wanted to tell you what happened, you were there for me. I knew if I told you what made me feel this way, it would be better. But I didn't want to tell you what I had done. I knew you wouldn't ever tell anyone but I didn't want you to despise me. That's why I turned away and stared at the wall and finally you patted my shoulder and left. I woke up in the night—I wake up in the night a lot now—and knew I had to do something. I can't do anything now, I don't have that much time, but maybe if I tell you, you can make her stop. I know she's still hurting people, taking money. She's good at finding kids who can't fight back and she figures out a way to force them to help her. I held down two jobs so I could go to school. I was a waitress at the cafeteria and then I got a work-study job in the Dean of Students Office. I thought that was a real honor. I never had any extra money and sometimes I was hungry but I thought if I worked hard, I would get my degree. Now I won't have my degree. It doesn't matter, does it? Maybe nothing matters. When I die, I hope I don't care anymore. I guess I hate myself, too. I should have done something when it happened, told somebody. But who would believe me? She had a picture of Jill's billfold in my drawer. We each had a drawer to keep our things in when we were there to work. I won't ever forget that day. She called me into her office. I never liked her. I always had a bad feeling about her but I needed work study. It was fall a year ago, an ugly, cold, dreary day with leaves coming down and pretty soon it would be winter. My last winter. I got sick in January. But that day in November, I went into her office and she told me to shut the door and my stomach kind of squeezed because of the way she was looking at me. I thought I'd made some big mistake and I was going to get fired. I was scared because I didn't have enough money to pay my share of the rent unless I got my check. I sat down. She stared at me and I thought how cold her eyes were, like little slivers of ice. She smiled. It wasn't a nice smile. It was kind of pitying, like she was looking at some sort of scum. She didn't say anything. It was awful, the silence went on and on. Finally I asked what was wrong. She shook her head real slow like. "JoLee, I wouldn't have thought it of you." I asked what was she talking about. She said, "When things disappeared, I thought someone must be slipping in the office and taking them." I knew what she was talking about. Mike's lunch was gone one day, Emily's cell phone a week later. She shook her head again. "When someone told me what they'd seen, I didn't believe it. But when I opened your drawer, there was Jill's billfold." I jumped up and said it was all a lie and nobody saw me take anything because I never did, never would. She just listened with that awful smile, then, it was like she'd had this sudden idea. She looked at me. "But there is a way out. I've thought of something you can do for me and if you do what I ask and never say a word, why, it will be like this never happened." I knew then that it was all a lie and she was behind it. I couldn't believe it when she told me what she wanted me to do. I can still hear her voice: "Since you are a drama major, it won't be hard and it's all a harmless joke that will just be between us, but if you agree to help me, why, I will help you and I'm sure nothing will ever be taken again." She laughed, a real satisfied laugh. Susannah, you are real strong. I knew that after you'd come to see me only a few times. But she would have known that, too, and she would never have tried it on you. I guess she figured me out. I don't have any family to help me. I didn't even have many friends because I worked all the time and I didn't have money to go to the city or to concerts or anything. Once a guy took me to Dallas for a concert but that was the only one I ever went to. I wonder what would have happened if I told everyone about her? But I know. No one would have believed me. She knew I wouldn't fight back. That's why she gets away with it. She finds out things or—and this is worse, this is what makes me feel awful when I remember—she waits until she finds a kid she can bully, or maybe with some of them she pretends it's a joke and promises cash. I figure she's been doing it for years. Each time it would be different. For me, well, she had me wear this real sexy red teddy. It was cold that night so I wore a raincoat over it. Anyway this guy's wife was out of town and she got a key to the house someway. She had me go inside and wait in their bedroom. When he came back from dinner, I called out to him. He came running into the bedroom and I was there in this teddy and I grabbed him and kissed him and he was trying to push me away. She was waiting just outside the house but I had opened the window so she got pictures. She was all in black and you couldn't even see her face. She had on a mask. She yelled something like, "Hot pictures." He turned

toward the window and I ran and got outside the house. I
don't know what happened after that. But I think I hate
her the most because of Mike. He was such a nervous, gen-
tle guy, really thin and he always looked scared. I was
already sick and out of school when I heard what happened
to him. I don't know what she made him do or maybe she
was leaning on him to do something awful. Mike was a
sweet, sweet guy. I think about him going out to the lake
and walking into the water and it must have been cold and
he was scared and I feel so sick I want to die. But I am go-
ing to die. But if I had told somebody about her, maybe
Mike would be okay. But I didn't. I don't know if you can
do anything. But you know people. You're important. I'm
sorry. Sorry for everything.

JoLee's signature was smudged. Perhaps by her tears. Perhaps by Susannah's. Perhaps by mine.

JoLee was right. Susannah was a fighter. Did she know the identity of JoLee's tormentor when she went to the office that September day? I rather thought she did. JoLee had told Susannah on one of her visits how much she hated . . . someone. She never told Susannah why. On the day she died, Susannah received JoLee's letter and learned the reason for JoLee's anger. A distraught Susannah tucked the letter in her purse and went directly to the Dean of Students Office. Susannah saw the woman JoLee hated. Was there anyone in the office who could testify that Susannah came that day and saw the dean or assistant dean? It would be useful confirmation, but it was not proof of the contents of the letter. I was sure Susannah saw either Eleanor Sheridan or Jeanne Bracewell because JoLee wrote that "she" called JoLee into her "office." There were two offices, one for the dean, one for the assistant dean. One or the other, Sheridan or Bracewell.

I slipped the sheets back into the lavender envelope. A woman with power and authority forced JoLee to act as an accomplice in creating a compromising situation for an unnamed man. I suspected this was a pattern of behavior, the woman pinpointing possible blackmail victims, using students to frame the victims. Was Mike forced to set up a romantic encounter with a male professor? There could be other scenarios, drugs perhaps, or gambling or underage sexual encounters. I had no doubt the brains behind the scheme found it easy to ensnare victims. The subjects of blackmail weren't the only victims. The students used were also victims. Perhaps the woman usually chose students who faced drug, alcohol, honor code, or sexual accusations, promising the records would be destroyed if they cooperated. In the case of JoLee, she'd taken advantage of a student who had to have a job and had no defense against a false accusation.

A sexy red teddy and a man photographed in an embrace likely spelled a man in the upper reaches of the college administration or a professor who could afford payoffs to avoid scandal. Blackmail can be very profitable. If the right victims were chosen, it would be possible to milk them for years.

The haunting strains of Ravel's *Boléro* combined with the sylvan setting to create a sense of exotic release on the wooden porch of Eleanor Sheridan's A-frame. A petite blonde stretched at ease in a hammock. Loose in her lap was a trade paperback. I skimmed close enough to see the title: *Collected Poems* by Louise Bogan. On this sunny October morning, shaded by oaks and sycamores that crowded close to the porch, she appeared comfortable and relaxed, lips curved in a slight smile. She appeared to be a woman without worries or cares.

Inside the A-frame, all was light and color: a brightly patterned Navajo rug hanging on one wall, a large canvas with brilliant splashes of orange and red on another. The furniture was Western in style, but there was a spartan simplicity to the decor. I didn't see many personal knickknacks. Tucked on either side of the front door were a bathroom and a large storage closet. An open loft contained a queen bed, dresser, closet, and bath.

The open area downstairs contained a sofa, easy chairs, a fireplace, a dining room table, a kitchen with an island and tall stools, and an office area. On a desk was a studio portrait of a man with a thatch of dark curly hair, Robert Taylor—handsome features, and a confident smile. Keeping an ear attuned for the sliding door to the porch, I checked the contents of the desk, a personal checkbook with a balance of $4,265. Folders for insurance, medical bills, car title, receipts, warranties, and investments. *Hmm.* Her stock account amounted to almost three hundred thousand. A tidy sum for someone her age. However, she was a well-paid administrator, single, and possibly savvy at investing.

I pulled open the central drawer. Pens, postage, a calculator, stationery, a campus telephone directory.

The sliding door from the porch moved in its metal frame. I eased the drawer shut.

Eleanor strolled inside. She placed the book in an empty

space in a bookcase near the fireplace, walked toward the kitchen area.

I spotted a turquoise cloth handbag on an entryway table. As she stood at the refrigerator and ice plunked into a glass, I eased the handbag open. I found her cell phone, tapped the phone, found the number. I slid the phone into the bag.

Suddenly she turned. She stared at the bag, her face puzzled. She must have glimpsed a movement. There was a sharp, intent expression on her face.

It was time for me to leave.

§

Storms had spattered wind-driven mud against the peeling facade of the small-frame house. A portion of the picket fence leaned inward. Cracks marred the concrete sidewalk to the front porch. Large pottery vases on either side of the front door held humps of dead vegetation in dry brown dirt. The screen door sagged, one bracket loose at the top.

I found Jeanne Bracewell in an immaculate small living room. She slumped against the cushions of an overstuffed chair. Perhaps everyone is vulnerable when observed in solitude. I was saddened by what I saw, a middle-aged woman whose face offered no defense against the world, dark brown eyes staring emptily into the distance, muscles flaccid. She was neat and crisp: short iron gray hair neatly combed, a touch of pink lipstick, a fresh white polo and tan slacks, but it was as if a wax mannequin rested in the chair. Her expression and posture revealed sorrow and defeat.

"Jeanne." The cry was faint, scarcely audible, but Jeanne was on her feet immediately. She moved quickly down the hall to the first bedroom. By the time she stepped inside, her face was transformed by care and kindness.

An emaciated figure lay beneath a single sheet. The woman, her head bald, looked up weakly. ". . . feel so sick again. Please, Jeanne, hold my hand." Pain and suffering marked her face, but the thin hands on the coverlet were unwrinkled. She was likely in her forties.

The bedroom held the scent of illness yet it glistened with cleanliness, not a speck of dust. Buttercup yellow curtains framed windows with sparkling clear panes. An iPad lay on the bedside table, and music sounded softly: Johann Strauss's "Voices of Spring."

"Let me fix you an ice. I'll flavor it with blue raspberry. Like the time we went to Hawaii."

The woman shook her head, a tiny suggestion of movement. "Can't do any more."

Jeanne sat in a straight chair close to the bed, gently grasped limp fingers. "The doctors are encouraging. Only four more treatments, Bebe. Please. I'll help you. You know I'll be with you."

Bebe gazed up. "Need to let me go."

"No." Jeanne was brusque, her voice deep. "You can do it, Bebe. Please. For me."

Bebe moved uncomfortably. "Tried . . . so . . . hard. Last year. Now again. And the money. It costs so much mo—"

"Damn money." Jeanne was harsh. "What's money when it's your life? We're managing. Everything is fine. I've got enough money."

Bebe closed her eyes, sank deeper into the pillow.

When I'd seen the shabby house, I'd almost turned away. Black-mailers can afford to keep a home in good repair. I'd expected to step into slovenliness, but the interior of the house reflected care and thought and effort. Jeanne would do everything in her power to maintain nurturing surroundings for this very sick woman. Did Bebe notice the disarray of the exterior? Perhaps Jeanne brushed off any queries with reassurances: *Those repairs would make too much noise now, be disruptive; you need peace and quiet.* Bebe was too frail, too ill, to press her.

I found a businesslike metal desk in an alcove near the kitchen. It didn't take long to see that bills were stacked high and that some creditors were pressing her. Could the fruits of blackmail have been her answer to the ravening need for money?

A little cuckoo clock marked the quarter hour. Fifteen minutes after two. Minutes and hours fled before me. If I had time, if I had the resources of the police, I could determine the financial backgrounds of Jeanne Bracewell and Eleanor Sheridan, though it was quite possible that a canny blackmailer had very effectively hidden any unexplained sums of money. I didn't have the luxury of time and financial inquiries.

Tomorrow morning the acting chief would order Michelle Hoyt's arrest, this time on suspicion of shooting Ben Douglas, unless I discovered and trapped JoLee's *she.*

Perhaps I could lure Ben's killer out of hiding if I set a trap with irresistible bait.

⟡

Going from there to here in a heartbeat is a ghostly perk. Uh-oh. Wiggins does abhor the term *ghost.* Excuse me, Wiggins. In case you are listening, I meant simply that incorporeal travel moves one instantly to the desired location. Think and go. Which has a nice ring to it.

The instant I entered Chief Cobb's office, I knew all hell—excuse me, Wiggins—had broken loose. Howie Warren looked like he'd been plucked from the golf course in a watermelon pink polo over pink and green tartan Bermuda shorts. His face was red from both sun and irritation. He paced up and down, jabbing a stubby forefinger occasionally toward Detectives Smith and Weitz, who stood stiffly in front of the blackboard. Smith was as tall, dark, and handsome as ever but his lips were closed in a grim line. Weitz stared stonily in front of her. She stood with her shoulders back, her dark eyes hot with anger.

". . . and somebody's going to get canned. Who the hell's been using my computer?"

I raised an eyebrow. *His* computer? That would be news to Chief Cobb.

Warren's amber-colored pig eyes looked at Smith and Weitz, then swung toward a half-dozen officers crowded near the door. "Who's tired of being a cop? I want fingerprints made of everybody in this building and we'll run them against the keyboard—"

Honestly, I was surprised at Howie's acumen. If a wayward cop had been responsible for the e-mails I'd signed as acting chief, likely the culprit would have been revealed by fingerprints. However, Howie wasn't going to find any prints on that keyboard other than his and those that remained from Sam Cobb's last use.

"—and somebody's going to get his butt kicked big-time."

Chief Cobb would be appalled at Howie's language. "Crudity diminishes a message." My tone was stiff.

Howie's head jerked up. He looked at Weitz and three uniformed female officers. "Who's being cute? That's what I want to know. Which one of you said that?"

Smith's face folded in a frown. "Not Weitz. I'm right here. I would've heard her."

A tall, thin woman with sharp features was brusque. "None of us said a word." She looked at the male officer nearest the door. "That right, Jed?"

Jed looked like he wanted to be in the break room, but he took a quick breath, and said quickly, "Not a peep from over here, sir."

I couldn't resist. I intoned in my best sepulchral voice, "Tomorrow all will be revealed. Await instructions."

Howie's round face puckered in fury. "Okay. The joke's over. I'm not stupid. I'll find the ventriloquist, but right now I want an APB out for that student. Wanted on suspicion of murder. That cock-and-bull story about somebody trapping her in a house is so much crap. She stole that book. They found it in her apartment. She must have gone back to get something else when she shot the night watchman . . ."

I didn't have time to make the phone calls from the police station that I felt sure would lure *she* out of hiding. I had to find Michelle. Before the police did.

∾

Inside Michelle's apartment—I didn't wait on the nicety of appearing and knocking—I called out, "Michelle? Joe?"

George lifted his furry head from a cushion in a window seat and regarded me sleepily.

No answer. No movement.

Thunderous knocks sounded at the door. My heart lurched. An APB must have gone out already and a nearby patrol dispatched.

George flew to the floor.

"No problem for you, buddy." I took a moment to give him a reassuring pat.

I felt a huge sweep of relief when I reached Old Ethel, high on its hill, and saw no flurry of official activity there, no police cars, no officers on foot surrounding the building. Detectives Smith and Weitz might eventually remember Michelle's association with Joe Cooper, but right now Michelle should be safe in Joe's office, if indeed that's where she was.

A yellow Beetle slammed to a stop in front of Old Ethel, ignoring the adjacent fire hydrant. Moki's Pizza was splashed in psychedelic letters on the passenger door. The motor was still running and a radio blared: "Just in from the news desk. Police are looking for a Goddard student in conjunction with murder of night watchman. Police identify the suspect as Michelle Hoyt. The police said Hoyt is five foot seven and has black hair and brown eyes. Police said she was last seen wearing red-and-white-striped blouse and red slacks. . . ."

I popped into Joe's office. Michelle looked fetching in the red and white cotton blouse and red slacks, although her expression was strained, her dark brows drawn down in concern as she stared at a laptop balanced on her knees. If the pizza delivery man saw her, she was all but in jail.

Redbrick columns adorned the porch to Old Ethel. I paused behind a pillar long enough to appear in a dark gray pinstripe blouse, black slacks, black huaraches with the most attractive cutout at the toes. I opened a shoulder bag in matching gray and pulled out a change purse. I hurried down the steps. A pudgy balding man in his early twenties schlepped up the sidewalk with a pizza box.

"Thank you. I'll take it for Joe." I stood squarely in his way, reached out for the box. "How much do I owe you?"

He looked startled. "Like I told Joe. Fourteen bucks. That's the double crust with everything."

I found a ten, a five, and two ones—Wiggins always provided what I needed—and took the box.

"Yeah. Right. Hey, thanks." He looked toward Old Ethel. "Yeah, I was going to ask Joe if he heard the news—"

The car radio blared: "Police are asking anyone with knowledge of Michelle Hoyt's whereabouts to contact them immediately. Police said the suspect may be armed and dangerous. . . ."

I gave a casual wave, rested the pizza box on one hip. "He's on it. Don't know if he's alerted the cops yet, but the word is that she went to Lake Texoma with friends this weekend."

The deliveryman's eyes glistened. "Wow. The campus is swarming with cops. I got stopped four times between Moki's and the bottom of the hill, cops asking if I'd seen her around."

I looked down the hill. A black-and-white cruiser came around the corner. "Good luck getting back to Moki's." I turned and moved fast, not quite at a run, up the walk. I pushed the door. Locked. I glanced over my shoulder. The Beetle was making a U-turn. I disappeared, moved through the door, pulled it open from the inside, and grabbed the pizza box. The Beetle was running up over the curb, the driver hanging out the driver's window, staring at the door and the box that appeared elevated by itself in the air. I reappeared, gave him a jaunty wave, slammed the door.

A siren wailed.

I ran toward the newsroom, skidded around desks, reached Joe's office, yanked the door open.

Joe Cooper held his cell. ". . . take a look at that JPEG. Did you see—" He broke off, stared at me.

Michelle's head jerked up. "You're back."

Joe looked irritated. "Hey, I may have a lead—"

I reached over the desk, grabbed the cell, swiped, handed it back. "You can call them back. Cops are coming to arrest Michelle. Is there any place she can hide?" The police would surround Old Ethel, might be approaching as we talked. I felt frantic. Even if we hid her in a closet with a lock, she would be found.

"Downstairs. Quick. I know a way." Lorraine's high, well-modulated voice clearly came from near the ceiling. "A hidden tunnel leads into the woods. It was an escape route for men when the police raided the boarding house in the twenties. A portion of the wood paneling behind the press opens. You pull on a knothole in the center. Charles was with the police—he was mayor of Adelaide then—the night they raided Old Ethel and closed it down as a bordello."

I shook my head. "That was a long time ago."

Lorraine spoke in a quick staccato. "Tunnels don't go away. No one today is likely aware it exists. That doesn't mean it's disappeared."

Joe was half out of his chair, frozen in a posture of shock as his eyes sought the speaker but, of course, Lorraine wasn't visible. Michelle's dark eyes stared upward.

Another siren.

It might not work, but anything was better than standing here waiting for the police. I jerked a thumb toward the newsroom. "Joe, show us how to find the press. We can try."

Another siren rose and fell very near now.

Joe took a breath, came fully upright, and charged around his desk. "Never heard of a tunnel. The press is in the basement." He pulled Michelle to her feet, yanked open the door. Hustling her ahead of him, he hurried us through the newsroom and out into the hallway. Running now, we pounded down the hallway to a door at the end of the hall. He reached for the knob.

I grabbed his arm. "We'll take it from here. Get back to your office. Distract the police for as long as possible. Tell them it's been a while since you've seen Michelle, ask why they're looking for her, delay them with questions." By this time I had the door open. I flipped on the lights. "Come on, Michelle."

She started down the steps.

"Try to go a little faster." Lorraine's soft voice was encouraging.

Michelle stopped, grabbed my arm. "Why do you talk in two different voices?"

"Don't worry about that right now." My tone was soothing. "Hurry. We don't have much time."

The pressroom was full of shadows. We moved in half darkness. I followed Lorraine's quick calls. "Down this corridor . . . past the newsprint rolls . . . keep to your left."

I was holding Michelle's arm. She flinched every time Lorraine spoke.

Finally we came to the far reaches of the basement. There was almost no light here. Lorraine was murmuring, "I wish I'd paid more attention. Charles said the tunnel was in the center of the far wall. After the war, when it was a residence hall, Charles joked that he would be a popular man if he told the vets of a secret way in and out. I shivered and told him I wouldn't want to go into an old tunnel no one had used for years—who knew what might be in there—but he said vets wouldn't be afraid of bats."

By this time we were edging behind the huge press that towered almost to the ceiling. There wasn't much room behind the press. As I slid my palms across the wall, I bumped into Lorraine. "Sorry, didn't mean to step on you."

Michelle gave a ragged laugh. "Who did you step on? Or should I ask?"

The texture of the wall changed from plaster to wood. Was it possible that I was feeling a wooden panel that was almost a hundred years old? "Oh, good Heaven," I exclaimed.

"You stepped on Heaven?" Michelle's tone was plaintive. "Do you know, I can believe almost anything at this point, but that's a stretch."

"This has to be the panel." Lorraine's voice was exultant.

Michelle said frantically, "Two different voices again. Stop that, please."

"I'm talking to Lorraine." It was time to give up pretense.

Lorraine said firmly, "Michelle, don't worry. We'll take care of you."

"We? There's only one of you." Michelle's voice wobbled.

"We'll explain later." I hope I sounded patient. "Lorraine, the wood is smooth so far."

"Take your time. I doubt the knothole is very large."

"Do I want to know who Lorraine is?" Michelle was clearly disturbed.

I spread my fingers wide, moved a few inches at a time. I heard distant shouts. The police had opened the door and found the lighted stairway to the basement.

I poked a finger into nothingness. "I found the hole." I hooked my index finger inside the opening and pulled. Nothing happened. I thought about a mechanism that would move a panel.

Men shouted. Heavy footsteps thumped. Soon they would be

down the stairs and searching the basement, but we were screened from view by the huge press.

I moved my finger inside the hole and felt a spring. I pressed and heard a click. Putting my shoulder against the wooden panel, I pushed. Slowly, creaking, a portion of the wall swung forward into impenetrable darkness. A dank odor swept over us.

Michelle stood stock-still. "That smells awful. What's in there?"

"It may be a bit"—I hesitated—"challenging." I could disappear in an instant if the floor was rotted or the walls caved in, but Michelle didn't have that option.

"Don't be frightened." Lorraine sounded confident. "I'll get a light."

"Don't leave me." Michelle grabbed my arm.

"I'm not going anywhere."

Michelle's fingers dug into my arm. "I don't know that I want to know, but you've got to tell me. Why are you talking in two voices, and how can you go somewhere and still be here?"

"Lorraine went for a light."

"Who's Lorraine and when did she join us? Why didn't I see her?"

A muffled shout sounded on the other side of the press. "Hey, who took my Maglite? Hey, what's it doing up there by the ceiling? Hey—"

I looked up. A bright beam rose toward the ceiling, abruptly disappeared. Good for Lorraine. Once she turned the flashlight off, no one could follow its path. I whispered, since the police were now on the other side of the press. "Don't worry. Everything's going to be fine. Lorraine got us a light and now we can go into the tunnel."

Michelle whispered, too, a ragged thin wisp of a whisper. "How peachy. Just like that, presto chango, Lorraine, who I never saw, went somewhere and got a light and she's coming back—"

"Now we can see." Lorraine spoke softly. A bright beam illuminated a narrow bricked tunnel. The floor of the tunnel was also bricked. Cobwebs hung in shimmery swaths.

Michelle was rigid beside me. "Nobody's holding the flashlight."

The Maglite, just inside the tunnel now, appeared to hang without support.

It was time to be frank. Surely Wiggins would understand. The girl needed reassurance. "Don't be distressed—"

"Distressed?" Now her whisper was frantic. "I'm not distressed, I'm hysterical. The police are after me. I'm down in a basement with a woman who comes and goes through locked doors—and don't think I don't know the front door to Old Ethel was locked, because Joe tried it three times, and here you came with pizza—and you keep talking in two voices and I don't know who Lorraine is and now that flashlight's hanging there by itself."

"Lorraine, join us."

Although not clearly visible in the dark, colors swirled and Lorraine held the Maglite. She looked crisp and elegant in a white blouse, a long blue skirt, and matching blue slippers.

Michelle let go of my arm and sagged against me. "I'm not hysterical. I'm crazy."

The shouts were louder, the sound of feet pounding on the far side of the press. Soon the police would fan around the press, find this narrow space.

I spoke quickly, but still softly. "Actually you are quite sane. You heard two voices. One is mine and one is Lorraine's. We will introduce ourselves at greater length another time. Come." I took her elbow.

Michelle stiffened. "If you think I'm going in there, you're the one who's crazy."

Lorraine handed me the Maglite. "I'll see to the cobwebs." She disappeared and in the bright yellow beam cobwebs fell away to each side. "Come now," she called softly.

I took a firmer grip on Michelle and propelled her ahead of me. "Here, hold this." I handed the Maglite to her and turned to swing the panel shut behind us. As it clicked into place, Michelle shuddered.

I took the light. "The faster we move, the sooner we will be out of here."

Without a sound, Michelle turned and gingerly picked her way forward.

I tried to keep the beam steady, but occasional twists and turns illuminated portions of the tunnel walls. I had no doubt Michelle was well aware that they were slimy. She made a clear effort to stay free of entangling shreds of cobwebs.

The tunnel angled to our right then abruptly ended. The Maglite clearly revealed a brick wall with no apparent exit.

Michelle stumbled to a stop. "It's a dead end."

Lorraine's voice floated to us. "I'll find a way."

Michelle stood with her arms tight across her front. "Night-mares are kind of funny, aren't they?" Her tone was conversational. "I mean, obviously I must be asleep. When I wake up, George will be curled at the end of the bed and everything will be back like it was: I'm going to school and I have a paper to write and I don't know this guy named Joe and I'm not really trapped in a tun-nel . . ."

We waited and it seemed an interminable time. I knew Lor-raine wouldn't desert us, but the exit might be well hidden. Michelle looked back the way we'd come. "Do you think you can open that thing from the inside?" Her voice was shaky. I hoped she wasn't beginning to feel claustrophobic.

"Certainly. But we'll get out at this end." I maintained a confident tone. I needed to give Michelle a boost. I decided it was a nice moment to recite "If." "'If you can keep your head when all about you / Are losing theirs and blaming it on you, / If you can trust yourself when all men doubt you, / But make allowance—'"

A sudden shower of dirt and dust, with pieces of wood and clods of dirt, enveloped us.

Michelle sounded scared. "The ceiling's falling."

I swung the Maglite beam up.

More dirt fell. Dust swirled.

Lorraine's voice was excited, pleased. "I knew there had to be a way out. It's cleverly camouflaged. You know those stone ruins in the woods on the other side of the hill from the campus? There's a wooden cover in the ground that looks like a top to an abandoned well. It's rather splintery and worn and may not have been moved for years. It didn't want to budge, but I found a broken branch— green wood and quite strong—and I managed to prize up the lid."

Chapter 13

As the dust cleared, light streamed through a round opening about five feet above us.

"Disappear, Bailey Ruth. Between us, we can lift Michelle."

Michelle clamped her eyes shut as I took one arm. With Lorraine on the other side, we rose and lifted Michelle through the opening and onto a patch of ground in the midst of tumbled stone. Late afternoon shadows made the ruins dim and dusky.

Michelle took a deep breath, opened her eyes. "All right. I give up. There are two of you and you come and go. I don't know which is worse: when you're here, when you're not here, or when you're in between."

We reappeared on either side of her. Lorraine gave her an encouraging pat on one arm, then knelt to push the weathered trapdoor cover back into place.

Michelle's gaze flickered from Lorraine to me. "You"—her tone was faintly accusatory—"called yourself Theresa Lisieux. She"—her head nodded toward Lorraine—"called you Bailey Ruth. Who are you?"

Lorraine beamed at Michelle. "Bailey Ruth's very special. She's an agent for the Department of Good Intentions. She's here from Heaven to help you. And me."

Michelle tried to breathe evenly. "Heaven?" But her voice squeaked.

I patted her other shoulder. "We don't have time to explain everything."

"Ghosts. You're ghosts." Michelle whirled toward Lorraine. "You're Lorraine Marlow. You've been dead for years. I've seen your portrait in the library. You throw roses around." She began to tremble.

Lorraine raised a delicately arched brow. "I would scarcely call delivering a rose to a young man or woman *throwing* them."

"Michelle, be calm. Breathe in. Breathe out." I smiled at her. "Everything is fine. Lorraine is most particular about the recipients of roses. That's why she felt you and Joe definitely were due roses. As Lorraine said, we're here to help you, so please don't worry."

"Am I dead?" Michelle's voice shook.

"Not for a long, long time." Of course, this was simply a guess on my part. I certainly didn't know when Michelle would be summoned, but the dear girl needed a boost and I am always willing to be positive. "Now, enough of this. Lorraine and I aren't at liberty to say more. And you and Lorraine can have a long talk about roses at Rose Bower."

"Rose Bower?" Michelle stared at me.

"What a splendid idea." Lorraine clapped her hands together. "Why, it's only perhaps a half mile from here through the woods." She turned to Michelle. "Did you know Rose Bower adjoins the campus? That's one reason Charles left the estate to the college. It's hardly any distance at all."

⁓

As I expected, Chief Cobb's office was still crowded, though Detectives Smith and Weitz were absent. Several plainclothes detectives and uniformed officers stood stiffly near the door, faces blank. Howie Warren looked small in the chief's chair—small, beleaguered, and pressed.

Neva Lumpkin, Adelaide's mayor, arms folded, glared down at the acting chief. Her blonde hair was an impressive beehive over a plump face congealed with distaste. She looked like a Wagnerian soprano upstaged by the tenor. "Traffic was a nightmare. Those leaving the concert were harassed, intimidated, obstructed. I was stopped four times." Her voice quivered with outrage. "Despite the fact that my Lincoln clearly has plates front and back that read *Mayor*." She swung toward the line of expressionless officers. "I called you in here because you are sorely lacking in tact and responsiveness to the public." She turned back to Howie. "I told them who I was." A ringed hand plunged into the capacious pocket of a blue pantsuit, pulled out a note card. "Officers Kerry, Bitterman, Sweet, Laswell, McKay, French, Jarvis, and Kramer. To add to my outrage, I learn the stop-and-search nonsense was apparently in error, that the student has escaped to Lake Texoma. Now"—her voice dripped sarcasm—"I'm sure you can explain how it happened that this criminal was in custody on Saturday and then released?"

Howie made feeble gestures at the computer. "Somebody used my computer, told the officers she was cleared."

The mayor's tone was icy. "Of course, I'm sure an investigation has revealed how that happened?"

Howie stared at the keyboard. Obviously, no vagrant prints had been found. "We're trying to find out."

Neva drew herself up, an unfortunate maneuver that emphasized her over-endowed bust. "Adelaide looks like a laughingstock. What if the papers get hold of this? I am replacing you with Detective Weitz. You are on leave for the foreseeable future."

"Woo hoo." I clapped a hand over my lips.

Howie glared at the officers near the door.

The mayor swung toward the door. "Excuse me?"

A bald-headed officer standing with his arms behind his back looked puzzled. "Ma'am, we didn't say anything."

Mayor Lumpkin's nostrils flared. She flapped a hand. "Out. Attend to your duties—if that can be done without imposing on the public."

I wouldn't say Adelaide's finest scuttled, but they were out the door in an instant.

Mayor Lumpkin turned back to Howie. She jabbed an index finger at the computer. "Summon Detective Weitz."

I didn't stay to witness the transition of power or observe Howie Warren's departure. The mayor would direct Weitz to redouble efforts to apprehend that master criminal, Michelle Hoyt.

In an instant, I was alone in Detective Sergeant Hal Price's office. The desk was bare, though his in-box was stacked high with papers. It was late afternoon now. I felt a quiver. Saving Michelle from arrest had delayed executing my plan to flush out the identity of the woman who used students in blackmail schemes. I pulled out a city directory, scrawled down two numbers, and reached for the phone. It was important that both calls be made from a police department telephone.

"Eleanor Sheridan."

Perhaps she always answered with her name. Perhaps she noted the Adelaide Police Department on caller ID.

"Ms. Sheridan," I used my most homespun Adelaide drawl, "Officer M. Loy calling."

"Yes, Officer." Her tone was pleasant, slightly patronizing.

"Ma'am, are you the dean of students out at the college?"

"Yes."

This was not a woman to say more than was necessary—no excited demands to know if there was a problem, nothing more than a level pleasant voice that exuded authority.

"Yes'm, we had a message left on Crime Stoppers. That's a number citizens can call to anonymously report—"

"I'm aware of Crime Stoppers." She sounded amused.

"Oh, yes'm. Good to know the community is generally aware. Anyway, this message was a little garbled. I just got a printout of the call."

"Officer, I doubt I can be of help. Perhaps you should contact the campus police."

"You're the person named in the search warrant. It's your office."

"Search warrant?"

"Yes'm. The chief wanted to make sure you'd be there at nine o'clock in the morning so the warrant can be served."

"Search for what?" She was impatient.

I gave an apologetic chuckle. "Like the chief said, anonymous tips usually don't amount to much but they have to be checked out. We'll be in and out real quick tomorrow."

"What are you looking for?"

"The chief didn't say exactly. Something about blackmail. I guess it will be spelled out in the warrant. The chief will probably come along and explain everything, seeing as how it's an office at the college. Anyway, appreciate your cooperation. See you tomorrow. Nine a.m." I hung up, made my second call.

Jeanne Bracewell answered with a gruff "Hello."

"Officer M. Loy here. Are you the Bracewell who's the assistant dean of students out at the college?"

"Yes. How can I help you, Officer?" The assistant dean sounded prepared for some kind of bad news.

"Will you be at your office at nine tomorrow morning?"

"Yes. Is there a problem with a student?"

"Not sure, ma'am. A search warrant's been issued for your office. Just want to be sure you'd be there——"

"Search warrant? Why?"

"Suspicion of blackmail, ma'am."

"That's absurd." Bracewell was crisp, definitive. "Clearly there's been a mistake. However, we will certainly cooperate with any investigation."

"Thank you, ma'am." But she had already hung up.

I made my third call. "Please connect me with Sam Cobb's room."

The phone rang a half dozen times, switched to voice mail inviting me to leave a message. Late on a Sunday afternoon, a honeymooning couple might well be out and about, enjoying a walk along the seawall. I thought fast and spoke rather formally, "Chief Cobb, this is Officer M. Loy. Officer Weitz is now acting chief and has been instructed by Mayor Lumpkin to apprehend Goddard student Michelle Hoyt on a charge of theft and murder at the library. The evidence against Hoyt has been fabricated. Hoyt is currently with a reliable friend of mine. By this evening, I will provide you with the identity of the woman behind a series of crimes, beginning with the murder September seventeenth of Susannah Fairlee." I always opt for the positive in making a statement. I paused, then said warmly, "Congratulations on your marriage, and I hope you and Claire are having a grand holiday."

⁊

I made quick trips between Eleanor's A-frame and Jeanne's house.

Eleanor sat in a cushioned swing on her deck. Her face was thoughtful. She looked into the trees, a faint line between her brows. Once she looked at her watch. But she appeared settled on the porch. She was not en route to the Administration Building. Finally she reached over to a wicker table, picked up a book with a bright jacket. She opened to a bookmarked page, began to read.

Jeanne stood at a counter in a narrow 1950s-era kitchen. She looked into a cupboard, lifted a hand to pluck a box of melba toast from the shelf. She opened the package, drew out the dried brown toast, looked down at it with a shudder of distaste. After a moment, she sighed, turned to the refrigerator. She spread a thin layer of marmalade on the toast, placed the piece on a small bright pink plate. A tea whistle blew. She hurried to the stove, poured water into a teapot. In a moment, she had a tray fixed. It was only as she left the kitchen that she paused, gave a hard stare at the wall phone, then pushed through a swinging door into the hall.

✍

There would be another hour of daylight. However, I didn't intend to wait much longer before I went to the Administration Building to see if either Eleanor or Jeanne stepped into my trap. First I decided to check on Lorraine and Michelle. They should have arrived without incident at Rose Bower. I felt confident Lorraine had been able to admit Michelle and slip into the upstairs suite without being noticed. However, Michelle likely was still high strung and nervous, worried about the police search and frantic to know if she had any hope of escaping prosecution. I wanted to reassure her that progress was being made.

Indeed, the suite for Lorraine and Charles did afford a hospitable sanctuary. The chandelier's prisms glistened and the room appeared large and comfortable. The sound of the softly strummed harp charmed me. Lorraine looked quite lovely sitting on the brocade stool. Soft lighting emphasized the gold of her hair and her flawless complexion. She had changed into a pale ivory gown that had an enchanting shimmer.

Apparently the soothing music had done little to relax Michelle. She sat stiffly on a loveseat, fingers tightly twined together. Her gaze shifted from Lorraine to the portrait on the near wall. The color of Lorraine's dress matched the dress in the portrait. Perhaps that accounted for Michelle's haunted expression. But she should understand that ivory is always complimentary to blondes.

I chose a coal-black top and silver leggings as I appeared. I thought I was a good foil for Lorraine. Black, of course, sets off red hair quite nicely. Wiggins felt I was too often preoccupied with fashion, but how can a woman do a good job if she doesn't look her best?

Michelle watched as colors swirled and shifted into substance. She waited until I was fully present, then said, almost without a tremor, "Good to see you."

I laughed. "You haven't lost your sense of humor."

"Not yet." She managed a flash of a smile, then sat up quite straight. "I want to text Joe but Lorraine says it would be a mistake."

Lorraine's fingers slipped from the strings. "I've never used one of those phones, though they don't look like phones to me, more like elongated compacts. But I've heard students talk about them and how any use can be traced. Michelle is safe here, but what if the police have access to her cell phone? Right now she has it turned off. If she texts Joe, they could be here in an instant."

Michelle pushed to her feet. "The last time he saw us, we were disappearing into the basement of Old Ethel. In a text before I turned it off, he said police searched everywhere and when they left they told him to call them ASAP if he heard from me. He's frantic to know where I am." Her look was imploring. "I have to text him."

Lorraine was right. The police very likely did have access by now to her cell phone. "Definitely not. I'll drop by and tell him you're all right."

She sank back onto the loveseat, her face forlorn. She looked around the lovely room with a hopeless expression. "All right? Not very. I'm a fugitive. What do they say? I'm on the lam. Except I'm in a room nobody ever comes into except ghosts." Her voice was shakier. "I can't stay here forever. For one thing, I'll starve."

I hadn't thought about dinner. I turned toward Lorraine. "If Michelle promises to stay here and keep her cell turned off and not text, you can go to Lulu's and pick up dinner."

Michelle studied me thoughtfully. "Is there anything you two can't do?"

"Quite possibly. But dinner is easy."

Lorraine looked doubtful.

I reassured her. "Arrive on the side street. Find a shadowy area and appear. Imagine a lovely purse to match an outfit." I thought fast, something appealing that wouldn't look too 1940s but Lorraine would find acceptable. "A white crochet blouse and a pale lavender short jacket and a maxi skirt with a pattern of lavender swirls and matching lavender heels."

"How can I pay for a meal?" Lorraine's blue eyes were concerned.

I smiled. "The purse will contain a billfold."

Lorraine said eagerly, "Do you suppose I could have the change purse I last carried in a bag? It was about five inches long and three inches deep, a silk brocade with a phoenix and a dragon. I haven't thought about it in years. Charles bought it for me in Hong Kong."

"Imagine that change purse. It will be there."

"That will be such a delight for me." Lorraine came to her feet and threw me a kiss. "You have the loveliest ideas. I see why Paul thinks highly of you."

I quailed inside. I wasn't sure Wiggins was thinking highly of me at the moment. Precepts Two, Three, and Four had been jettisoned along the way.

Lorraine beamed at Michelle. "I'll be off at once. You will be a good girl and wait quietly for me." Her dark blue eyes fastened on Michelle's face. "I'm trusting you." And she was gone.

Michelle brushed back a tangle of dark hair. "Crazy. That's all. I've tried not to think about it. But there's no doubt. She's here, then she's gone. You're gone, then you're here. But hey, I'm hungry and if she comes back with something good, I will not look the gift ghost in the mouth."

"Perhaps it would be better not to trouble yourself with details."

"I am troubled about a detail: me. My future. We aren't any nearer knowing who's behind everything that's happened. If we don't find out, I'll go to jail and be there forever."

This girl needed encouragement. Quickly, I explained what I'd done. "So I should learn who's behind everything tonight. The greatest help you can give is to stay here out of sight. Don't call or text Joe. By tomorrow you will be vindicated."

If all went as planned . . .

∽

Joe jumped to his feet, rushed around his untidy desk, knocking off a pile of folders. Papers cascaded onto the floor. "What'd you do with her?" His bony face was anxious.

"What one doesn't know, one cannot reveal."

"Like I'm going to tell the cops?" His jaw jutted and he gave me a ferocious glower. He loomed over me, big, powerful, and riled.

"Cool down. Michelle is safe. She's with a friend of mine."

"Somebody you can trust?"

"Absolutely. Michelle understands that she must remain there until the case is solved. She didn't text because her cell might be traced. It won't be too long now. Everything's under control."

"Under control?" It was almost a sneer. "Oh sure. The cops keep popping in here and glaring at me. There's an APB out for Michelle. I'm sure AP and the *Oklahoman* have picked up on the story. Even if she ever gets cleared, she's been labeled a fugitive. How's that going to work out for somebody who wants to be a historian? I've been going nuts. Michelle went down into the basement, though I told the cops I didn't know where she went when she left here, but I know where she went and I've been down there and looked into every closet and under the press and if there's a tunnel, somebody hid it awfully well. You can stand there and tell me about forgetting to lock doors but I know the doors are locked and here you are. Who are you and how come you have keys to Old Ethel?"

I heard a faint throat clearing.

Joe was too intent on my answer to be aware of that unmistakably masculine harrumph.

I picked my words carefully. I wanted Wiggins to realize that my intention was always to honor the Precepts. Joe's assumption that I entered with a key inspired me. I couldn't claim to be Adelaide Police Officer M. Loy, but maybe I could convince him I was another kind of investigator. "You're too smart for us." I sounded regretful and admiring at the same time. "I'm Special Officer M. Loy, undercover for the FBI. We have a case of blackmail that crosses state lines." I was definitely spinning a big one. "Michelle was picked to be the patsy. But we're close to cracking the case. If you want to help, here's what you can do."

He listened intently. When I finished, he quirked an eyebrow. "You want me to manufacture evidence?"

I feigned shock. "Definitely not. The film isn't intended ever to be used as evidence." Certainly that was true. "But we can create material that will lead the Adelaide police to look for the right person."

His thick dark brows bunched in a tight frown. He rubbed knuckles along one jaw.

I liked him a lot. He was an honest guy who believed in following the rules.

"All I can tell you"—and this was certainly true—"is the result will faithfully reflect what happened Friday night."

Joe turned away from me, paced back and forth in the small office.

A tap on my shoulder suggested Wiggins was getting impatient. I said softly, "Meet you in the newsroom." Then I immediately spoke loudly and clearly to Joe. "If you help me, I'm sure the police will investigate further and there will be some compelling evidence for them to find." If and when I placed such evidence advantageously, but I didn't intend to tell Joe everything. "We are not falsifying evidence. We are going to create a dramatization of what occurred Friday night at the library. As for false evidence, that's what was planted on Michelle, her entry code used the night of the theft at the library, the rare book placed in her apartment."

"Yeah." His voice was tight with anger. "You got that right. Michelle never did a thing to land in the kind of trouble she's in. Ben Douglas was nice to me. He shouldn't be dead."

I opened his office door. "You'll do as I ask?"

Slowly he nodded. "I'll be there."

I stepped into the newsroom and pulled the door shut before I disappeared. I whispered softly, "Wiggins, please meet me on the roof of the Administration Building."

"Very well." His tone was crisp and definitely contained no pleasure.

It was almost dark. From the roof of the Administration Building, the campus was a patchwork of shadows illuminated by spots of golden light. I balanced on a parapet, felt a gentle breeze stir my hair. Leaves rustled in a nearby elm. I patted the brickwork next to me. "It's a lovely night, Wiggins."

"I suppose so." He spoke from beside me.

I wondered how he could always find me, and, I assumed, his other emissaries, while I could not see him unless he appeared. Oh well, there are more things in Heaven and earth than I will ever understand. Possibly a kind of Heavenly GPS. I giggled. I doubted Wiggins was au courant with the world's electronic marvels.

"You are amused?"

"Forgive me." I was contrite. "I was thinking of worldly things like GPS—"

"Lorraine was quite clever to be aware of the dangers of using a cell phone when avoiding detection." His voice exuded admiration.

I had underestimated Wiggins. Maybe there was a Heavenly GPS. What did I know?

"Lorraine shouldn't have appeared, of course, but she wanted to console the young woman." His voice was soft. "The lovely harp music took me back so many years. As always, Lorraine tries to bring peace and calm. However"—his voice was edged by frost—"there has been wholesale disregard for Precepts Two, Three, and Four. I have reached my limit."

Coal smoke tickled my nose. Wheels clacked on steel rails. I spoke hastily. "Wiggins, *we*"—I emphasized the plural; after all, I represented the Department of Good Intentions as honorably as I knew how and never saw myself as playing a lone hand—"are very near a solution. I understand you prefer that emissaries and others, such as Lorraine, remain unseen, unnoticed, unsung, but surely you understand that Lorraine and I had to disappear so that we could lift Michelle through the trapdoor to safety. Each of us took an arm and up we went. Think how dreadful it would have been for Michelle to be trapped in that dark tunnel." I hoped he was envisioning rats and spiders and bats.

"Certainly I understand that would upset her."

Encouraged, I said firmly, "Had Lorraine been aware of the Precepts, she would have refrained from making her presence known. But what is, is." I was a well-meaning emissary, dealing with the vagaries of the world. "I know you understand we needed to reappear and reassure Michelle after her rescue." That Michelle was also distressed by our appearing and disappearing wasn't a matter I intended to pursue. I was cheery. "I rather think Michelle will be reticent about her experience." Would she and Joe compare notes? Quite likely, but as Michelle had said in another context, it was better not to look a gift ghost (or two) in the mouth.

The woo-woo of the whistle was almost deafening.

I shouted. "Tonight the woman who shot Ben Douglas and struck down Susannah Fairlee and implicated Michelle Hoyt will slip into this building. Is justice to be done?"

A defeated harrumph. "Someday, Bailey Ruth, you will be too clever for your own good." His voice held a mixture of irritation and acceptance, possibly overlain with a tinge of admiration. "I'd say you offered me Hobson's choice. Very well, stay here. Do your best. But try"—his voice was growing fainter—"to observe the Pre . . ."

The scent of coal smoke was gone. A distant whistle faded. The rooftop was silent. I was alone.

Whew.

✍

I like to be active. I am not fond of solitude. I am sure the Desert Fathers had no difficulty remaining distant from the world as it was then, but right now time seemed interminable. I'd slipped Joe into the building as soon as it was dark. We'd only been here about two hours, but I felt like a caged tigress. Not that I claim that sort of beauty. To me, nothing in this world or the next is more beautiful than a big cat. There's a particular lion I last saw . . . Oh yes. Precept Seven ("Information about Heaven is not yours to impart. Simply smile and say, 'Time will tell.' "). Those who insist Heaven is only for humans should recall Saint Francis and Isaiah 11:6. I entertained myself by recalling images of feline grace but, finally, unable to remain still an instant longer, I popped to the roof. I breathed deeply of fresh air, but I felt a flicker of shame. Joe Cooper had neither moved nor spoken the entire silent time despite the tedium. Likely he had learned immobility during his tour in Afghanistan. Joe was hidden behind the counter near the swinging gate. His camera was braced on a box, since longer exposure time was essential for photos in near darkness. The only light in the office was a faint radiance that spilled through the windows from outside lighting. However, our quarry could no more see in the dark than we. I doubted an overhead light would be turned on, so a flashlight would be necessary. I remembered quite clearly the thin beam of the pencil flashlight Friday night in the library.

I peered down into shadows. A faraway dog barked. Leaves rustled in a brisk breeze. Neon glimmered through the trees, a reminder that cafes and bars brimming with activity rimmed the campus. I saw movement on a side path. A dark figure rode a bicycle without night lights. The bike slid to a stop. The rider stood motionless. Several minutes passed before the rider moved the bike behind a shrub and ran lightly toward a back entrance. I was rather sure there would be the use of someone else's entry code. Criminals follow a pattern, especially ones with past successes. If all went well, the subterfuge would not matter, because no one would be focused on an entry tonight. I had never doubted the killer was prepared to manage an entrance without revealing her identity.

A thump as a door closed.

In an instant, I was back in the Dean of Students Office, standing just inside the door in the long narrow space between the interior wall and the counter. "She's coming." My whisper was faint. Joe neither moved nor spoke.

I stood tensely, listening.

The door opened. A thin narrow beam looped back and forth, skimmed the entry area, touched the counter, flicked around the administrative area, swept over the heavy red velvet drapes. Slowly, cautiously a dark figure stepped inside. The door closed. Again the beam explored the room.

I held my breath. Perhaps, as Wiggins had warned, I'd been too clever in bringing Joe and his camera with me. But the intruder moved no closer to the counter. The thin beam illuminated desks and chairs and the wall of filing cabinets. If the intruder had walked to the counter, swung the beam down to the floor, Joe would have been found.

Instead, the black-clad figure turned away from the door, walked swiftly to the dean's office. A click. The door opened and the figure entered, walked to the desk, bent down to place the pencil flashlight on the floor by a filing cabinet. As she knelt by the cabinet, I saw Eleanor Sheridan in profile, the planes of her cheek sharp, angular, tense. She was dressed in a black turtleneck, black slacks, black gloves, black sneakers, hair hidden beneath a black stocking cap. This was the figure I'd glimpsed when Ben Douglas turned on the light in room 211.

I perched unseen on the edge of her desk as she pulled keys from her pocket. She inserted a key in the bottom drawer of a filing cabinet, twisted. The drawer squeaked as it rolled forward. A thin hand reached toward the back to pull out a bulky accordion folder. Quickly she flicked past tabs, then pulled out a slender folder. She lifted the cover, removed a small manila envelope about six by nine inches. The large folder and its contents were replaced in the drawer. A push, a twist of the key, the contents once again under lock. She picked up the manila envelope and stood. I saw that the flap was securely sealed with a strip of packaging tape.

Eleanor ripped open the envelope, tipped out a flash drive into her right hand, tucked it into one pocket. She carried the empty envelope with her as she stepped out of her office. She walked toward the counter.

And I knew Joe was filming her every step of the way. My breath caught in my throat. If she saw Joe . . .

In the backwash of the pencil beam, her eyes were narrowed,

her expression preoccupied. She reached the counter, crumpled the envelope, and tossed it toward a wastebasket, turned, and was at the door.

Taking advantage of the faint illumination provided by her pencil flashlight, I swooped to a desk, plucked a flash drive from the CPU.

Eleanor opened the door and stepped into the hall. As the door closed, I waited a moment, eased open the door, heard the whisper of steps near the end of the hall. Holding the flash drive I'd taken from a secretary's CPU, I moved into the hall, eased the door shut. I caught up with Eleanor at the stairway. I had instructed Joe to remain silent and hidden for at least ten minutes after the intruder left. I had no doubt he would do precisely as directed. He understood chain of command. Eleanor opened a side door, looked out cautiously, waited to be sure no one was about. I was right behind her as she slipped from the building. She kept to the shadows as she walked to a bank of shrubbery and pulled the bicycle from the shadows.

I hovered near enough to touch her, intensely aware of her every movement. There were many ways she could dispose of her flash drive if that was her intent. If her hand dipped into the right pocket of her black slacks, I was prepared to act. But she swung astride the bike, both hands gripping the handlebars.

✑

Light spilled cheerfully from all of the A-frame windows. A golden bulb glowed on the porch. She unlocked the door, stepped inside.

I waited until the door closed, then I slipped my flash drive inside the letter box, a good hiding place for the moment. Now unencumbered, I joined Eleanor inside.

She tossed the black stocking cap onto the hallway table. She drew off the gloves, dropped them next to the cap. Her hand returned to the pocket, came out with the small flashlight and the flash drive, added them to the pile on the table. Finally, she tugged up her turtleneck and pulled a small pistol from the waistband of her slacks. She placed the gun on the table, too.

I felt a sudden emptiness in my chest, as if my lungs had been squeezed of all air. That's why she'd worn gloves for her surreptitious visit to her office. There was no reason for her to fear leaving her fingerprints anywhere in the Administration Building, but she had gone prepared to shoot anyone who challenged her. I was struck by the methodical coldness she exhibited. I was sure the gun she carried the night she shot Ben Douglas was fingerprint free, or she could not have placed it in Michelle's car trunk to implicate her. Sheridan was prepared at any time to remove anyone who threatened her. I wondered if she had obtained this gun to replace the one used to shoot Ben Douglas, or if she customarily owned two guns.

Her attractive features were set in a hard mask of concentration. She looked slowly and carefully around the room, then her mouth spread in an amused smile. She retrieved the flash drive and strolled to the office area. She opened the center drawer in the desk, dropped the flash drive into one of the compartments.

There is no hiding place so successful as no hiding place at all.

Unless a searcher knew to look for a flash drive, there was no reason for a flash drive in a desk drawer to attract attention.

Still smiling, she lifted a hand to fluff hair pressed down by the cap. She was relaxed as she walked to a minibar in the corner of her living room. She poured two shots of Scotch in a glass, added ice, club soda. She stood by the counter, took a deep drink, no doubt a woman pleased with her night's work.

My night was just beginning.

Chapter 14

The tower bell tolled midnight as I reached the library. An occasional car sped past, headlights briefly illuminating the imposing Gothic structure, emphasizing the darkness of its windows. The front steps glimmered in light from tall golden-globed posts. I went instead to the rear of the building and steps that led down to a basement service door. "Joe?" Had he followed my instructions, waited to leave the Administration Building ten minutes after the dean departed?

"I was beginning to wonder if you were coming." The tone was just this side of combative. "I've been here long enough that I can see in the dark like an owl. Funny thing is, I don't see you."

"It's good not to be observed. I intend for neither of us to be noticed."

"I know a brush-off when I hear it. Mine not to reason why,

right?" He kept his voice low but his irritation was obvious. "Okay, you aren't visible—what else is new?—but somebody dressed all in black slid into the dean's office. All I know for sure, it had to be a woman. Guys don't move like that. Who was she? Where—"

I felt a whoosh of satisfaction. He'd seen enough to know the figure was that of a woman, which meant his video should work perfectly for my purposes.

"—did she go? What was going on?"

Joe was an invaluable assistant, but I wished he didn't immediately fall into reporter mode and pepper me with questions. "She was there to remove a file containing blackmail material."

"I didn't miss a move she made. She wasn't carrying a file when she came out. On the video, I wasn't able to get much." He sounded discouraged. "I'll tell you right now that there wasn't enough light to be able to pin the shots to that office. The only light came from that little flash. You can make out the leather glove and a dark sleeve, but the video could have been taken anywhere. All I really got was a dark figure—"

"Great." That was wonderful news.

"Great?" He was exasperated. "What's the point then? This looks like a bust to me. I was getting somewhere with my calls to the kids who work in that office—"

"I told you not to stir anyone up." My voice was sharp.

"I don't work for you."

Uh-oh. Time for a little feather smoothing. "Of course you don't." I couldn't have sounded more agreeable. "But you want to get Michelle out of a deep pit."

"Making a dark-as-ink video that's worthless?"

"Not worthless. Perfect for our purposes."

"Oh, yeah. Dark on dark. If she filched a file—"

"A flash drive. She put it in her pocket."

"Oh, great." He mimicked me. "She does the deed and we don't get a shot. I stayed where I was like you told me to. I almost came out. I could have caught her by surprise, turned on the light, got a picture nobody could dispute."

"Ben Douglas turned on a light and got a bullet in his chest. She had a gun with her tonight." I gave him time to digest that.

"So I guess I'm a lucky dude I didn't storm out and corner her, like I thought about doing." It was the first time he had ever sounded subdued.

"You're alive."

"She shot Ben Douglas?"

"She did. Your video is going to place her at the scene of that crime. Wait here until I open the basement door."

"You got keys to the library?"

"I'll open the door." If Joe assumed I had keys, I certainly hadn't intentionally misled him. In an instant, I was inside the library. I fumbled for the light, turned it on long enough to unlock the door. I plunged the basement back into darkness, turned the knob, pulled. "Come in."

"Said the spider to a damn fool."

I laughed, closed the door behind him. "Did you bring a flash-light?"

"I follow instructions. You told me to come prepared to film in the dark and to bring a flashlight." I heard him open his backpack.

I'd forgotten I was invisible, to facilitate entrances and exits, but I remembered and appeared just as the beam of a Maglite turned toward me.

"Funny." His voice was conversational. "You looked kind of blurry there for a moment. Guess my eyes aren't used to the light."

I held out my hand. "If you'll give me the flashlight, I know the way." That was a fib, but it didn't take long to find stairs. He followed. I cupped my hand over the light, afforded a narrow beam so we could see to climb up one flight and another. On the second floor, I turned off the flashlight and gently opened the door. The hallway was dark except for a faint luminous patch that marked lighting on the central stairway. I flicked on the flashlight, shaded it again, providing just enough illumination. I took care to walk softly, though I hoped we had the library to ourselves. Joe didn't make a sound behind me. We passed the opening to the wide central stairway.

Two doors farther and we reached room 211. Crime tape crisscrossed the door. "Here we are."

Joe stepped toward the door.

I grabbed his elbow. "We can't break the crime tape."

He folded his arms. "You know some magic way to open the door and not disturb the tape?"

"Wait here." I sped to the next door, turned off the flashlight, placed it on the hall floor. Hidden in the almost complete darkness of the hallway, I disappeared. Inside the room, enough light came through the windows to find my way to the connecting door to room 211. I unlocked the door, took an instant to release the lock on the other side as well. I popped back into the hall, reappeared, picked up the flashlight, turned it on, and rejoined Joe. "We can go in through the connecting room." Once again I was careful to cup my hand over the beam, allowing the smallest amount of light possible.

He followed me. "I keep having this funny feeling something really weird is going on."

"Think about Michelle."

"Right. What happened to her is definitely weird, too weird for cops to believe—taken prisoner, kept in a vacant house, her keypad code used to enter the library, the stolen journal found in her apartment, Michelle coming to the police station just in time to be accused of theft and also of shooting Ben Douglas. Somebody—the gal in black?—set that up. You claim to have a scheme to trap the lady in black. All right. I'm your guy. I took the video that nobody can pin to a place, which makes it pretty worthless, but I follow orders. What next?"

"You brought food and water?"

"I got orders. I followed them." He shrugged out of a backpack. "Got it all in here: video cam, night vision goggles, beef jerky, raisins, granola bars, thermos of coffee, bottled water."

"Make yourself comfortable. I'll leave the flashlight, but don't use it unless it's absolutely necessary. I hope not to keep you waiting long."

⟳

The interior of Eleanor Sheridan's home was dark, though night security lights glowed under the front eaves and on the deck. I stood silently in the entry hall, listening. Through open windows came the rustle of tree limbs, the distant whoo of an owl, a nearby barking dog. Although the A-frame wasn't an old structure—probably built within the last fifteen years—there was an occasional creak.

Mostly there was the silence of sleep.

I wondered about the dreams of a woman who had twice killed.

Was she so self-absorbed that any action seen as necessary for her safety seemed reasonable, with never a moment for regret? Was she fully asleep, that first heavy sleep of the night, when cares and concerns are lost in a plunge deep beyond consciousness?

For my present purposes, I hoped so. Although I love being *in* the world, it is obviously helpful to remain unseen and enjoy the safety of movement above impediments like furniture. As my eyes adjusted, I distinguished the darker bulk of furnishings in the glow from the deck. I reached Eleanor's desk. Slowly I pulled out the center drawer. She had dropped the flash drive into the third compartment. I felt cautiously, found the drive. I held it firmly in my hand, closed the drawer, and returned to the entry hall. I thought for a moment. I wanted her flash drive easily accessible to me but I had to be sure I didn't confuse it with my flash drive in the letter box. I cautiously felt the items she'd placed on the table, found one of her leather gloves, and tucked the flash drive in a finger. I placed the glove on the floor by the door. I unhooked the night safety chain, popped the lock on the knob, eased the door open an inch at a time.

Creak.

My heart thudded. I pulled the door open swiftly, bent, grabbed the glove with the incriminating flash drive, placed it in a shadow on the porch.

A light flashed on upstairs, spilling down into the living area.

I moved fast to open the letter box where I'd earlier hidden my flash drive. I ignored the clang, grabbed the flash drive I'd taken from a secretary's desk. Back in the entry hall, I closed the front door, looped the chain.

Light flared in the living room.

The flash drive was small but discernible. I had to keep it from her view.

She leaned over the railing of the loft. She carried the gun she'd previously left on the entry hall table. That she was obviously at ease with guns didn't surprise me. That night at the library, when she jerked around from the desk, she had fired without hesitation and struck her target.

She surveyed the empty room, wary, intent, suspicious.

I reached a sofa near the desk and dropped the hand with the flash drive behind the sofa back.

Eleanor was slender in a blue shorty nightgown. She eased down the steps, eyes flicking right and left. On the ground floor, she turned toward the front door.

With her back to me, I felt it was safe to move to her desk. I waited until I heard the door open and Eleanor step out onto the porch, then quietly eased out the center drawer, placed my flash drive in the third compartment, closed the drawer.

Immediately I arrived upstairs in the loft. I didn't know if she had gone around the house to be sure everything was secure, but I didn't have any time to waste. Quickly I looked around the room. There was something alien to me in the immaculate neatness. She hadn't tossed the black pants and top she'd worn that night carelessly on a chair. I sped into a small tiled bath. A straw hamper sat against the wall beneath a towel rack. I lifted the lid. A neat woman. Tidy. Not likely to wear clothing more than once. Huddled on the bottom of the hamper was a mound of dark clothing. I reached inside, grabbed the long-sleeve black cotton turtleneck and black spandex pants.

I heard the creak of the front door. I reached the railing of the loft, carrying my booty, and judged distances. I jammed the clothing into a tight bunch, was over the railing and downstairs crouched behind the sofa by the time the door slammed shut.

The chain jangled. Footsteps. The stairs creaked.

I watched her climb, the pistol still firmly in her grasp. I rose near the ceiling and eased through the air to the now dark entry hall. Her weight on the stairs masked the creak as I opened the front door and placed the wad of clothes outside. In another instant I plucked the stocking cap, remaining glove, and pencil flashlight from the table, added them to my pile. More creaks upstairs as she crossed the floor.

I closed the door and secured the chain, making sure there was no betraying clink. Once outside, my heartbeat slowed to normal as I gathered up my booty, especially the glove I'd left in darkness at the edge of the steps, the precious glove with the incriminating flash drive. Should Eleanor rouse again and come downstairs, she likely would see that the items she'd earlier dropped on the entry table were gone. But I intended to be quick.

First I went to the dean's office. I placed the bundle of clothes, the glove with the flash drive, and Eleanor's pencil flashlight on a window ledge and moved inside. I unlocked and opened the window, retrieved the flash drive. In a moment more, the flash drive, nestled inside the crumpled envelope Eleanor had tossed in a wastebasket, was safely resting in the desk of Dean of Students Eleanor Sheridan. I returned to the window, locked it, moved outside, and picked up the pencil flashlight and Eleanor's clothes.

My next stop was the unlocked basement door of the library. I was glad to have Eleanor's pencil flash to find my way. I still carried the clothing. I waited until I was inside the connecting room to 211 to appear. It wasn't pleasant, but I pulled on the turtleneck, stepped into the trousers. They weren't a bad fit, though Eleanor might be a bit taller than I. I wasn't wearing her black sneakers, but that was an easy addition to the wardrobe. I tucked my hair beneath the stocking cap, drew on the leather gloves.

I opened the connecting door quietly. "Joe, I'm back." I stepped inside, the pencil flashlight beam pointed at the floor.

He blinked his light on, off, illuminating me for an instant. "Hey, you look just like the woman in the dean's office. Where'd you get the costume?"

"The look should be the same." That was all I said.

"I don't see how—"

"The point now is to get a new video." The less he knew, the better. I don't know if my actions constituted breaking and entering, but the result was the same. "Friday night the woman in black came through the hall door. She held a pencil flash." I waggled the flash in my hand. "She crossed to the table." I aimed the light at the table. "In the dean's office, you got shots of her in the area between the hall wall and the counter. I want you to get pictures of me walking toward the table in here and doctor the video to make it look like it's a video of her in here."

"You want me to Photoshop the video of her and make it look like it was taken in here?"

"Exactly. I'll walk across the room, and when I get to the table, I'll hold the flash to look in the box that holds Susannah Fairlee's papers."

"Yeah. That'll work." He did several takes.

When he was done, I studied the table. The wood was smooth. I needed a protrusion, a splinter, something sharp.

249

"Oh, hey, Joe. Film me again at the box." I lifted the lid. The night Ben was shot, Eleanor's arm had caught for an instant on the edge of the lifted lid. I leaned near the box, then swung around to face the door as Eleanor had when Ben turned on the light. The right sleeve of the turtleneck snagged on the corrugated edge of the box lid, leaving behind a long black thread.

⌒

The truck stop on the outskirts of Adelaide was the sort of place where strangers occasioned no notice. I wore a denim jacket, gray trousers, and black ankle boots. I felt I'd earned a late evening cheeseburger and fries after taking my time getting in and out of Eleanor's house without arousing her. It had taken patience, but I had been determined that no vagrant noise would alert her. I put the clothing in the hamper and left the stocking cap, gloves, and pencil flash on the side table in the entryway. In the morning, there would be no evidence her home had been entered.

I enjoyed each bite of the cheeseburger. I took a last swallow of good black coffee. I imagined lights burned at Old Ethel as Joe finished his assignment.

I walked outside as if going to a car, made sure I was unobserved, disappeared. Back inside the building, I found a small office that likely was used by the manager. I used the telephone to call Crime Stoppers. Bobby Mac always described my voice as Lauren Bacall with a touch of June Allyson. *Eleanor Sheridan shot Ben Douglas. She's hidden the murder weapon behind books in the second shelf of the bookcase in her office. Look for a flash drive in a small manila envelope in her center desk drawer. Blackmail material is contained in the flash drive.* I hung up. I had yet to install the murder weapon, but as soon as it was daylight, I would retrieve the gun and deposit it in her office. Until then, I was off duty. Had I forgotten anything? I hoped not.

I found an empty room in a nearby motel rather than returning to Rose Bower. I settled in for a quick nap after setting the radio alarm for five. I appeared long enough to wash my face and put on fresh makeup. I returned to the truck stop for breakfast. I was ready for a full day when pink tinged the eastern horizon.

It was the half light between dawn and daylight when I reached the abandoned train trestle near the cement plant. Dark columns of smoke rose from two massive chimneys. Rusted steel girders were still shadowy. I moved to the middle of the bridge. I felt behind a girder, continued to search until my fingers touched the ridged butt of the gun Eleanor Sheridan carried when she shot Ben Douglas.

I truly felt buoyant when I stood in Eleanor's office, pulled some books out of the shelf behind her desk, and carefully nestled the weapon there.

⌒

I turned on the lights in Chief Cobb's office, settled behind his desk, checked his Outlook Express in-box. I found, as I'd expected, an e-mail from the *Bugle* with an attachment.

> To: Chief Cobb
> From: Joe Cooper, Editor of the *Bugle*
> Subject: Anonymous video

Chief Cobb, an anonymous source left a flash drive on my desk in an envelope marked: *Urgent—Send to Adelaide Police Chief Sam Cobb re murder of Goddard Library night watchman Ben Douglas.* I have not looked at the video—

I understood this was an artful statement. Joe could quite honestly say he hadn't looked at the video since he finished editing it and therefore his claim was accurate as far as it went.

—and cannot vouch for its contents.

I grinned. Joe was uncomfortable with Photoshopping.

A note inside the envelope contained this message: *Video depicts intruder in room 211 at Goddard Library immediately prior to arrival of night watchman Ben Douglas.* There was no signature. The video is attached to this e-mail. The envelope and the flash drive are here in my office. I will be happy to bring the envelope and the flash drive to the police station if you wish. The *Bugle* stands ready to assist the police in any way in its investigation to discover the murderer of Ben Douglas.

Best Regards,
Joe Cooper
Editor

"Pretty interesting video." The deep voice was behind me. I looked over my shoulder.

Sam Cobb stood next to the old leather couch near the front windows. He was much as I remembered: six feet tall, burly build, broad face beneath grizzled black hair. He was unshaven and his hair was untidily sprigged, but his dark eyes were alert. A slight smile pulled at his lips. "Figured you were here when I heard my chair squeak." He stood in his stocking feet, arms akimbo. He jerked a thumb over his shoulder. "Not the first night I've sacked out on the couch. Got here about three a.m. I told Claire we had to get back—a big case—and she got us packed in twenty minutes. We picked up some fish tacos and Dr Peppers on the way out of town. Takes about eight hours to drive up from Galveston. Dropped Claire off at home. Figured I better get over here. Picked up an interesting call to Crime Stoppers. Anonymous tip called in from the truck stop out on Highway Nineteen. Enough substance to get some search warrants. Been looking at all the e-mails to and from the acting chief. Unusual. And the files. Smith and Weitz have done a good job. APB for Michelle Hoyt so far unsuccessful. Haven't canceled it yet. The mayor has a scanner. Better not to rile her up. I figure the girl will keep out of the way."

His voice was dry. "Almost spooky how she's nowhere to be found." His broad mouth quirked in a grin. He lifted his arms above his head in a waking bear stretch. "Couple hours of sleep. Ready to line things up. Got a bunch of pictures out of the file from the crime scene when Douglas was shot. The box on the table in the *Bugle* video looks like the box in room 211. The lab can verify that. No proof the figure in black shot Douglas, but it puts her on the scene of the crime late at night."

"Chief, I am so glad to see you."

"Wish I could say the same." His mouth again quirked.

I was shocked for an instant, then understood. I laughed. "I would appear, but——"

"You're on good ghostly behavior?"

"The best I can manage."

That brought forth a deep chuckle. Then he was serious. "Fill me in. I gather there's lots for me to do."

"There is." I, too, was serious now. I talked fast, describing Susannah Fairlee and the terminally ill girl she visited.

Sam's big face creased in sympathy. "Always thought it'd be damn hard to die all alone. That poor kid. So you found a letter from her at the Fairlee house?"

"The letter from JoLee Jamison arrived the day Susannah was murdered. The letter was in Susannah's purse. It's still there."

"I'll see that it's taken into custody." He frowned. "Too bad the girl didn't use Sheridan's name. A defense attorney will say the girl was dying, probably confused. The letter offers no proof that Sheridan was involved."

"JoLee didn't need to tell Susannah. Susannah already knew from their visits."

Sam jammed his hands in the pockets of his baggy shorts. "You figure Susannah got the letter and went straight to Sheridan?"

"Exactly. A friend of Susannah's saw her leave the Administration Building that day. She will testify that Susannah was obviously upset and angry. I think Susannah confronted Sheridan. Maybe she demanded that Sheridan resign. Susannah probably didn't want to hurt the people who'd been set up by Sheridan, even if she'd had a way to find them. Maybe she saw her best hope was to threaten to take the letter to the college president, tell him. JoLee had made it clear to Susannah that she hated Sheridan. Susannah didn't know why until she received the letter that told about the blackmail scheme. Susannah may have said she'd remain quiet if Sheridan agreed to write out a confession, give it to Susannah, and quit her job. Sheridan likely decided then that Susannah had to die. Maybe Sheridan asked for twenty-four hours to think about it. Maybe she said she'd write the confession, mail it to Susannah, and offer her resignation the next day. Something—anything—to keep Susannah quiet until that night."

Sam nodded. "I saw in the reports that a back-alley neighbor saw someone on a bicycle. We'll talk to him again. Maybe he'll remember something else about the rider."

"Sam, have you had much rain the last few weeks?"

Sam looked bewildered. As well he might. "You know Oklahoma. Rained off and on all summer. Only a couple of days of rain since then."

I rushed on. "Sheridan has a bike. I saw her on it last night. It isn't quite a month ago that Susannah was killed. Check for tire tracks in the alley and in the Fairlee backyard. Maybe there will be some trace."

"We'll look. Be better to have the neighbor in to take a look after we get her in custody. He said the rider was a woman. Maybe he saw enough to be able to identify her." He strode to his desk, then stopped and cautiously reached down to make sure the chair was empty, though of course no one was visible in the seat. I had already moved. Reassured, he dropped heavily into the swivel chair. Face puckered in thought, he sent off a series of short e-mails, then picked up the phone, punched a number. He moved the chair until he could stretch his legs out comfortably. "Yo, Teddy." He glanced toward the clock on his desk. It read a few minutes after six. "Hope I didn't get you up." He reached out, punched Speaker.

"—already run five miles. Got to get you out for some PT, Sam. Hey, how come you're calling from your office? Thought you were out of town this week."

"Got a murder to solve. That night watchman shot out at Goddard didn't make it. A slug in his chest Friday night. I need a couple of search warrants. Can I meet you at the courthouse in an hour?"

"Sure. Sallie Mae'll already be there. She takes off at three to pick her grandkids up. You got probable cause?"

"Anonymous tip but credible, a video that shows there may be some fibers at the crime scene, and if we match them up with clothes from the suspect's home, we'll have something. At the home we're on the lookout for a black stocking cap, black top and slacks, black gloves. At the office, we're looking for a flash drive that contains blackmail material and the Douglas murder weapon. Need warrants for the home of Eleanor Sheridan, Goddard dean of students, and her office."

"The dean of students?" Teddy's voice had lost its easy air of camaraderie.

"That's the tip."

A deep breath. "Mayor Lumpkin will have my ass if you're wrong."

The answer was quick and firm. "I'm not wrong."

Bless Sam. He was coming on strong because he trusted me. It wouldn't only be the judge's ass if the evidence didn't jibe. Mayor Lumpkin would trash Sam quicker than a skunk can stink.

There was silence on the line. Saving Michelle now depended

upon an elected judge who was likely a political animal, quick to avoid danger. The search warrants would make all the difference.

Finally: "This will be a pretty big deal, Sam. Meet me in my chambers. Twenty minutes. I want to know exactly what I'm dealing with."

The line clicked off.

His Honor Teddy Cooley was even bigger than Sam, probably six four, a big face with a hooked nose and full lips. He was slick bald, ruddy, made a good-sized office appear small as he paced up and down next to a conference table. He was still in his warm-up from his run. His Adidas shoes looked expensive.

Sam stood at parade rest, equally imposing in his own way, broad face resolute, brown eyes steady, jaw firm, even though his aloha shirt was crumpled—there might have been a couple of taco stains down the front—and his cotton knee-high shorts revealed sun-reddened knees. He had the solid, tough look of an old fullback, still in shape and ready to rumble. Sam continued in his deep voice, ". . . won't know how far back the blackmailing scheme goes until we get the flash drive. Think of it like a 'gator swimming in muddy water: All you see for starters is the ripple he leaves behind as his tail moves back and forth. We kind of came in on the back of what had been happening. It started with Susannah Fairlee's murder."

The judge stopped, stared at Sam. "Susannah drowned. It was an accident."

Sam held up a broad, callused hand. "That's what we were supposed to think. Let me tell you what we know. Some of it we can prove, a lot of it we can't. Susannah Fairlee was friends with JoLee

Jamison, a student who had worked in Sheridan's office. Susannah visited her as a Stephen Minister. That meant she was there to listen and be kind. After the girl died, Susannah got a letter."

Teddy Cooley's back was to his desk. I hovered over the desk. His secretary obviously knew how to keep a happy boss. In the center of the bare desktop lay a fresh legal pad with a pen beside it. Keeping a careful eye on the judge, I picked up the pen, wrote swiftly: *Tell him Susannah went to dean's office after she read the letter.*

Sam broke off. His face stiffened as he watched the airborne pen point at the legal pad before it returned to the desk. He took two quick steps, reached past the judge to pick up the legal pad. "Think of it like this." He ripped the sheet off, his eyes scanning the script, then folded the sheet like a letter. "Susannah receives a letter." He waggled the folded sheet.

The judge looked a bit puzzled, possibly wondering why Sam felt it necessary to illustrate the form of a letter.

Sam saw his expression, talked faster. "The letter," Sam tapped the folded sheet for emphasis, "said a blackmailing ring was being run out of the office of the dean of students. Fairlee went straight to that office after she received the letter."

Sam tossed the legal pad back on the desk, apparently absentmindedly stuffed the folded sheet into the pocket of his baggy cotton shorts. "Susannah Fairlee confronted Sheridan. That night Sheridan went to the Fairlee house, took Susannah by surprise, knocked her out, pushed her face into the pond. That's not the murder we can prove, but I'm telling you about it because everything that happened flowed from the blackmail ring and Susannah's visit to the dean's office."

Cooley's frown was intense.

Sam met the judge's stare directly. "Here's the guts of the case, Teddy: Last week the *Bugle* ran a story about Michelle Hoyt, a senior scheduled to begin research Friday on materials donated to the library by the Fairlee family. Those materials included Fairlee's diaries. After the story ran, a series of odd incidents occurred at the library, roses mysteriously appearing, a gargoyle knocked from a niche. Meanwhile, Michelle Hoyt was decoyed to an empty house and held captive. Thursday night her entry code was used to enter the library. A rare book was stolen. A tip implicated Hoyt. The book was found in her apartment and Hoyt was nowhere to be found. That's the sequence: *Bugle* story, roses, vandalism, student taken captive, robbery, student's code used. The result: The student did not appear at the library Friday morning to open the box in room 211 that contained Susannah Fairlee's diaries. Friday night the library was entered by a woman dressed in black. She went to room 211, was confronted by Ben Douglas, shot him. Fairlee's diary for this year is missing. Sheridan couldn't take a chance Hoyt would find passages written after Susannah visited JoLee Jamison, passages describing JoLee's hatred of Sheridan. Sheridan was willing to do whatever she needed to do to take out that diary. There was no way she could have explained her presence in the library late at night to steal Susannah's current diary, so Ben Douglas was shot. We need search warrants to hunt for the outfit Sheridan wore the night she shot Douglas, the flash drive that proves blackmail, and the murder weapon."

Cooley looked toward the window, his face stern. When he turned back to Sam, his jaw was tight. "Sheridan knocked Susannah out, drowned her?"

Sam met his gaze directly. "That's what happened."

Cooley rubbed his chin with the knuckles of one hand. "Susannah—I spent one summer trying to get her attention. I was sixteen. She was a couple of years older. God, she was exciting. I almost broke my neck in a swan dive at the pool. She wasn't even watching. Years later, Corinne and I played a lot of bridge with Susannah and Jonathan." He slowly expelled a deep breath. "You can have your warrants, Sam."

Chapter 15

I gently tugged open the silver blue drapes. Early-morning sunlight spilled into the suite at Rose Bower. Lorraine was curled on her chaise longue. She looked very appealing, her face kind even in sleep. She wore a blue nightgown. A lime-and-teal-striped afghan was drawn up to her waist. I knew she had remained present in the suite to reassure Michelle.

I glanced at the four-poster. Michelle slept with a pillow snuggled against her face. I felt a bit frazzled after my active night. I appeared so that Michelle would not be startled should she awaken. And, yes, lovely clothes would be a boost for me. I chose a peach boat-neck sweater, white twill trousers, and peach ankle boots. I glanced into the full-length mirror in the wardrobe and nodded in approval. The colors were almost as energizing as black coffee brewed with chicory. I was quite pleased to find one hand held a mug of steaming coffee. I took a refreshing swallow, strolled to the chaise longue, and gently touched Lorraine on her shoulder.

She woke at once. "Bailey Ruth." She looked across the room at the four-poster bed, spoke softly. "I'm glad Michelle is getting some rest. I'm afraid she had a very troubled sleep. Do you have good news?" She sat up, patted the end of the chaise longue. "My, that coffee smells wonderful."

I settled beside her. Possibly I could imagine coffee for Lorraine. I squeezed my eyes shut, opened them. No luck. Perhaps she could give it a try. "Sometimes our thoughts can work wonders. I was hungry for very strong coffee and the mug just came."

She looked at the table. A cup and saucer in Limoges china appeared. She lifted the cup, beamed. "Twinings. Good strong black tea. One night after the ambulances were unloaded and we'd tended to the wounded, Paul and I rested for a moment behind the surgery tent. He was going to go back, but I put my hand on his arm and asked him to stay long enough to have some tea, to make him stronger to drive through the night. We took our mugs and sat on some empty wooden crates. He was afraid my apron would get snagged. I told him snags didn't matter. I knew the hem was stained with blood." Slowly she replaced the cup into its saucer, stared across the room, her dark blue eyes haunted. "Blood on my apron . . . The night they brought Paul in, I was there, and I knelt beside him and his face was gray. Blood matted one shoulder. I struggled to get his tunic loose and I found my letter." Tears brimmed, spilled down pale cheeks. "The envelope had been opened. He had received my letter, read it—and went out to die. I killed him." She lifted her hands, pressed them against her face. "They made me leave him. My fault . . ."

I knew better. Wiggins had never doubted that, after the war, when he and Charles were back and safe, he would win her heart. "Lorraine, you—"

Abruptly she pushed up from the chaise longue, whirled away from me. She walked across the room, touched the harp. When she turned back to me, her face was smooth and her eyes defied me to speak.

"Lorraine, Paul—"

"Tell me what you've done. Is there hope now for Michelle?" Her gaze was resolute. She was determinedly in the present. She didn't want to go back to pain and loss and heartbreak.

If she would listen, I could reassure her that Wiggins hadn't de- liberately put himself in danger after reading her letter. He had seen his duty and done it and the shell struck. But she was convinced she had caused him to die. Nothing I said would alter that bleak certainty. Now I knew why she had chosen to remain on earth.

"Tell me." Her tone was imperious. She sat on the stool beside the harp, waited.

I knew better than to speak again about Wiggins and, at the moment, we needed to do our best for Michelle. Perhaps another time I could find the right words, tell her he loved her still. I de- scribed my night.

She sat for a long moment, sunk in thought, then looked at me directly, as I knew she'd often looked at life, facing hard truths. "Will search warrants be enough?"

Lorraine understood the challenge. Even if warrants uncovered clothing Eleanor wore and a second careful search in room 211 found matching threads, the evidence was circumstantial. The threads did not place Eleanor Sheridan in the room the moment

Ben Douglas was shot. The discovery of the flash drive might prove blackmail, but would any of the victims or the students used to entrap them be willing to testify? Ballistics could prove the gun was used to shoot Ben Douglas, but I knew it had to be bare of fingerprints. Eleanor would have made sure it was shiny clean before she placed the gun in Michelle's trunk.

A good defense lawyer might scissor away any links to Sheridan. Where was proof that the thread from her blouse was snagged that fateful Friday night? It wasn't up to Sheridan to explain the thread. The video likely couldn't be introduced into evidence because its origin was unknown. Even if it were accepted, again, the video was no proof that Sheridan was in room 211 when Ben Douglas was shot. Others besides Sheridan had access to her office. What proof was there that she had hidden the gun behind the books?

I'd worked hard this night. I'd done my best. Sam Cobb was gambling his job security on my efforts. He trusted me. Michelle Hoyt's freedom hung in the balance. I faced Lorraine. "The evidence they find may not"—it was hard to get the words out—"be enough. She's hard. Tough. If she rides it out, keeps her mouth shut . . . Oh, Lorraine, it may not be enough."

Lorraine's gaze was searching. Finally, she nodded. "You'll think of something, I know you will."

Across the room, the bedclothes rustled. Michelle bolted upright. "Joe—"

Lorraine was on her feet, hurrying to the bed. "It's all right, my dear. Everything's fine."

Michelle swept back dark, tousled hair. She tried to smile. "I'd forgotten." She buried her face in her hands. "I wish I hadn't remembered."

I joined them. "Everything's under control, Michelle. The police are definitely working on the case."

Her gaze was weary. "Are they still hunting for me?"

I waved a dismissive hand. "Don't worry—"

She gave a strangled laugh. "Worry? Who, me? Why should I worry? My name's mud, my reputation's ruined, and I may go to jail forever, but hey, not to worry."

I touched her arm.

She stiffened, but didn't pull away. That was progress.

"I know what happened and why." I told her about Susannah and JoLee and the woman who fashioned the trap for her.

Michelle looked at me with stricken eyes. "That poor girl. I would hate to die angry and bitter."

Lorraine's face softened. She gave an approving nod. I knew she was quite pleased that she'd given roses to Michelle and Joe. Michelle's own life was in utter disarray because of Eleanor Sheridan, yet her thoughts were for JoLee Jamison, who died alone.

Michelle laced her fingers together. "When I walked into the house on Montague, that woman was there, waiting for me to go down the stairs. What if I hadn't gone down into the basement?" Her voice was thin. "I had a bad feeling. I almost turned around to leave. I thought, all that time when I was trapped, that nothing could be worse. But I was wrong. If I'd looked around, if I'd seen her, she would have shot me, wouldn't she?" Her gaze mirrored horror.

I was solemn. "I rather think she would."

Michelle reached out, gripped my arm. "You think the police will get her, but I'm afraid she'll be too smart for them. If nothing goes right, if they arrest me, please tell Joe"—she paused, took a deep breath, blurted out the words—"tell him I think he's wonderful. Please."

I tried to sound utterly confident—"You'll be telling him yourself"—but I had a stark memory of Eleanor Sheridan's smooth, expressionless, pitiless face.

෪

The door to Joe Cooper's office was closed. It was no impediment for me. Once inside, however, I hesitated. Some light slipped through the window, but it was too dim to see the desktop well. Moreover, no miracle of organization had occurred since I was last here. Papers and files and books rose in stacks and mounds. I found the goosenecked lamp, turned it on, aimed the beam quickly toward the floor behind the desk. Joe's open backpack, contents half in and half out, rested precariously atop one mound. Joe sprawled half in, half out of his sleeping bag, one arm crooked over his face. I settled in his chair and tried to filch a sheet of paper from the near stack. The papers wobbled, tilted. I grabbed as pages fluttered downward.

A sudden thump. Joe was on his feet and in a crouch. He stared, slowly straightened. "Maybe there's a formula in physics. Papers at rest times invisible force equals mess on the floor."

I felt it was necessary to keep up appearances. So to speak. I went through the door, appeared, still in my fetching peach ensemble, and knocked.

The door opened. He looked out at me, poker-faced. "Why am I not surprised?"

"May I come in?" I smoothed back a tangle of hair and hoped I looked presentable.

He rubbed a bristly cheek with the knuckles of one hand. "What if I said no?"

"Chief Cobb got the video. He's getting search warrants this morning, one for Sheridan's home, one for the office."

He gestured with a big thumb. "Come on in. Find a seat." He looked faintly perplexed, finally moved a birdcage off a crate, shoved the crate toward me. "Did a feature on this guy who collects birdcages. He insisted on giving me one."

I turned the crate on end, pulled it closer to his desk, sat down gingerly. "I've talked to Michelle."

He leaned against the edge of his desk, looked at me soberly. "The APB was still out when I crashed about three." He nodded toward the sleeping bag.

"After the warrants are served, I'm sure the APB will be canceled."

"Maybe." His voice was heavy. "It depends on what they find and whether they can tie crimes to a woman who has to have the guts of a gambler and the instincts of a mafia don."

I understood why he was worried. I was worried, too. "I know. Sheridan will walk into her office sure that nobody can pin anything on her."

He rubbed the stubble on one cheek. "The flash drive might lead to the blackmail victims and the kids she used as stooges. You can bet there's no trace of anything about Sheridan. No confirmation of payoffs. Her fingerprints will be on the flash drive but she can claim she had the stuff because she likes to keep an eye on people, maybe she'll claim she foiled some bad actors, made them toe the line. Hell, that's crazy, but she can say anything she wants to unless one of the victims sings. People who pay blackmail won't be eager to spill their guts. So the cops get the flash drive and nobody can prove anything. As for the black outfit, even if fiber ties the black turtleneck to that box in 211, there's no fake time recorded on the video. It's all circumstantial. I can see where a DA would be leery of filing a charge. You need something more." He pushed up from his desk, folded his arms. "You need something that will shake her story." His eyes narrowed. "Listen, there's a chance . . ." He leaned forward, talked fast.

I'd warned him against talking to students and employees in the dean's office. Maybe it was time.

He looked at his watch. "Almost eight o'clock. The warrants are served at nine?" He moved behind his desk, shuffled through several files, finally flipped one open. He scanned a sheet, running his fingers down a list of names. He yanked his cell phone from his pocket. "This is Joe Cooper, editor of the *Bugle*. Hey, sorry to call so early, but you may be able to save the day at the dean's office. . . ."

∽

My palms would have been sweaty had I been present. The unoccupied bathroom held a faint scent of lilac. The mirror was still steamy from the shower. Breath bunched in my chest as I eased open the clothes hamper just far enough to see the hump of dark clothing lying inside. I put down the lid, hugely relieved. The black turtleneck and spandex pants were there.

Eleanor had begun to reach mythic proportions in my mind. She had so far been successful in everything she had attempted. There was no reason for her to know that the presence of the clothing in the hamper mattered.

Through the open door I heard her moving about. I stepped into the loft room and appraised her.

She adjusted a navy silk scarf at the throat of a heather gray blouse. I saw her in the mirror, short straight gold hair framing a finely sculpted face, smooth forehead, straight nose, lips perhaps a trifle thin, sharp chin, flawless complexion, clear eyes of a deep sea blue. I thought of Marlene Dietrich in *Witness for the Prosecution*. Neither the actress nor the film would likely be meaningful to Michelle or Joe, but I felt a chill. The same calculating intelligence. The same deceptive appearance of ordinary humanity. The same arrogant confidence.

Eleanor applied a stroke of blush to both cheeks, raised one perfectly darkened eyebrow, nodded in satisfaction. She returned the brush to a makeup tray, closed the lid. She rose, brushed a piece of lint from flared-leg navy trousers. Navy alligator flats appeared new.

She was unhurried as she walked down the steps. She didn't glance toward the desk. Had she looked, a flash drive lay innocently in the third compartment. She would not know it was a substitute. She picked up a large leather shoulder bag from a window seat, strolled to the front door.

Outside she closed the door firmly, moved lithely down the steps and across a short patch of lawn to the graveled drive. The shiny silver BMW coupe had been recently washed. She swung into the driver's seat, dropped the bag on the other seat.

I squeezed in beside the bag, moved it just enough to be comfortable.

She turned on the CD player, lowered the driver's window. The car purred, a beautiful machine in top condition. As she drove, she smiled contentedly as she listened to Dave Brubeck's "I'm in a Dancing Mood." The breeze stirred her short blonde hair. An attractive woman in an expensive car on her way to an excellent job. I studied her face and felt a wrenching misgiving. I knew she was guilty, knew she had connived and brought misery, including death, and yet there was no hint of cruelty and greed in her smooth features, nothing in her demeanor to betray her. The phone call yesterday had informed her there would be a police search of the offices this morning, but she was en route with an aura of invincibility.

We were nearing the campus on a tree-lined boulevard. She appeared in no hurry. Her expression was untroubled as she made two right turns. As she drove past Goddard Library, her gaze checked for an instant on the police crime van parked in front.

I knew Chief Cobb had dispatched the unit for intense scrutiny of what was now a murder scene

Did she know Ben Douglas had died? Possibly she'd heard on the news, but that didn't concern her. She could feel confident he had not seen her clearly enough to offer any identification. Not only had she moved fast in her all-black costume, the shots had caught him by surprise and he likely had only a confused glimpse of his attacker. Eleanor abruptly smiled a cold, satisfied smile. She didn't think of the library as the place where she had shot a man to escape. She saw it as a monument to her cleverness, all the incidents leading up to the theft of the rare book to implicate Michelle Hoyt.

Two more blocks and the Administration Building was directly ahead. Two police cars and an unmarked cruiser were parked in front. She glanced at her watch. A few minutes before nine. But the early arrival of the police caused her no alarm.

She parked in the slot marked *Dean of Students*. As she turned

270

off the motor, a blue Lincoln slid into the next slot, marked *Provost*. Eleanor was unhurried, gathering up her purse, strolling to the sidewalk, then turning to wait for the other driver.

Tall, thin, and lanky with short white hair and a thin white mustache, he joined her on the sidewalk. "Good morning, Eleanor. How are you?"

She touched the scarf at her throat. "Couldn't be better. And you, Reggie?" Her voice was clear, relaxed, good humored.

"Excellent, excellent." He clapped well-manicured hands together. "Looks hopeful about our rank in the next college ratings. I don't mind saying I put in a good effort there. The regents should be well pleased." The clear implication was that his good offices had made a substantial difference. Then his narrow chiseled face drooped. "But"—he leaned forward, his voice confidential—"I may have to put out some fires if what I hear is true."

They were at the steep steps to the back entrance. Eleanor looked at him inquiringly. "What have you heard?"

"That dreadful crime."

"Crime?"

"The night watchman at the library. Campus Security called me. Well, awful to have a crime on campus, and I understand the fellow was a good chap. Hard for the family, but"—he spread slender fingers in dismay—"ghastly if it involves anyone on campus. They said in the next breath there was a search on for a student. Hoyt, I think that was the name. Can't imagine the circumstances. Why would a student shoot a night watchman? Have to wonder if it was—"

They were at the top of the stairs now and he held the door for Eleanor.

"—a drug deal gone wrong."

"Such a shame," she murmured.

His face drew down in a petulant frown. "If all my good work goes for nothing . . ." He gave a vexed sigh.

I thought about Ben Douglas and priorities.

He continued his complaint as they curved around the back of the stairs, started up old worn treads. At the top of the stairs, Reggie smoothed his mustache. "No point in borrowing trouble, but it does seem hard to have some scandal drag us down when we're set to go up five spots."

"I'm sure everything will work out." Her tone was soothing. As he turned to his left, Eleanor strolled toward the end of the hall and into the Dean of Students Office.

Her stride didn't check as she walked into the space fronting the counter even though Detectives Smith and Weitz stood waiting. Smith was long and lean in a blue blazer and gray slacks. Weitz—if only I could take her under my fashion wing—looked dumpy in a tight red jacket and tan slacks. Her poofy brownish blond hair would have looked inviting to starlings seeking a nest.

It was rather like seeing a still shot from an action scene. At one desk, a woman with an intense expression clutched a cell phone in a heavily veined hand and watched the officers with unblinking intensity. At the other, a white-haired woman with a high forehead, strong jaw, and blunt chin held a coffee mug halfway to her mouth. The twenty-something receptionist moved from foot to foot, obviously excited at the prospect of a police procedural show unfolding in real time. A skinny student in a pink top and red leggings pretended to sort incoming mail but her eyes jerked toward the police every few seconds. The other student worker stroked a barely discernible mustache, uneasy and tense.

Detective Weitz, her face bland and unrevealing, stepped forward. "Dean Sheridan? I have a warrant here for a search of your office."

Smith stood to one side, his expression pleasant. He softly jangled coins in one pocket. He held a video camera under the other arm.

Sam Cobb was a foot behind Weitz. He was as big and burly as always. He'd found time to go home, change into his familiar brown suit. As usual it was wrinkled and a little tight across his chest.

Eleanor took the sheet of paper, glanced down. "It seems in order." She lifted her eyes, her face pleasant. "The college always hopes to be helpful to the authorities, though I'm puzzled at the cause for this. However, please feel free to look wherever you wish." Her tone was utterly relaxed.

Jeanne Bracewell came through her office door, a tight frown on her face. "Eleanor, glad you're here. I told them there has to be a mistake. They said they're looking for evidence of blackmail. And a murder weapon."

Eleanor's cool blue eyes sharpened. She looked toward Weitz, who was plunging the fingers of one hand into a plastic glove, drawing it tight, then doing the same with the other hand. For an instant, uneasiness glimmered in Eleanor's gaze. Her lips parted. Was she going to ask about a murder weapon? The call yesterday had said nothing about a weapon. She apparently decided not to speak, but her face looked sharper, more intent.

Sam Cobb took a step forward. "We appreciate your cooperation,

Dean. I'm Sam Cobb, chief of Adelaide police." His face was genial. He gestured toward the nameplate to his right. "We'll start in your office."

Eleanor frowned. "Why my office?"

His heavy face was stolid, almost bovine. "Information received."

Eleanor flicked a glance toward her door, and it was almost as if she reminded herself that she had no reason to worry. The flash drive was far from here. She gave a dismissive shrug, "Of course. Search where you please."

He moved his big head toward the door, but his eyes never left her face. "You'll come with us." It was a statement, not a request.

Her thin lips quirked in a cool smile. "You want me to be present?" Her tone was amused.

"Protocol."

Eleanor again shrugged. She walked to her office door, used her key. She pushed open the door and stepped inside.

Sam was right behind her, almost a little too close. Smith and Weitz followed. Smith held the video camera in his hands.

Eleanor walked past her massive desk and dropped onto a brown leather sofa, glanced at her watch. "Perhaps you can expedite this. I have an important meeting at nine thirty."

Sam nodded. "We'll do our best. Detective Weitz will conduct the search. Detective Smith will film the investigation." Sam gestured at Smith and Weitz.

The office was perhaps twenty feet deep and thirty feet in length. Above paneled wainscoting behind the desk, two upper bookshelves held an assortment of history books, primarily of the Old West, and a collection of what might be original publications of Louis L'Amour titles. The lower bookshelf was filled with an assortment of antique American millefiori paperweights, each an object of beauty.

Eleanor leaned back against the cushion, watched with a half smile. Heavy purplish red drapes framed the two windows in the wall behind the couch.

Smith stationed himself in the center of the room opposite the desk. He lifted the video camera, filmed Weitz as she stepped behind the desk, her face intent. She moved the chair aside and pulled out the top left drawer. She took her time, lifting out files, checking them. There was an air of certainty in her movements, as if she had a clear idea of what she sought.

Sam stood to the right of the door with his back to the wall. From this vantage point, he had a clear view of Eleanor on the leather couch, Smith facing the desk, and Weitz methodically thumbing through the contents of each drawer. She finished the top drawer, began on the lower left.

Eleanor ignored Chief Cobb and the detectives. She appeared comfortable on the couch, hands loose in her lap, legs crossed, purse on the cushion beside her.

Officer Weitz reached for the center drawer.

Eleanor looked amused. "I keep a very tidy desk. You said you were looking for blackmail material. I'd be interested to know what blackmail material consists of. I believe I have a student directory and—oh, yes—some throat lozenges. I had a little trouble with allergies—"

Weitz stood stiff and still, looking down into the drawer. "Chief." Weitz's tone was steely. "Looks like the tip was right."

Eleanor broke off. Her face was abruptly empty, her eyes alert.

Sam walked toward the desk, his footsteps heavy on the wooden floor. The lens of the video camera followed him.

Using the tips of her gloved fingers, Weitz lifted out a small wrinkled manila envelope, held it out for him to see.

Cobb craned his head. "The envelope was once sealed with packaging tape. It has been torn open, then crumpled."

Eleanor must have felt as if she were caught in a nightmare. She recognized that envelope. She herself had ripped it open last night, dumped out the flash drive. Then she had crumpled the envelope into a ball and thrown it into a wastebasket in the secretarial area. How could it be in her desk? Who had found it? Who knew? How much did they know?

It was a testament to her control, to her iron will, that, though she was silent for too long, she finally raised one black eyebrow, inquired, "I can't quite see what you have there. But"—now her voice was stronger—"I can tell you that envelope wasn't in my desk when I left on Friday." She took a deep breath. "If someone put the envelope in my desk, perhaps taking an envelope I'd used at some time, certainly its presence there now has nothing to do with me."

Sam's brown eyes studied her as if she were a beetle discovered in his soup.

He jerked his head at Weitz.

The detective lifted the flap, held the envelope at an angle. A flash drive slid into Weitz's gloved palm. "A flash drive, Chief."

Eleanor's face revealed nothing. She'd put the incriminating flash drive in her desk at home. How could it possibly have reached her office? But she couldn't claim the flash drive shouldn't be here. She could only, her mind darting and twisting, brazen her way out of what she now realized was a prearranged trap. Her fingerprints were on the flash drive, but she could claim someone had taken a drive she'd previously used, deleted files, added files of which she knew nothing. Was she flipping through images in her mind? She had to know the police would contact the people in the pictures. Would any of the students dare expose her? As for the victims, were they unaware of the identity of their blackmailer? Perhaps she was nothing more than a voice on a telephone, describing in detail compromising photos. She was a clever woman. Had she arranged for money to be dropped at certain sites and always been sure she was unobserved when she arrived to retrieve the payments? The police would make every effort to try and unearth undisclosed sums not accounted for by her income. But the chicanery possible with figures is truly remarkable.

Eleanor managed to affect a puzzled, but pleasant expression. Her blonde hair shone in the light from the window behind her. Her posture was that of a woman at ease on a sumptuously comfortable leather sofa. The only indication of stress was the finger that flicked against a silver bracelet on her left wrist, turning it, turning it.

Cobb flicked a glance at Weitz.

The detective cleared her throat, held up the flash drive between two gloved fingers. She turned to face Detective Smith and the video camera. "Officer Weitz, taking into custody a flash drive found in a brown manila envelope in the desk of Eleanor Sheridan, dean of students at—"

A sudden timid knock sounded on a panel of the open door. The student in the pink blouse and red tights stepped inside. "Excuse me. Please. I want to help. I didn't know I could help, but I got this phone call from this guy at the *Bugle* and he said"—she looked toward Sam Cobb—"that I needed to tell the police chief what I knew."

Detective Smith turned the video camera toward the doorway.

The girl stopped, a pulse fluttering in her throat. She barely managed the words. "Are you Chief Cobb?"

Sam didn't frown at the interruption. His brown eyes saw the uncertainty and shyness in the little figure who faced him with fingers laced tightly together. "Right. Can I help you?"

"I'm Daisy Butler. I'm a work-study student." She looked across the room at Eleanor Sheridan, her gaze timid but eager. "I'm glad to help out, Dean Sheridan. I was here that day, September seventeenth. I was working on name tags for the tea for the student activities fair and I was down on the floor behind the counter. Most everybody had already gone out of the office for lunch. People like to go at eleven thirty but they come back at twelve thirty so it isn't like they take more time than they should. Anyway, I was down on the floor sitting cross-legged. I learned it in my yoga class. I don't think anybody knew I was here, but I heard the door open and real fast footsteps. I popped up, thinking I could be, like, the receptionist, but I saw the lady and she looked scary. I mean she was actually a nice-looking older woman, her hair was brown with some silver streaks, and she had blue eyes and the kind of face like my aunt Margaret, sort of round, but I could tell she was really upset. I thought maybe somebody was in big trouble and she'd come to see about it. She came in from the hall, and she didn't even look toward the counter. She knew right where she was going. I mean, she came right to this door"—Daisy gestured—"and she didn't knock. She turned the knob and went right in, and before she slammed the door she said, 'I'm Susannah Fairlee. I told you—'

Then the door closed. The *Bugle* guy said somebody was saying that this woman—Susannah Fairlee; he sent me a picture on my cell and I knew it was her—wasn't here that day, but I can swear she was." She stopped and looked pleased.

Eleanor sat immobile. Her right hand gripped the silver bracelets on the opposite wrist.

I could imagine the questions pummeling her mind. *Why does the* Bugle *editor think it matters that Susannah Fairlee came to my office that day? No one else knows what happened to Susannah. Her death was officially deemed accidental. Why did that idiot girl come in and talk about Susannah? Do they know? How could they know?* Eleanor took a quick breath, said coolly, "Thank you, Daisy. That will be all for now."

Daisy blinked, aware that her willingness to help was somehow unwelcome. She looked deflated. She shot a questioning glance at Eleanor then at Chief Cobb.

"Close the door behind you, Daisy." Eleanor's tone was sharp.

Daisy shrank a little, hunched her thin shoulders. She nodded and stumbled a little as she turned.

Eleanor again seemed to draw on an inner reservoir of command.

I wondered how much effort it took as she managed to look exasperated. "I'm sorry for the interruption. I hope this exercise is soon coming to an end."

When the door clicked shut, Chief Cobb said brusquely, "We'll take her statement."

Eleanor's expression was one of puzzlement. "That is your prerogative. But I can't imagine why. As for that day, people come here all the time. I don't remember that particular incident. I can look at my daybook." Her lips curved in a mocking half smile.

"Perhaps that will refresh my memory."

Cobb spoke heavily, coldly. "The investigation into Susannah Fairlee's death has been reopened and she is now considered to be the victim of a homicide."

Eleanor's features hardened. She looked predatory and dangerous and very, very wary.

The chief jerked a thumb at Weitz. "Resume your search." He glanced at Smith.

The video camera followed Weitz to the windows. She pulled a wine-colored plush red velvet drape forward, checked behind it, carefully scanned the lining. She stepped to the next drape.

A short beep. Sam unsheathed his cell phone, held it up, listened. His face tightened. "Taken into custody?"

I tensed, moved near enough to hear an excited voice. ". . . found her by the fountain in front of the building. Listen, Chief, this big guy's raising hell, saying she's innocent, insisting we don't take her in, that he'll get a lawyer and—"

"Ask Ms. Hoyt and her friend to remain where they are. Tell them I will soon have information for them." The chief's deep voice carried well.

I was watching Eleanor. Her patrician features exhibited boredom in addition to long-suffering forbearance with idiotic officialdom. I had no doubt she'd heard and knew Michelle Hoyt was in custody, even if not under formal arrest.

Behind that facade pulsed a quick brain. She would bend her intelligence to discovering who and what lay behind the arrival of the police, but for the moment she was triumphant. No matter what was found, no matter if Susannah Fairlee was seen entering her office, she would insist the materials had been placed in her office by someone else and that she simply didn't recall Fairlee's visit, had no reason to recall it. Even if a search of her house yielded the clothes she'd worn the night she shot Ben Douglas, she wasn't in a corner. If the forensic team found a thread from her sweater on the fringe of the box containing diaries belonging to Susannah Fairlee, Eleanor could blandly shrug, insist she had no possible idea how that could have happened. But, of course, the box had been in the room for some time, hadn't it? And there was no way of knowing when a thread might have caught there, and perhaps she'd visited the library and inexplicably somehow a thread was snagged from her sweater. Certainly that was no proof she'd been in room 211 the night Ben Douglas was shot. She would be horrified at the suggestion. All the while a smug, catlike smile would mock her questioners.

Trials often were decided on circumstantial evidence, but a defendant had to be definitively linked to a crime by a witness, physical evidence, or a weapon.

That was my ace in the hole: The revolver that killed Ben Douglas would soon be found.

Cobb's craggy features furrowed in a deepening frown. He knew full well what she was thinking and knew further that so long as she maintained her bland dismissive attitude, they could not prove anything against her.

Detective Weitz completed her search of the last drapery, turned toward the bookcases.

On the second shelf, behind the fourth book—*Adobe Angels: The Ghosts of Santa Fe and Taos*—she would find a Smith & Wesson .357 Magnum revolver with six chambers, two of them empty. When test-fired, the cartridges would match the bullets that resulted in Ben Douglas's death.

My feeling of satisfied expectation abruptly evaporated.

Eleanor's fingerprints were not on the gun. Eleanor knew her fingerprints were not on the gun. She would have made certain the gun was shining clean before she placed it in the trunk of Michelle's car. I had no doubt she would recognize the gun when Weitz found it. I could predict Eleanor's response: shock, astonishment, anger that someone had placed a weapon in her office.

Weitz lifted books out, scanned the empty area, returned the titles.

Eleanor placed her fingers over her lips to smother a small yawn. She was a vision of boredom.

Weitz neared the end of the top shelf.

I slipped past the searching detective, careful not to brush against her. At the end of the bookcase, I looked up at the second shelf to the book about long-ago ghosts. I'd been pleased with myself when I'd tucked the gun there, enjoying the title, thinking— all right, pride goes before a smashing fall—how clever I was.

Weitz lifted out the last three books. In an instant, she would re-shelve them and move in her deliberate fashion, face expressionless, to the place where I now stood.

Eleanor smoothed back a strand of golden hair. She glanced at her wristwatch. Ah, yes, she had an important appointment in another ten minutes and likely would suggest that the search was a matter that the police would surely soon conclude, perhaps even rise and stroll toward the door, murmuring she had an appointment and she knew they didn't need for her to be present any longer.

Chief Cobb's stolid look didn't quite hide his uneasiness. What was he going to do about Michelle, now in police custody? If he found nothing here to justify arresting Eleanor Sheridan, if he couldn't pull together evidence to entrap the dean, Michelle would be placed in a cell and murder charges would be filed, his job would be in jeopardy, and a killer would be safe.

My eyes dropped to the third shelf, with its collection of expensive and beautiful millefiori paperweights. I remembered with a sharp stab of anger JoLee Jamison's single varicolored marble, so tiny in comparison, not of value to anyone but her. The dean's collection of heavy glass paperweights in contrast likely cost thousands of dollars, a luxury made possible by blackmail. No doubt the dean had held each one, turned them in bright light to enjoy the almost iridescent flashes of color, cupping each paperweight in long slender fingers.

My eyes lifted to the second shelf and the book about New Mexico ghosts. I had an empty feeling deep inside. Detective Weitz would find the gun where I'd so carefully placed it and the discovery would do no good. There were no fingerprints—

If Eleanor's fingerprints were on the gun, she would never be able to explain away that fact. I looked again at the shelf with its gorgeous paperweights.

Weitz raised her hand to the first books on the second shelf. Her back was to me.

Eleanor once again used the index finger of one hand to flick, flick, flick a silver bracelet. She gazed at the shining circle of silver.

Sam Cobb folded his arms, watched Weitz intently.

Detective Smith aimed the video camera at the bookshelves. He was leaning back against the wall, likely thinking this was boring and would Weitz get a move on, he wanted some coffee.

The leather couch and Eleanor were not in range of his lens.

Careful again not to touch Weitz, I slipped past her, reached down to the lower shelf. My fingers closed around a gorgeous paperweight, with blue, green, pink, yellow, and white ribbons of glass curled in the ball to a millefiori design at the top. The paperweight was designed in the shape of a ball that tapered to a small two-inch base. I eased the paperweight over the edge of the shelf, moving down, down, down.

Weitz continued to pull out books, return them.

Keeping my hand below the top of the desk to hide the paperweight, I once again passed Weitz. I bent down and with a sidearm angle a couple of inches above the floor threw the crystal ball as hard as I could. The paperweight crashed with a resounding whack on the opposite wall.

Weitz whirled, hand on her holster. Her brown eyes scanned the far side of the room.

Detective Smith straightened up from the wall, the video camera loose in his hand. He stared at the paperweight as it wobbled to a stop near his feet.

Cobb turned toward the sound in a flash, gun in hand, a quick move for a big man.

Eleanor's head jerked around and she stared at the floor.

I reached up, pulled out the book, grabbed the gun, and tossed it directly into her lap.

Caught by surprise, Eleanor gave a sharp cry. Her hands flailed, grappling with the gun. As her hands closed around it, she looked down. Her face changed. She recognized the gun, the weapon she had so carefully cleaned and placed to entrap Michelle and which she now held in her hands, and her fingerprints were all over the cold steel barrel and grip.

"Someone threw this at me." Her voice rose in a shout. She

gripped the stock in one hand, came to her feet. She looked from Smith to Weitz to Cobb.

Face cool and determined, Weitz held her service revolver with both hands, feet planted, aim steady. "Drop the weapon. Drop the weapon now."

Cobb was moving. The video camera crashed to the floor as Smith yanked his gun free.

Eleanor's face convulsed in rage.

Weitz was across the intervening space and her hand closed on Eleanor's wrist. "Drop it."

The gun clattered to the floor.

Eleanor had maintained her insouciant attitude each time the unexpected occurred: The recovery of the flash drive from her desk in an envelope she knew she had discarded. The work-study student's artless revelation about Susannah, which was utterly shocking because Eleanor had no inkling anyone knew of a link between her and Susannah. After each blow, she must have struggled with flickers of panic. Who put the envelope and flash drive in her office desk? Who alerted the Adelaide police? And now the gun that killed Ben Douglas, lying on the floor with her fingerprints.

Eleanor Sheridan no longer looked confident. "The gun—" But she knew what the gun would reveal. She stared at Cobb with an expression of horror. Red stained both cheeks. Her mouth twisted.

"Eleanor Sheridan, we are also serving on you a search warrant for your home—"

She drew in a deep ragged breath.

I saw terror in her eyes, terror and a sickened realization of doom. I was puzzled for an instant and then I knew. The police would find more than the clothes she'd worn to kill. The police would find Susannah Fairlee's diary. I felt certain of that discovery, read that knowledge in her desperate gaze. Why had she kept the diary? A trophy? Defiance? A macabre toast to her own cleverness?

"—and I am taking you into custody on suspicion of the murder of Ben Douglas. Anything you say may be used . . ."

I had no doubt she would remain silent and insist the evidence found in her office had been planted there. But with time, the police would painstakingly discover more and more. Perhaps the neighbor who saw the bicyclist the night Susannah was murdered would describe the clothing. Perhaps a tire track of her bicycle would be found in Susannah's yard. Perhaps a blackmail victim, if reassured a compromising photo was revealed to be fake, would speak out. Perhaps a careful financial analysis would show Eleanor had large sums that could not be accounted for. Most important of all, if Susannah's diary was in her house, Eleanor was finished.

Chapter 16

Chief Cobb stood on the front steps of the Administration Building, squinting a little in the bright morning sunlight. The light breeze stirred his grizzled hair. His craggy face gave no hint that he'd grabbed only a few hours' sleep on his office couch.

TV cameras whirred. Cameras flashed. Reporters, both TV and print, jostled for a place on the steps. I recognized Joan Crandall, the straggly, brown-haired fiftyish crime reporter from the *Adelaide Gazette*. She had a face that had seen everything, but her huge eyes glittered with excitement. Her voice had the staying power of a baying hound, rising above the other shouted questions. "Chief, we got a shot, officers escorting Eleanor Sheridan to a patrol car. What's the charge?"

Cobb was patient. "Joan, we are investigating the death of Ben—"

"Yeah. yeah, yeah," she rasped. "Cut to the chase. What about Dean Sheridan?"

"Dean Sheridan is a person of interest in the murder of Ben Douglas. The investigation is in its early stages—"

"What about the APB for Michelle Hoyt?" Joan obviously hadn't missed the alert.

"Ms. Hoyt is no longer of interest to the Adelaide police except insofar as she can help us determine who held her captive for several days in a scheme to implicate her in the theft of the rare book from Goddard Library. Hoyt has been cleared—"

"Captive! Where? When? What happened? What does this have to do with the murder at the library?" Joan quivered with eagerness.

Chief Cobb gestured to the base of the steps, where Michelle stood with Joe's arm tight around her shoulders. I was sure Lorraine was there, too. Smiling.

The chief sounded almost ebullient. "I suggest you speak with Ms. Hoyt. She and Joe Cooper, the *Bugle* editor, can explain the odd incidents at Goddard Library and how they have been working with law enforcement to solve the murder of Ben Douglas. I'll hold a news conference tomorrow morning—"

I reached the foot of the steps and Michelle and Joe before the pack of newshounds. I was behind Joe. I appeared, celebrating success with a tropical-design blouse, swirling blue skirt, and matching heels.

Michelle was looking up at Joe, her heart in her eyes. "You never gave up trying to help me."

He lifted a hand to touch a strand of shining dark hair. His grin was lopsided. "A man has to do what a man has to do when a girl stands him up at the Brown Owl. I'm counting on that date— and lots more of them." He pulled her close, bent his face toward hers.

I disappeared, but not before I felt a light touch on my arm.

Lorraine burbled in my ear. "A match made in Heaven, wouldn't you say?"

Reporters formed a tight circle around Michelle and Joe. Video cameras filmed. Cameras flashed. "What about those roses? . . . Who smashed the gargoyle? . . . What's behind the theft of the rare book? . . . How does the book tie up with the murder of Ben Douglas? . . . Who held you captive? . . . What's the deal with the dean? . . ."

I eased close to Michelle, spoke softly in her ear. "You and Joe take all the credit. Those who helped you wish to remain"—I paused for emphasis—"invisible."

I believe Michelle has changed her view about me and Lorraine. At least, that's how I would interpret the brief thumbs-up she made with the hand that rested lightly on Joe's arm. The gesture was quite subtle, and neither Joe nor the reporters noticed.

Again I felt a touch on my arm. I heard a quick whisper in my ear.

The central landing on the main library steps was deserted. Lorraine's portrait was lovely in the soft white beam from an antique brass light above the painting. When I'd first seen the portrait in the light from Ben Douglas's torch, the library was quiet and dark with the silence of late night. The old building was silent and deserted now because of the excitement outside.

I didn't bother to whisper. There was no one to hear us. "Joe will have quite a story to write."

"The important story is their story." Lorraine's voice was soft.

I offered her a tribute. "Their love began with the roses."

Lorraine was once again Goddard Library's kindly ghost in residence. How many hearts would she bring together? But now there was no one with whom she could share moments. Ben Douglas would never again stump up the stairs, big light in hand, and stop to talk to Miz Lorraine. Although I knew I'd often disturbed her, wouldn't the suite at Rose Bower seem too solitary now?

I felt a sweep of sadness. There was no time in Heaven, but on earth days roll on and on, month after month, year after year, decade after decade. How long for Lorraine?

I scarcely knew what I intended to say, but words came fluttering out, like rose petals thrown at a wedding. "Paul loved the letter you sent him."

I heard a catch of breath. "I told him I was going to marry Charles."

"Paul thought you were the sweetest, kindest, most wonderful girl in the world because you knew Charles needed that promise to keep him safe. Paul was sure you loved him, and after the war he intended to compete man-to-man. Paul never doubted he was the man you'd marry. It wasn't to be. He went out, brave as always, responding to his duty to get a badly wounded man, and Heaven called him home. He loves you still."

A racket and a rumble, wheels clacking on steel, the smell of coal smoke. I could feel the trembling of the landing as the Rescue Express came near.

"Lorraine, come with me. Come now. Come home to Heaven."

The rush of the Express overwhelmed me and I whirled away, touched with sadness at the silence I left behind.

∽

When we went somewhere special, Mama always made sure we wore our best. She'd say, "Bailey Ruth, honey, put on a smiling face and the nicest dress you have. That's how we show how happy we are to be asked."

As I came aboard, I was thinking about Bobby Mac and the sea and a stroll hand in hand on a beach next to crystalline waters. I appeared and snatched a peek in the shining metal of the caboose. The wind stirred my red curls, fluttered against my graceful cotton smock dress, an enchanting Mediterranean blue splashed with bright hibiscus. I wiggled my toes in sandals.

I hoped Wiggins would understand I truly wasn't being vain. Well, maybe a little bit. But mostly I wanted to look my best. I turned to see—

Wiggins stood at the back rail, reaching out. He wasn't dressed in his usual white shirt, the upper sleeves puffed by black garters, and heavy flannel trousers with wide suspenders and a wide black belt with a silver buckle and black shoes. Absent too was his stiff dark hat. This was an eager Wiggins with shining reddish brown hair and muttonchop whiskers and a smaller mustache. He was handsome in a dun-colored belted wool tunic buttoned at the throat and flared over matching uniform trousers and knee-high leather boots. On the left arm was a white armband with a Red Cross.

The wind stirred Lorraine's golden hair, too, lifting tendrils away from a face made even more beautiful by the love in her dark blue eyes. He had last seen her behind a hospital tent and now she was on the steps to the Rescue Express's caboose in a long gray cotton crepe dress with a white piqué collar, white cap, and white pullover apron with a Red Cross emblem.

"Paul." Her voice was tremulous, eager, uncertain.

Wiggins reached out, took her small hands in his huge ones, and pulled her aboard with a flourish. They stood together at the rail, wheels clacking on silver tracks, the woo of the whistle a triumphant cry. He looked down at her with the love of a lifetime shining in his face. "Welcome home, sweet Lorraine."